THE SKIN HUNTERS

A HARRIET HARPER THRILLER

DOMINIKA BEST

THE SKIN HUNTERS
Harriet Harper Thriller series - Book 5

Copyright © 2021 by Dominika Best

ISBN: 978-1-949674-14-9

www.dominikabest.com
First Edition

For Dave
without you, none of this would be possible

And for Peter Russell
Thank you for all your knowledge

I'd been searching for Jared since I woke up early this morning. I'd gone through ten more tents, and no one had seen him. I couldn't believe Jared would disappear like this. He was too smart and careful. I stood staring at the small island in the center of the concreted LA River contemplating my next move.

Last night had been a hard one. Screams and shouts from outside my tent woke me up at an ungodly hour and I recognized the signs of someone overdosing. The gurgling sound of retching came from somewhere to the left of me and I'd had to listen to someone's pain for close to an hour. Another reason why it was good to be inside my tent by six at the latest.

Every neighborhood changes after the sun goes down. This ragtag community is no different. Things always got a little hairy once it got dark out. The drinkers kept drinking into the night and the users still scrounged for their next fix. Things got rowdy, sometimes dangerous. I'd been on the streets for close to three years now and I knew when to keep myself hidden.

1

Our camp was down in the LA River and that helped keep things somewhat safe. We were far enough away from Skid Row in downtown Los Angeles and all that crazy. It was one of the reasons why I'd chosen this camp. Jared told me he'd made the same calculation. Plus, the view of course.

I was happy he'd chosen to pitch next to me. His being there made me feel safer, too. I was proud of how both of us got our shit together. Well, for being homeless, that is. Or rather, the unhoused. That's what we're called now.

I still couldn't believe I was where I was.

Falling through the cracks didn't take much for me. It was a series of unfortunate events, as they say. First, I lost my job and couldn't find another one to pay the rent. My parents died years ago and my grandpa and my brother were dead as well. I had no other family to help me. My friends tried to help out with job referrals, but the jobs never came through and my friends started getting too busy to take my calls. I tried to hang on with credit cards and unemployment in the six months it took my landlord to evict me. In the end, he took me to court. I'd sent out close to four hundred resumes in those six months and didn't get one damn bite the whole time.

Once I lost my place, that was it. An address is necessary to get through normal everyday life. It didn't take long before I was drinking away the day in shame and embarrassment. I'd done things I wasn't proud of, but I was still standing. At least I had that.

Jared and I bonded over our love of science fiction. He saw me reading Kurt Vonnegut and it got us talking. We'd both been working through the steps and when things got hard, we leaned on each other. I felt like I'd known him forever and it had only been a month.

I needed to keep searching for him.

I poked my head into another tent.

"Hey Donnie, you seen Jared today?" I asked.

"How you doing, Whitey? No, girl. Not since yesterday. But I ain't been out much today," Donnie said.

He scratched his white hair, and I could see the dried drool on the edge of his mouth.

"Thanks," I said.

"You look worried," he said as he peered up at me.

"It's not like him. He's been sober for weeks. Just hope he hasn't fallen off the wagon," I said.

"Happens to the best of us," Donnie said. "Hope you find him."

"Me too," I said and stood up. It was close to eleven and I still had thirty tents to get through.

Jared had been clean for the last couple of months, he'd told me. We made sure to check in on each other.

I'd been lucky to find this community when I did. I'd been living at a bus stop on the corner of Vermont and Sunset for weeks when the crews came to take down the stop. I'd put all my things in my cart and hustled out of there before they started messing with me. I didn't want to watch them throw all my stuff away again.

When I saw the community under the bike bridge along the river, I couldn't believe it. The main island had large trees and the small trickle of river glinted in the sunlight.

It was beautiful.

I pitched my tent in a good spot an hour after that. The garbage on the edge marred the picturesque view but I ignored it. Beggars couldn't be so choosy. The people surrounding me had their fair share of problems, but who didn't? And for the most part, they were friendly enough. During the daylight hours, at least.

There was Frankie in the last tent at the end, who I was pretty sure was a schizo. The lady next to him, a scrawny gal named Molly, had a pretty hardcore smack problem. Then came Matty, Rufus, and Junior who were all garden-variety alcoholics and addicts like me and Jared. We had our fair share of fights and troubles. Mostly at night, though. I was friendly to everyone during the day. For my own safety, I kept myself to myself at night. Even with Jared.

I checked my watch. It was already close to five in the afternoon. I'd been going through the camp all day and hadn't realized.

My stash of water and snacks was enough for tonight, but I'd have to stock up tomorrow. I couldn't leave the camp tonight. I'd already shooed off three looky-loos from getting into Jared's tent. I planned to eat my dinner outside his door, but I wasn't sure how long I could keep people away from a nice empty tent. I'd already taken his library books and his little black note-book out of there, just in case. If Jared didn't show up by tomorrow, his tent and gear would be lost. I was only one woman and keeping his stuff safe was hard enough for even a day.

I tried to keep my anger at him from raging like I'd been doing all weekend. I was terrified he'd slipped up somehow and didn't want to tell me. He'd been going to AA meetings almost every day and I just couldn't imagine him drinking without telling me. It didn't feel like him.

I pulled my granola bars and soda out of my pockets and set up my small dinner on a blanket in front of

Jared's tent. As I ate, I looked up and down the bike path, meeting the gazes of a good number of people. They knew what I was doing. I could tell by the looks I was getting that I'd have a new neighbor by morning. No way could I try defending his tent overnight. I ate my granola bars and drank my soda, my mind racing.

Jared was nowhere to be found and I could feel in my gut something was wrong.

The others had disappeared like this, too. They were there one day and then, all of a sudden, they were gone. Me and Jared had just talked about that a few days back. Big D had gone missing and left all his stuff behind. And then there was that guy, Artie. His girlfriend was convinced something happened to him, too.

We'd agreed we would watch out for any strange people down in our camp and I'd seen a bearded man a couple of times. But I wasn't sure if he was one of the outreach workers that came around every week to see if we needed food or had medical needs. Sometimes they even gave us vouchers for places to stay.

The bearded guy looked a little creepy to me, so I kept away from him, but Jared laughed it off. He hadn't taken it seriously. Maybe that was his mistake and he'd found himself a bag of trouble.

It was also possible he could've fallen off the wagon and just ended up going on a bender. Anything was possible out here. Even though that explanation didn't sit right with me, I knew it had to be considered.

The day turned into dusk and a brisk wind picked up along the river. I shivered. The sun would disappear completely in the next few minutes.

I folded up my blanket, unzipped my tent, and went back inside, closing it behind me. I snuggled into my blanket and was thankful once again I'd found that twin mattress off of Griffith Park Boulevard some weeks back. It really helped keep the cold of the concrete away from my butt. I clicked on my flashlight and took a sip of water. My stomach grumbled. The granola bars were not enough. I felt nauseous, but that could also be my nerves.

Something had happened to Jared. I was sure of it.

Should I go to the police?

Maybe I'd wait another day just to make sure he wasn't out on some bender somewhere.

I heard voices and could tell a party was starting. Some younger people had moved into the tent next to Donnie's. I didn't like the newcomers much because they were always on something and that made them unpredictable. I wasn't crazy about unpredictable people because they could really hurt me.

I listened for Jared's voice in the crowd, but he wasn't there.

"Jared, where did you go?" I asked.

My guilt resurfaced as I remembered the last two conversations we'd had. I'd been such a jerk to him and we'd fought both times. I knew something was up with him and he wouldn't tell me what it was. His being so secretive hurt my feelings. Now, he was gone.

I needed my friend.

It was lonely out on the street. It took me some time to open up to him. But when I finally did, it all came gushing out. The pain, the heartbreak, the eventual ending up on the streets like he had. We all had stories about how we got here. It was safer to have friends nearby, but you also had to be careful who you let come close. Now one of my only friends had disappeared.

Raindrops pattered on the tent fabric above me. I hadn't even noticed the clouds rolling in. I was distracted all day in my search for Jared. Rain was dangerous to our little community on the edge of the LA River. Most days, Los Angeles was sunny without a cloud in the sky. But every once in a while a storm would come along and dump a whole ton of rain onto the city.

The city wasn't built for a lot of rain and the drains all emptied out into the washes and eventually ended up gushing into the Los Angeles River. On a typical day, the LA River was a trickle of water in a vast cement canyon.

Once the rainwater came, the LA River turned into a dangerous place to be. It became a churning, fast-moving waterway, rushing toward the ocean and taking everything it could with it. When the homeless first came to the banks of the LA River, some of the people decided to put up tents on the little islands that formed in the center of the huge concrete space. It was easy to walk over the trickles of water on each side of the island.

But then the rains came one night and swept the entire island away along with the people living on it. One of them had drowned and another one had been rescued by the fire department.

When Donnie arrived, he and some of the others decided to go on higher ground to make sure that wouldn't happen to them.

I squeezed into the corner of my tent and pulled my blanket and sleeping bag around me. It was going to be a long night. I'd tried to patch all the holes I could find in the tent, but there was no way that some of my stuff wouldn't get wet inside here.

The rainfall came down harder and I wished for the millionth time that I had a real home with a real roof.

DAY 1 – MARCH 6, 2019 - MORNING

The skyline was starkly clean this morning, rare for Los Angeles. The air even smelled fresh. It really was a beautiful city, Detective Harriet "Harri" Harper thought as she drove down Sunset Boulevard towards Los Feliz and the Los Angeles River on an early morning call.

The epic storm the night before brought down three inches of rain within an hour. Los Angeles was not designed for that kind of rain.

This morning, however, the rain was all but gone. In its wake came the clear blue skies and fresh air.

It almost made up for Harri having to cut her vacation short.

She'd had many sleepless nights working on a task force in the Los Angeles Police Department's Robbery-Homicide Division trying to uncover a team of bank robbers in East Los Angeles. She'd watched countless hours of footage to track the getaway cars from four different robberies. It had taken her all month and she didn't think she could watch a minute more.

The task force, led by Detective Tom Bards, found their robbery crew and she'd taken the opportunity to take some needed time off. She and Jake Tepesky, her boyfriend, had bought a house together, and moving in was always a pain.

Harri slowed her Audi as she neared the police cordon and surveyed the scene in front of her. Whatever was down in the LA River was big. Special Services had constructed a gate as a checkpoint and shut down East-bound traffic on Los Feliz Boulevard. She saw both LAPD and news helicopters over the scene. Numerous LAPD vehicles lined the road including a Coroner's van and Scientific Investigation Division vehicles.

Tom Bards had called her early that morning as she was finishing up her breakfast to join him at the crime scene down in the river. She was thankful he'd included her in the case. She'd had her fair share of big cases in the last year and Jake thought she should slow down but she'd been trying to get into RHD for years and had finally made the transfer. She wasn't going to miss an opportunity to prove herself worthy of the position.

She parked her personal vehicle behind a cruiser and grabbed her crime scene kit from the trunk of her car. She'd already dressed for the trek down to the river in jeans and hiking boots. She had gloves and her protective gear in a small backpack with a flashlight, evidence bags, and other things she might need.

Harri stepped up to the patrol officer manning the checkpoint. She gave him her name and credentials and he directed her to the bike path to his right.

Harri followed a well-worn trail to the entrance gate

to the bike path and looked down at the circus below. She could see no discernible path down to where the crime scene was.

The waters had receded from the night before and the river was back down to being a trickle of tranquility. Decades ago, a large island had formed in the middle of the vast expanse of concrete that now supported four or five tall trees and a mound of dirt and detritus from the river that spanned about five hundred feet.

Harri Harper was a native Angeleno and grew up in the South Bay, specifically El Segundo, and hadn't paid much attention to the Los Angeles River. El Segundo was right on the Pacific Ocean and the only time she ever encountered the Los Angeles River was when she went through the Ballona wetlands on her way up to Venice Beach and Santa Monica. The LA River wended its way toward the ocean through the wetlands and had been paved over throughout the city in the 1930s.

Harri had always assumed the government paved over the river because men coming out of the Great Depression needed a job. She'd later watched a documentary segment about Los Angeles and found out that in fact, the Los Angeles River was extremely deadly when it rained.

Before the Army Corps of Engineers redirected the river and paved its embankments, it flooded its banks and caused tremendous damage. Any structures within range were destroyed and many deaths, including entire families, were attributed to those flash floods. On most days, the river was a trickle going down the very center of the paved channel. When it rained, the water roared through the channels, sometimes breaching over foot-bridges.

When Tom had called her, Harri asked if it was a

homeless encampment that washed away but Tom said it was more complicated than that and she needed to get there as quickly as she could.

Los Angeles County was in the midst of a homelessness crisis and tent cities were popping up everywhere there was space. Skid Row in Downtown had spread its regular borders, enveloping streets around it and encroaching into Little Tokyo.

Even wealthier neighborhoods were now seeing tents coming up wherever there was pavement space and not a lot of police presence.

New policies had been enacted by the state of California that categorized the temporary tent cities as private residences and now police couldn't enter them without a warrant. They also couldn't get rid of people's personal property, even if it was on public land. It was a complicated situation that wouldn't be resolved anytime soon.

Five months ago, they'd had a similar rainstorm that washed an entire encampment away. Rotating patrols kept pushing people off the islands that developed from all the silt that washed down the river, but they kept coming back. Four homeless people died during that storm and three others were never found.

"Can I help you?" a voice from her right interrupted her thoughts. She hadn't noticed the patrol officer approaching her from another path.

"What's the best way to get down there, Officer Radley?" she asked, reading the name on his uniform badge.

He pointed at a small trail to the right of him.

"That's the way I've been going down and back," he said.

"Looks steep," Harri commented.

"It's not too bad once you get going," he said.

A smell of urine wafted by and Harri made a face.

"It's from over there," Officer Radley said pointing behind her. "I keep having to move whenever the wind changes direction."

Harri looked to where he was pointing and saw a line of tents extending down under the bridge along the chain-link fence.

"That's a big one," Harri said.

"Thirty-two tents, in fact."

Harri whistled. Those poor souls, she thought.

Movement on the island caught her eyes. She needed to get down there.

"Thanks for the help," she said and made her way down the incline. The sound of the helicopters thundered above her as she inched down the concrete. The sound rebounded against the concrete embankment and made her ears ache. She could see more news helicopters had joined the single LAPD helicopter. What in the world had they found?

Five minutes later she had joined Detective Tom Bards and Dr. Grimley, the Coroner for the County of Los Angeles, and several people from the Scientific Investigation Division. The group surrounded Dr. Grimley who knelt next to a body. A man's head and shoulders were visible from the top of the cocoon of plastic sheeting covering it.

"I don't know how you've been able to stand the noise for longer than a minute," Harri said pointing to the helicopters above them.

"It's hard to think," Dr. Grimley shouted over the noise.

Tom leaned over to Harri.

"This is going to be another one of those cases," he said in a loud voice.

Harri squinted her eyes and looked at him. What kind of case? A serial killer? Had they found any other bodies while she was gone?

"Is this our only victim?" she asked, looking around. She saw a different group of SID techs clustered around another portion of the island.

"No," he said.

"Another body?" she asked.

"Sort of," he said and tilted his head toward the other scene.

Harri turned back to the corpse in front of them.

"Morning, Dr. Grimley," Harri yelled, and her voice rang out in the sudden quiet as the air space above them finally cleared. Her ears buzzed in the silence. She shook her head to clear the ringing. It took several more moments before she could hear over the sound in her ears.

"Hope we didn't get hearing damage from that," Dr. Grimley remarked. "And it looks like you have your voice back."

"It's taken some serious self-care to get here," Harri said.

Harri had recently been involved in a case where the killer had come after her in her own home. He'd tried to strangle her and that left deep-tissue damage to her neck muscles and vocal cords. It had taken a good three months for her to get her voice back. Thank goodness she didn't have any permanent damage. At least physically, she thought.

Harri bent down to examine the corpse alongside the coroner.

"I'm glad to hear you recovered," Dr. Grimley said never taking her eyes off of their victim.

"Was he found like this?" Harri asked Tom, motioning to the head sticking out of the plastic sheeting.

"That's what the witness said," Tom said.

The man's shoulders indicated he was naked at least from the waist up. His arms looked oddly deflated and his skin held a red tinge almost like a sunburn.

The plastic had come undone around the shoulders while duct tape held the plastic wrapping in place around the rest of his body.

"Is that a sunburn?" Harri asked.

"Not sure yet," Dr. Grimley said.

"And do those arms look weird to you?" she asked.

"They do," Dr. Grimley noted. "But I won't be able to know more until I get him unwrapped. I'll perform the autopsy this afternoon."

"That's expedited," Harri said in surprise.

"I'm curious about this body too," Dr. Grimley admitted.

"Who found him?" Harri asked Tom.

"A woman named Darlene who lives in the encampment up there," Tom said and gestured to the tents above.

"What makes this an RHD case?" Harri asked.

The Robbery-Homicide Division was an elite detective squad that investigated high-profile cases throughout Los Angeles County. The types of crimes they usually picked up were serial murderers, high-profile murders that dealt with celebrities and politicians, and any notable death that was going to end up in the media. This death, although tragic, didn't look like it would be necessary to go to the Robbery-Homicide Division. A regular detective could have been assigned. The other body must be the reason, although she didn't understand why Tom was being cryptic about it.

Harri turned toward the other SID techs.

"Is that body wrapped up in plastic as well?" Harri asked.

"You should see them for yourself," he said. "Excuse us, Dr. Grimley."

"I'll meet you over there," Dr. Grimley said. She turned back to the victim as Tom and Harri walked to the other crime scene.

"Do we have an ID on him?" Harri asked.

"We do. His name is Jared Atkinson. Darlene said he was one of her neighbors in the encampment. Said he'd gone missing about three days ago," he said.

"That's a lucky break," Harri said. Some victims were never identified because they had no relatives or no record on file.

Tom didn't say anything. Harri stole a look at her partner.

"Are you okay?"

Tom wasn't typically queasy about crime scenes.

"I am. Just wasn't ready for another one of these cases so soon."

"What are you not telling me?" she asked.

"Look for yourself," Tom said.

Harri looked down and saw three arms and one leg scattered haphazardly in the mud.

"Could you all give us a moment?" Tom asked Paul Gibson, the SID investigator standing closest to him.

Paul motioned to his crew, and they left the two detectives to it.

The body pieces were swollen from the river water and had a strange tinge of blue-green coloring them. Judging by the appearance of the fingernails and toenails, Harri guessed the limbs belonged to women. The limbs also had a strange marking all over them, like a brand. It had two slanted circles that formed a bigger circle. A cross was formed at the noon spot and a small triangle was formed at six o'clock. Tom made a sketch of the brand and held it up to Harri.

"That's pretty close," Harri said. To Harri, the brand reminded her of a bird's face. The brand was two inches in diameter and each limb had about ten of them burned into the skin.

"There are people out in the city missing some parts," she said with a shudder.

Dr. Grimley appeared behind Tom.

"I'm done processing the victim. My team is ready to take him. Have you seen what you need to see with him?"

"Yes," Tom said.

Harri nodded.

"These parts are female?" Harri asked.

"Yes. The shape of musculature and also the appearance of the toenails and the fingernails suggest female limbs. I wouldn't say the same woman for any of those arms."

Harri looked at the branded limbs again. "What are you seeing?"

"Different lengths for all three arms. The muscle mass appears different too," Dr. Grimley said. "I won't know for sure until we run the DNA."

"You can tell all that even with the putrefaction?" Tom asked.

"I'm that good."

"Putrefaction cause the color?" Harri asked.

"And the water. They must have been in the water for days," Dr. Grimley said.

"The brands? Do you think they were done pre or post-mortem?" Harri asked.

"With the way the skin reacted, the victims were alive when they were branded," Dr. Grimley said.

"Were the victims alive when these limbs were removed?" Tom asked.

"I can't say one way or another yet. I'll do the autopsy right after our guy over there," she said. "On first look, they've been in the water longer than our guy. He died in the last forty-eight hours. These had to be submerged longer than that for this level of decomposition. I'll know for certain in the lab."

"Thank you very much, Dr. Grimley," Tom said.

Dr. Grimley nodded and waved Paul Gibson over.

Tom and Harri let the SID investigators get back to work and walked to the edge of the island. The homeless encampment was shadowed by the street above it.

"Shall we go talk to this Darlene?" Harri asked.

"I asked Martinez to stay with her near her tent. She was pretty shook-up since she and Jared Atkinson were friends," he said.

"Could these be two cases?" Harri asked.

"Could very well be," Tom said. "The manner of

death is different. The treatment of the bodies is different, too."

"He still has all his limbs. Although did you see how his arms looked so strange? Almost deflated?"

"I did," Tom said.

Harri nodded and didn't say a word as they climbed up the steep embankment. Her breath came in short bursts and a heavy feeling made the climb even harder. She'd had the feeling of heaviness for weeks now. It felt as if her bones were made of lead. Her therapist said it was a sign of depression, but Harri wasn't sure about that.

Listening to that recording every night gave her nightmares. She wasn't sleeping well and, when she did sleep, she had nightmares of her time on that island from her memory. The island where she'd rescued a young boy and then found the remains of her sister who'd gone missing decades before. She wanted to find Jerome Wexler, her sister's murderer, as much as Jake did yet at the same time, she was happy to have picked up another case. She wasn't sure how much more her psyche could take.

The physical therapy for her vocal cords had been rough and her therapist had also diagnosed her with PTSD. She'd been cleared for duty, but she wasn't as solid as she'd been before her attack. She didn't want to admit that to herself, but she could feel the butterflies in her stomach at the thought of even being at a crime scene. Before, she'd get hopped up on adrenaline with a new case. Now, everything was muted, almost as if all the bright color had been sucked out and only a dull flatness was left.

"You all right?" Tom asked.

"I'm not in as good of shape as I should be," she said,

deflecting the question as they made it to the homeless encampment.

She turned her focus to the task at hand.

"There's Martinez over there," he said.

The smell of food and something else unpleasant wafted from somewhere to their right. She felt a pang of sorrow for all of these people who found themselves here and wondered what it really took to live like this.

2

DAY 1

U p close, some of the tents looked to be in almost brand-new condition. Different smells drifted by: cigarette smoke, alcohol, sweat, urine, and the stink of rotting garbage. A woman in her early 30s stood next to Officer Inez Martinez. Her blonde hair was cut short, almost in a pixie cut. She wore clean jeans and a t-shirt underneath a flannel shirt. Flip-flops finished up the ensemble. Her face was deeply tanned and blue eyes flashed back at them. Her face appeared swollen from crying. At least, that's what Harri assumed.

How did this woman end up living in a tent? If Harri passed her on the street, she'd never know she was homeless.

"Thank you for waiting to speak to us," Tom began.

He nodded at Officer Martinez, who took her cue and stepped away.

"Darlene, this is my partner, Detective Harriet Harper."

Harri scrunched her nose at a surprise bad odor that wafted from somewhere to her right. She tried to hide her reaction, so she didn't offend the woman in front of them.

"And this is Darlene Whiteman," Tom said.

"You can call me Whitey. That's my nickname around these parts," the woman said.

She had a pleasant voice and dimples when she smiled.

"You found the bodies this morning?" Tom asked.

"That's right. When I wake up, I usually have to go pee and the island is the perfect place for that," Whitey said.

"Around what time did you get down there?" Harri asked.

"Well, I left the tent at around seven, maybe seven-fifteen," Whitey said.

"How did you come by the body?"

"I do my business behind those trees over there," Whitey said and pointed at two trees on the end of the island.

"What made you go to the other end where the body was?" Tom asked.

"The storm was really bad last night. The thunder rumbled all night long and the sound of the gushing river was so loud. All of my stuff got wet," Whitey explained.

Harri wasn't following her logic.

"You went to the other side of the island because of the rain from the night before?" Harri asked.

"The river can wash up treasure. You never know what you can find," she said with a smile. Then, as if she remembered what she'd found, she winced and covered her mouth.

"Was the plastic open like that when you found him?" Tom asked.

"Yes, sir. It was," she said and then gave a sniff. "I was searching the ground and noticed the plastic. And then when I came closer, I saw, you know. I saw what it was. And then I saw Jared. Which really sucked."

Tears sprang into her eyes.

"Were there any other people down there when you found him?" Harri asked gently.

"I didn't see anyone," Whitey said.

"No one from the camp?" Tom asked.

"No. Most people don't get up that early," Whitey said, sniffing.

"And you knew this man?" Harri asked gently.

"He was my friend, and his tent was next to mine."

"When was the last time you saw him?" Tom asked.

He was the one taking notes this time.

"He'd been missing for days. Since last Sunday. I've been looking for him everywhere."

Something stirred behind her eyes.

"Why were you looking for him?" Harri asked, noticing how Whitey's eyes slid down to the ground.

"I reported him missing," Whitey said instead.

Harri noticed she didn't answer her question.

Whitey looked back up at her.

"He lived next to me. Jared had been sober for two months now and we were kind of each other's support system."

"When did you realize he was missing?" Tom asked.

Whitey turned to him. "We have breakfast together every morning since we're pretty much the only ones who wake up that early. He'd missed dinner Sunday night and then Monday morning came around and he didn't show. I thought maybe he might have fallen off the wagon the night before. I didn't hear him come home that night," she explained.

"And you didn't see him again?" Harri asked.

"No. I didn't. Tuesday came along and he still hadn't shown. That's when I got real worried. I knew something must've happened to him," Whitey said.

The way she'd said those words sounded strange to Harri.

"Happened?" Harri asked. "Why wouldn't you think that he'd fallen off the wagon?"

"It wasn't like him. He was in a rush when I saw him Sunday morning though," Whitey said.

"Tell us about your conversation Sunday morning," Tom said.

"It wasn't much of a conversation. I was already setting out our bagels when he rushed out of his tent. He told me he couldn't do breakfast because he'd over-slept," Whitey said.

"Did he tell you what he was late for?" Harri asked.

"He yelled back that it was an AA meeting," Whitey said. "I couldn't hear what else because he ran away so fast."

"Was he having troubles then?" Harri asked.

The moment it came out of her mouth she wished she could take it back. Of course, he had troubles.

He was homeless.

"More than the rest of us?" Whitey asked.

Harri nodded.

"I don't know," Whitey said. "He was keeping stuff to himself. He wasn't exactly himself that weekend." Whitey's eyes glanced from Tom's face to Harri's.

"Himself?" Tom prodded.

"We always had breakfast and dinner together. Always. That didn't happen this weekend. He wasn't talking to me like he was before. I don't know." She mumbled that last part.

"Which tent is his?" Harri asked.

Harri wanted to keep her talking and was worried that she was shutting down.

Whitey pointed to a brand-new-looking blue tent to the right of hers. "This one is my tent," she said and pointed to an older-looking red tent right behind her. "He moved here about a month ago. I was the end of the block back then."

"How did you know that Jared had gone missing?" Harri asked. Whitey's use of that word was bothering her for some reason.

"I know what you're going to say. People travel back and forth between different sites in the city. They tent up close to churches that give out food and shelter. No one leaves their stuff behind, though. Would you leave your house and never come back if you were moving across the city?"

Harri and Tom exchanged a look.

"When I say disappear, I mean that. They leave all their stuff behind and vanish. No one does that," Whitey said.

"And so that's how you knew that Jared was missing? Because he left the stuff behind?" Tom asked.

"That's exactly right," Whitey said.

"You said they?" Tom asked.

Harri had noticed the use of that word, too.

Whitey nodded. "He's not the only one that's gone missing. Big D disappeared that same way about three weeks ago. Left all his stuff behind."

Harri noticed Tom writing all that down. Missing men and one turned up dead. Maybe they were onto something bigger.

"Going back to why you stay in your tent at night?" Tom asked.

"I'm," Whitey started and then hesitated. "I'm doing the work. I'm doing my recovery, best as I can. I'm a recovering alcoholic and Jared was, too. When the sun goes down, the addicts come out. Sometimes this place is a party with drugs and alcohol flowing left and right. People can get violent. I don't want any part of that so I make sure my tent is zipped up and my lights are out so nobody bothers me."

"And Jared was the same way?" Tom asked.

"It's hard to be constantly living with temptation," she said. "It's not like you can go home and get away from all the noise and craziness that goes on all around when there's partying happening. But we do our best."

"How many others disappeared in this way? Where they left stuff behind?" Harri asked.

"Just Big D. I don't know his full name. And then I heard about a guy named Artie," she said.

Tom stopped writing and looked up at her.

"I never heard their full names," Whitey said.

"Who did you report the disappearance to?" Harri asked.

"I went down to the Hollywood precinct. I took the bus there," Whitey said.

"And was the missing person's report filed properly?" Harri asked.

"Yes," Whitey said. "I mean, I hope so. The cop down there seemed kinda annoyed because I didn't know Jared's entire life story. I know what cops think about us. You all don't really take us seriously. We're a nuisance."

Harri couldn't argue that point with her. The homeless crisis was a complex problem that politicians kept trying to solve but was left to the beat cops to deal with. There was a lot of ugly talk going around and a lot of frustrated people. She wasn't sure how the desk sergeant would have taken the missing person's report, but she had a general idea.

"Is there anything else you can tell us about Jared?" Harri asked.

"He kinda kept to himself," she said. "Kept a lot of things close to his chest. It sounded like he grew up in Los Angeles. He never mentioned any other places to me."

"What did you talk about then?" Harri asked.

"Books mainly. We both love science fiction. We have library cards and go to the Los Feliz branch. We can do a wash-up there. I could spend all day in that library. Especially on the hot days. We were all about Kurt Vonnegut," she said.

"Thank you so much for your information, Whitey. If we need to speak to you again, will you be around here? Do you have a cell phone?" Harri asked.

Whitey nodded and dictated a phone number to Harri. She jotted it down and put on disposable gloves.

"Has anyone moved into Jared's tent yet?" Tom asked.

"Not that I've heard," Whitey said. "I've made sure to keep it his. I guess now it'll be up for grabs."

"Thanks so much for all your info," Harri said.

Whitey nodded and turned back to her tent.

Harri didn't mention the services that were available for the homeless in the neighborhood because she was sure Whitey already knew all about them.

She turned back to Jared Atkinson's tent and Tom.

"You ready for this?" Harri asked.

Tom nodded and zipped open the tent. Wet damp air came floating out, but the smell wasn't too bad.

They both looked inside and saw there wasn't much in there. There was a sleeping bag and a bedroll, a flashlight, and a bottle of water. That was it. No other personal effects.

"Someone's been through here," Tom said. "Whitey would know if anything's missing."

Harri pulled her head out of the tent and called out to Whitey.

Whitey came out of her tent with a frown on her face.

"I heard you say it was cleared out. Last night his pack was still in there. I swear it," she said.

"Pack?" Harri asked.

"One of those big backpacks. He had one of those big camping backpacks. You know the kind people go out into the woods with," she said. Whitey stuck her head inside Jared's tent. "It's usually in that corner," she said and pointed to the back left of the tent. "He has all his clothes and stuff to wash with in there."

"Anything else missing?" Harri asked.

"Doesn't look like it. He only had his things in that backpack of his," she said. "His books, his wash-up kit, clothes, and his journal."

"Thank you, Whitey," Harri said.

Whitey nodded and left them looking at Jared Atkinson's meager possessions.

"So, he went missing on Sunday, March 3rd, leaving all of his stuff behind including his backpack."

"Which is now missing," Harri said.

"We need the techs to come in and pack up this tent. See if we can find fingerprints or any other type of evidence in it," Tom said and motioned to the nearest officer.

They walked away from the encampment and Tom gave the officer instructions for the SID tech team. He told the officer to protect the potential crime scene until they got there. Tom called Paul Gibson to send two SID technicians up to Jared Atkinson's tent.

"I have officers taking statements of everyone in the camp. Hopefully, somebody saw something Sunday night," Tom said.

"And then we have the random leg and arms," Harri said.

They had turned away from the tent city and started walking back to their cars.

"With the amount of putrefaction on those limbs, I'm wondering if we just caught two different crimes at the same scene," Tom said.

"Thanks a lot, Los Angeles River," Harri said.

3

DAY 1 - AFTERNOON

Harri had been tasked to uncover all she could about Jared Atkinson. They had a team of officers canvassing the homeless encampment and Tom was in constant contact with them for any new developments. Dr. Grimley had set the autopsy for three in the afternoon and Harri hoped to have a better handle on who Jared Atkinson was by then.

Her first problem was that the Jared Atkinson whose body they found didn't seem to exist. She'd called Tom over when she came up empty and they both searched all the databases they could.

Neither of them found anything under that name with Jared's face in the DMV database. He had no criminal record. No arrest record. They even tried social media but came up empty.

They still had no real name for the man they'd found.

"It's time," Tom said and Harri was relieved to get up and leave the bullpen. It had been an incredibly disappointing afternoon.

☞

Harri and Tom stood in their white protective gear, goggles, and gloves next to Dr. Grimley in exam room one in the basement of the morgue.

"This is one of the weirdest bodies I've ever examined but I think I have some answers for you," she started with.

"Weird in what way?" Harri asked.

The body had deep bilateral lacerations running from the ankles to the knees and then from the knees to the hips. The same long slashes spanned the entire length of the arms. The horror of what this man had endured made Harri look away.

"He didn't feel any of this. It looks bad but it was all done postmortem," Dr. Grimley stated.

"Any idea of a cause of death?" Harri asked.

"I found a pinprick at his neck. I should get the tox results back in three days. My guess is he was injected with something that killed him fast. Stopped his heart and then the killer could get what he really wanted from this body," Dr. Grimley said.

"That's a big leap of logic. You got all that from his body?" Tom asked quizzically.

"Yes," Dr. Grimley said. "His body told me why this time around."

Harri and Tom exchanged glances.

"You've seen bodies like this before?" Harri asked.

"Not exactly, but the pieces that are missing in this body make me believe it was harvested," she said.

"Organ harvesting?" Tom asked.

Harri wasn't expecting that.

"No." Dr. Grimley shook her head. "Organs need to be harvested fresh from a body. They require proper refrigeration. Organ harvesting requires a team specifically trained in organ procurement under a skilled surgeon. Not to mention the harvested organs need to be in the receiving body within hours. But that leaves everything else in the body. Have either of you heard of tissue retrieval?"

"Come again," Harri said.

"Tissue retrieval is just as profitable and way easier to do compared with organ retrieval."

"By tissue do you mean skin?" Tom asked.

"Anything that isn't an organ. That includes skin, as well as veins, tendons, heart valves, and bones," Dr. Grimley said.

"Is that what these cuts are?" Harri pointed to the long gashes on the arms and legs.

"Yes. The bones are missing. As are the tendons and cartilage," Dr. Grimley said.

"Where do these, um, tissues, end up?" Tom asked. Even he was turning a bit pale.

"Tissue banks. But they only accept tissue from registered tissue procurement companies. There must be some illegal pipeline going on here," Dr. Grimley said.

She pointed at large red patches on Jared's torso. She pushed him over to his side and pointed at his back. The skin looked as if it was badly sunburned.

"See this reddish tone to the skin? I've seen this before. This was done by a device called a Dermatone. It's a machine used by tissue procurement technicians to shave off the top layer of skin."

"Hold up, this guy's skin was shaved off?" Harri asked in disbelief. She'd never heard of anything like this.

"Cadaver skin is extremely versatile. It can be used for skin grafts, and severe burn treatment, which is the more noble cause. But most of the time it's used in plastic surgery. Like for penile enhancement," Dr. Grimley said with a grin.

Harri and Tom looked at each other in disbelief.

"Doctors aren't required to tell patients where any of the tissue comes from," Dr. Grimley said.

"What else is he missing?" Tom asked.

"Along with the bones in his legs and arms, the tendons, almost all the veins, cartilage, and scalp patches. The heart valves are gone, as well. This body was almost completely stripped of any tissue that could be reused," Dr. Grimley said.

"They didn't do a very good job of it seeing as how it looks so damaged," Harri said.

"Harvested cadavers aren't treated with respect. At all. They sometimes use hammers to get bones out. A body is nothing more than a way to make a profit."

"How much do you know about this? Have you seen this kind of thing before?" Tom asked.

"You'd think so in this city, but no," Dr. Grimley shook her head. "I went to a conference in Seattle a few years ago. There was an interesting case about a mortician who'd been caught stripping the bodies and salvaging tissue from the people he was supposed to be burying. The law enforcement officer gave a detailed presentation about how it all works. It was very eye-opening," she said.

"Is this industry regulated at all?" Harri asked.

"The industry regulates itself, which you know means there's really no guard on duty. Each tissue bank is registered with the FDA, but they don't really do much else. The FDA doesn't check up on them. There were some issues years back with drugs remaining active in the donated tissue. Some tissue was found to have come from people with toxic cancer medication or recreational drugs in the samples. Supposedly there was some tightening of the regulations. But…"

"But?" Harri asked.

"It's really an unregulated industry worth billions."

"Billions? Who are the main clients?" Harri asked.

"Plastic surgeons mostly. We all know how well they're doing," Dr. Grimley said.

"Have any other bodies turned up at the morgue like this?" Tom asked. His color had come back.

"I've checked and no. This is our first one. I'm surprised by that though," Dr. Grimley said.

"Why surprised?" Harri asked.

"Whoever did this knew what they were after, so where did they learn it? How did they learn it? It's not something just anyone can figure out how to do. This couldn't have been their first harvest. Where are the other bodies?"

"Could they have been cadavers from a mortuary like the other case?" Tom asked.

"Could be. But it would be risky. The case I was telling you about from the conference, the mortician used PVC pipe to replace bones so the families wouldn't notice, otherwise the body would look deflated, like our guy here."

"But someone did notice?" Harri asked. She couldn't imagine the horror the family must have felt to discover their loved one's body had been desecrated like this.

"Exactly. And since there's precedent, I'd imagine a mortician wouldn't want to take that kind of chance."

"We'll look up that case," Harri said.

"He most likely didn't suffer then?" Tom asked. He shook his head in disbelief. "How much is this tissue worth?"

"A single body can garner over one hundred grand for the tissue. Now, supposedly this is a non-profit industry and no one is supposed to make money from the tissue. But as always, people figure out some sort of kick-back scheme," Dr. Grimley added.

"Any chance for foreign DNA?" Harri asked.

"The guy was washed. They must have prepped the skin in some way. Then the river cleaned up the rest of him. I did swab all crevices. We'll see what comes back. He was pretty tightly wrapped."

"And the plastic and the duct tape?" Tom asked.

"All went to the SID forensics unit. You'll be getting a call from them," she said.

Harri stared at the body trying to process all that Dr. Grimley told them. Their case had turned on a dime with this news. She imagined she'd be learning everything there was to know about tissue donation and inwardly shuddered.

"And then we have the limbs. Another weird case," Dr. Grimley said as she turned to the table behind them, draped with a white sheet.

"Are the limbs harvested, too?" Harri asked.

Dr. Grimley took the sheet off the table and presented them with the three arms and a leg.

"No. Each of the arms and the leg have their bones intact. The skin doesn't show that it's been shaved. But whoever these limbs belong to was tortured. The brands were done while the victims were alive. I'm positive of that," Dr. Grimley said.

"The brands look like a crudely drawn owl, don't they?" Harri asked.

"I can see the owl, now that you mention it," Dr. Grimley said.

"There are so many brands on each one of these. That must have hurt like hell," Tom remarked.

"Definitely tortured," Dr. Grimley repeated again.

Harri and Tom glanced at each other again.

"So, two different cases then?" Tom said.

"You tell me," she said.

"Notice the bruising here and here," she said pointing at a purplish-blue splotch on each one of the wrists and the ankles of the legs. "These look like ligature marks to me. They were tight, too. I also took x-rays of each arm and the leg. The knee and each of the elbows have been dislocated. The wrists and ankle are dislocated, too."

"How would that kind of dislocation happen?" Harri asked.

"Your guess is as good as mine, but I will say they seem uniform, somehow. The dislocations are all similar, the angles of the stretching the same," Dr. Grimley said. "I cut open the joints and found snapped cartilage and ligaments. When I put the muscle fiber under the microscope it was completely stretched. No way would the victim be able to stand on that leg ever again."

Harri gulped down the bile that raced up her throat. She tried not to comprehend that level of torture, yet her mind was creating images she wanted no part of.

"How long have these limbs been in the water?" Tom asked. He was pale again.

"The level of decomposition on these two arms makes me think two weeks. This arm and leg," she pointed to the limbs to the right. "Are more recent. I'm thinking one week, tops."

"Were the victims alive when these were cut off?" Harri asked.

"They were already dead when the limbs were amputated. I've been attempting to figure out what method was used. Could have been a chainsaw by the rough edges but I'm going to need more time with that," Dr. Grimley said.

"How many victims were there?" Tom asked.

Harri noticed that each hand was missing some of its fingernails.

"I did a very quick analysis to see the sex. These limbs all belonged to women. Specifically, three women. She pointed to the leg and arm that were only a week old.

"These belonged to the same woman. Those two arms belonged to two different women. I sent the samples to the lab for testing, DNA, and a tox screen. The limbs show the same tool was used to dismember them. I've also taken all the relevant fingerprints," she said and sighed.

Dr. Grimley had been shaken by what she saw on the examining table, as well.

"The nails?" Harri asked, her voice cracking.

"They were removed while the victims were alive. I've never seen this level of torture before," Dr. Grimley said.

"The modus operandi changed if this was the same killer as the one who did Atkinson. And the motives look totally different," Tom said.

"And the sex of the victims and the treatment in life, too," Harri added.

"Looks like we picked up two cases then," Tom said.

"How long for the results from the lab?" Harri asked Dr. Grimley.

Dr. Grimley was staring at the limbs and didn't hear her at first.

"Dr. Grimley?"

"Oh, yes. Sorry. What was the question?"

"How long for the labs?" Harri said.

"Days. I'm going to do some research on what could have created the conditions on those arms and leg. I feel like I've read about this kind of damage before, but I can't place where," Dr. Grimley said.

"We'll work on our John Doe," Tom said. "Any idea where to start with the tissue banks?"

"They have an association. Start there," Dr. Grimley said still deep in thought. "I'll email you the notes on the case with the mortician. Save you some time on that front. I wouldn't be surprised if you're dealing with people active in the death industry. I thought the vic's name was Jared Atkinson?" Dr. Grimley said. "Wasn't he positively ID'd?"

"He was but we can't find him anywhere in the system under that name. We're going under the assumption that it's not his birth name. He was last seen on Sunday afternoon," Harri said.

"That fits the time of death. I'd put it in the Sunday night to Monday morning window," Dr. Grimley said.

"You've given us a lot to work with," Tom said.

"It wasn't me. I was just reading what these remains are telling us. Those women, though." She abruptly fell silent.

Harri and Tom looked at the dismembered limbs of the three women. Harri was sure all of them would be having nightmares tonight.

They left Dr. Grimley to the macabre scene and went to the changing area to get back into their civilian clothes. Neither of them spoke, taking in everything they'd just seen and heard.

Harri made a mental note to change her organ donation status on her driver's license to not being a donor. A chill ran up her spine at how all of these victims had been killed. It was a terrifying way to go. Especially for those women. The level of violence apparent in their remains made her blood run cold. At times like this, her mind went to her sister and what she must have endured during that year in captivity. Pain blossomed in her chest, and she pressed her arm against it.

"You all right?" Tom asked.

They had reached the car. It was still a warm day, even though it was close to five o'clock, and yet Harri shivered. "No. Are you?"

"Not really. Those bodies. They were all defiled. Who could do that to a body of a human?" Tom asked, his voice dropping.

"At least Jared wasn't alive for what happened to him," Harri said.

"Those women…" Tom fell silent again.

"I'm not ready to go back to the PAB," Harri said.

"Let's work this from home. I think I need a stiff drink and a change of scenery. I'll do some research on the tissue banks tonight. You finish up unpacking. The team should be done with canvassing sometime tonight. We can start piecing together Jared's movements and hopefully figure out who he really was."

"What about the branded limbs?" Harri asked.

"We need more information. Maybe we'll get a hit on the DNA or fingerprints. Or what could have caused so much damage? I'm not sure how else to proceed. With the river flowing the way it does, we can't even be sure where those limbs went in. It could have been anywhere upstream. And there is the brand. We can search around for what that symbol stands for."

"Thanks, Tom," Harri said.

"I'm sorry. It's going to be another weird one. A twofer this time. Those limbs. That's another serial."

"Should we call in the FBI for a profile?" Harri asked.

"Can't. We don't even know what we have yet. But I'll run it up the chain. Maybe we can get Mitzi sent out here again."

"We could ask Jake for a profile," Harri suggested.

"You know we can't afford him. Consultants cost way above what we have budgeted. The feds are free."

"True enough," Harri said.

She shivered again. She'd be happy to be home.

4

DAY 1 - NIGHT

Harri found Jake Tepesky in the middle of a sea of boxes in their new living room, sipping a glass of red wine. Jake had been her older sister's best friend in high school. They had reconnected on the Creek Killer case and he'd gone with her up to Oregon where they found her sister's remains. They'd been successful in bringing her sister home for burial and had been together ever since.

Her commute took her close to an hour and a half from downtown Los Angeles to their new neighborhood of Brentwood. Her mind looped through the information Dr. Grimley had given them. By the time she pulled into their drive, she was nauseous and afraid.

Jake took one look at her face as she walked in and knew something was wrong.

"Was it really that bad of a commute?" he teased, trying to lighten her mood. They had gone back and forth on whether it was wise to buy a home so far away from downtown. The Hollywood Hills would have been closer.

"I wish it was that," she said.

She dropped her computer case and bag down next to the couch and leaned over to kiss him.

"That Hollywood house sure looked good to me as I was inching along on the I-10," she said, attempting to cover her fear. Jake wanted her to take a leave of absence after her last case, but she'd received the go-ahead to return to work from the police psychologist. She had just been transferred into RHD, too. Harri knew she had to prove to everyone she'd earned her place there. She also had to prove it to herself.

She gestured to the glass of wine.

"Is there another one of those for me?" she asked.

"Of course," he said. He put his glass down and got up from the couch.

"I wasn't suggesting that you should go get it for me," she said although she was grateful that he had.

"You sit back and try to relax," Jake said.

She sank deep into the couch and took a look at the view outside. They had situated the couch right in front of the French doors looking out onto a beautifully manicured garden. They'd discussed how they hoped the tranquil view could help reset their moods once they got home from work.

Harri breathed in deeply like the psychologist had taught her, but she wasn't sure if it was helping any. The garden wasn't lifting the cold fear snaking along her spine.

She closed her eyes and focused on the sounds of Jake getting a glass out of a box and uncorking the bottle of wine. It didn't take him long to come back with a full glass.

"You sure you still want this? Want to hit the bed instead?"

Her eyes drifted open.

"We still have a lot of unpacking to do," she said. "Doesn't look like you've done so much."

She saw that he had his laptop open to the sound program again.

"Were you able to get any work done today?" she asked.

Jake Tepesky was a former FBI agent that had been with the Behavioral Science Unit. He'd been a profiler there for close to fifteen years and was now retired. He was in private practice and worked with different agencies and jurisdictions to help them solve unique and unusual cases. It wasn't much different than what he had done with the FBI but he was paid a lot better and he could choose what he wanted to work on or not.

His business had been bustling until they'd received the package with the memory stick inside.

The plain manila envelope had arrived the same day that Harri had closed her last big case. She hadn't slept in days and Jake had picked her up at the hospital where she was interviewing the survivors.

Instead of going to sleep, Harri had decided to listen to the sound file on the memory stick. It had changed everything. In the ensuing months, the envelope and its contents had been run through the FBI's labs for any evidence, DNA or otherwise, that could give them a clue as to who'd sent it. Both the envelope and the memory stick were clean.

Harri and Jake both knew it was from Jerome Wexler, the man they'd hunted ever since they discovered the graves on an island in Oregon. The island is where Harri and Jake had discovered Harri's sister, Lauren Harper's remains along with other victims.

Jerome Wexler's knowledge of their home addresses

prompted them to look for a new home the very next day. Within weeks, they found a beautiful home in Brentwood.

Harri had received a sizeable inheritance when her mother died. Her father still lived in a memory care facility, lost to dementia. His own trust covered all those expenses. Jake had done very well for himself so the combined funds from the sale of both their homes were more than enough to get them into their new place in Brentwood.

Neither of them wanted to retire yet, even though their financial planner insisted they could. Instead, they bought a gorgeous home in a fancy neighborhood of Los Angeles. One of the major selling points was the excellent security around the private community due to the celebrities and high net worth people that lived around them.

No one would get through the gates. Many of the security staff were ex-LAPD and all their neighbors had cameras all over their properties. After Harri had been attacked, she hesitated to leave her own home. She and Jake decided the extra cost was well worth the security. As a former FBI agent, Jake's personal information was scrubbed from the Internet and they still weren't sure how it had been uncovered.

"Find anything?" she asked as she sipped the wine.

"Let's talk about you first," he said. "If your mood isn't because of the commute, then what's up?"

"This new case is a weird one. Actually, two cases. A body and a bunch of limbs washed up after the rainstorm last night. Looks like the body was harvested," she said.

"Harvested how?" he asked.

Harri was grateful to be dating someone in law

enforcement. Jake understood the cases and the horrors that Harri dealt with daily. He'd seen much worse than she had in her career as a detective.

"Tissue harvest," she said. "Ever heard of it?"

"Yes, but I don't know about it," he said. "I'm assuming it's not organ harvesting."

"No, it's bones, tendons, skin, and ligaments. A lot of things that are used in plastic surgeon's offices," she said. "Definitely makes me think twice about organ donation."

"The body was that bad?" he asked.

"It was brutalized," she said.

"Pre or postmortem?"

"Postmortem, thank goodness. Looks like he died pretty peacefully, all things considered. Aside from being murdered, of course," she said.

"And what about the arms and the legs?" he asked.

Harri shivered again. "That was gruesome. The women were tortured and branded. Ripped apart. I..." she stopped and drank the wine he'd poured for her.

"It's set off my PTSD, I think. Let's not talk about it before bed. Maybe we can talk about it tomorrow," she said.

Jake frowned in concern, but he knew better than to push her on it. "Want some dinner?"

"No. Tell me what you've discovered on the file?"

A team of FBI specialists worked on the different sounds on the recording at Quantico but Jake and Harri were analyzing it, as well. Especially Jake.

The memory stick had only one file on it. A sound file. There was no better way of describing it. The file started with footsteps and background noise of people talking. Doors swished open and closed. Car doors slammed. Silence and then a wind picking up and rushing by. Waves and seagulls could be heard in the distance. At the very end of the tapestry of sound, Harri's dead sister Lauren could be heard saying 'My name is Lauren Harper'.

Her voice coming through so many years was stark and frightening.

Then a whispered voice said, 'Come find me.'

The creep factor of the sound file was at a hundred. Hearing Lauren's voice and the pain behind it from twenty years ago had slipped into Harri's dreams at night. There hadn't been many nights since hearing them that she had a reprieve from those five words.

"You look like you've figured something out," she said. She felt the excitement coming off him.

They had listened to that recording for a month and became convinced the first part most likely had happened at an airport. Then they started narrowing down what airports were close to places that had seagulls around the world. Jake had taken it on himself to figure out times between airports and the actual shoreline to see if it matched the amount of time that was on the sound recording.

"I've narrowed it down to Los Angeles Airport," he said.

Harri cocked an eyebrow at him. "Seriously?" she asked.

"I'm almost positive. The time matches more closely to that than the airport in San Francisco."

Jake had flown up to San Francisco the week before to see if he could record the disembarking and getting down to the escalators and into a car.

He was disappointed to find out that it did not match up. Harri knew he'd been planning to do the same thing at Los Angeles Airport, but with all the packing and moving that had taken up their time in the last week, he hadn't had a chance to go do it.

"Did you go down there today?" she asked.

"Yes, and it's a match."

Excitement crowded out Harri's fear. This was the first major break they'd had in three months. They had assumed the sound recording could have been done anywhere in the world and it had taken them months to go through each one of the airports along with their regular job duties.

"Jerome Wexler's here in Los Angeles?" Harri said with a catch in her voice.

"He can't get to us here," Jake reassured her.

The attack she'd survived last fall had done a number on Harri and she was seeing a therapist weekly to work through the PTSD. Harri had never been afraid of anything and now it seemed like she was afraid of everything which was a terrible place to be for a cop.

"Have you told anyone yet?" she asked.

"No. I have a call into Mitzi though," he said.

Mitzi had been one of his colleagues at the BSU and was still a profiler who flew around the country helping out various law enforcement agencies. She was also their point person on the sound file and was helping them track down Jerome Wexler.

"Are you hungry or do you want to do some more unpacking?" Jake asked.

"Let's do some unpacking," Harri sighed.

Jake groaned but nodded.

"We should hire somebody to do this for us," he said.

"Seriously?" Harri asked and Jake smiled.

Harri was glad he hadn't played the sound file again to show her how he had uncovered it was recorded at LAX.

She needed a mental break from searching for Jerome Wexler. They would find him. She was sure of it. But she also needed time to recover. Her voice had finally gotten back to normal just two months ago.

And she kept dreaming she was being strangled. But she didn't tell Jake about those nightmares. She didn't want him to worry any more than he already was. What good would it do anyway? He couldn't help her with that, and it would just stress him out even more. It was something to talk to the therapist about. Now she would also mention the fear that she'd experienced at the coroner's office when she'd heard about the torture those women endured. She didn't think her emotions made her a bad cop. They meant she was human and made her want to catch the bastards that did evil things to other human beings. It gave her drive and focus. Having emotions couldn't be a bad thing.

"Sure, you don't want to talk about it?" Jake asked.

"Let's unpack some boxes first," she said. She had a suspicion her days would only get longer from here on out.

5

DAY 1 - WHITEY

I checked my watch again. My heart was beating hard in my chest when I realized I was way later than I should be. I was on one of the streets north of Los Feliz Boulevard in the Franklin Hills.

It was the day before garbage day and all of the fancy people that lived in this neighborhood had put out the garbage and recycling. I could make a good twenty dollars on collecting cans if I got here early enough.

I hadn't slept well the night before. Thinking of what Jared must've gone through had kept me listening to all of the sounds around me. Matty and Junior got into another argument last night and both of them sounded trashed. I could hear Rufus trying to referee somehow but it didn't work out very well for him. At some point in the night, punches were thrown.

I heard crying and swearing and pushing, and I was happy my tent was completely zipped up. I hated the nights. Being homeless in Los Angeles was both hard and way easier than in other parts of the country.

I'd grown up in Northern California outside of San

Francisco and it was cold and damp there. All of your stuff always smelled like wet air. A lot of people said the climate was mild but cold at night. The kind of cold that got into your bones.

I opened up another recycling bin and picked through the plastic with bare hands. I had an okay haul, but it had taken me hours going up and down the hilly streets because I'd gotten there past two o'clock and some of the other scrappers had already been here before me.

It was slim pickings, but I had to cover so much more ground. I was getting dangerously close to arriving back at my tent as it was getting dark. Right as my neighbors were starting to party and things got dangerous for single gals like me. I didn't have Jared anymore to protect me. He was dead.

Tears sprang into my eyes as I remembered our dinners. We ate together at least five nights a week. The other nights he was in AA meetings.

Jared reminded me of my brother, Larry. He died six years ago from his opioid addiction. It started back in high school when OxyContin was flowing into everybody's medicine cabinets. Both me and my brother had lost our parents and lived with our grandfather in a suburb right outside of Silicon Valley.

The wealth growing around us over the years was incredible. My grandfather had lived there since the fifties, back when the neighborhood was way more working-class. That's what we were still. Definitely working class and just barely keeping up with everyone else at school.

Grandpa had a bad back and, like everybody else, Larry started sneaking his OxyContin. All the kids in our high school were raiding their parent's medicine cabinets for party favors and it didn't take too many pills for Larry to get hooked.

Grandpa threw him out of the house. I didn't begrudge him. He was right. Larry was stealing from him. He needed a lot more Oxy than Grandpa ever had. Heroin was much cheaper, and it wasn't long before he was shooting up. I did whatever I could to get him clean. Get him housing. Nothing worked. I didn't know what to else to do. And then Larry overdosed, and my grandpa died, and I was left all alone again.

Grandpa had mortgaged the house to the limit to pay for all his medical bills. As soon as he was gone, so was my home. I tried to keep my life on track, but I fell, too. Just as hard as Larry had. Picking up the bottle was easy after all of that and the other drugs came easier. At least I wasn't shooting up, I'd tell myself while snorting meth.

How stupid I was. I stopped drinking, though, and all the hard drugs. I did the program and it worked. It was too late to find housing by that time. I stayed on the streets hoping one day my luck would change. And it had when I met Jared. I had a friend again. We were keeping ourselves sober. We looked out for each other. And now he was dead. And it was my fault. I shouldn't have come at him so hard that weekend. What if I made him stay away from the safety of our camp? What if he'd been drinking and got himself in trouble? He was new to the streets. I could tell. We needed each other, and I'd failed him.

I was so dumb. I hoisted my garbage bag over my shoulder and the few cans clattered inside. I looked around to see if I'd disturbed any neighbors and that's when I saw the sedan.

I moved to the next recycling bin and watched the car out of the corner of my eye. It was black and it pulled into a parking spot at the top of the street. I could almost make out the figure of a man inside.

The street I was on was quiet and didn't have many cars parked at the curb since every house had a long driveway. I glanced to see if it was a cop car but it didn't look like it. I could only make out the man in the driver's seat. I didn't see anyone in the passenger seat.

I closed the bin and moved to the next one. I checked my time again. It was now 4:15. By the time I dragged my load back to camp it was going to be close to 5:30.

My haul was not going to net me more than seven to ten dollars. It had been a crap day. I started down the street and the hairs on the back of my neck prickled.

I was being watched.

I turned to look behind me and saw the dark sedan pull out of its spot. It cruised at a slow pace down toward me. I speed-walked toward Los Feliz Boulevard.

If I took a left turn onto Los Feliz, he wouldn't be able to follow me. It was a busy street and he'd have a hard time making a left turn. He wouldn't be able to track me, and I could dip back into the neighborhood and go the back way toward Griffith Park.

I looked behind me again.

The car was edging closer. It was maybe sixty feet away and it wouldn't take much to pull up alongside me. If that happened, I was a goner. I was sure of that.

I heaved up my bag of cans and raced down the rest of the street toward the Boulevard. The bag hit me on the back and the cans clanged in my ears.

My breath came out and gasps.

I put what little energy I had left from a long day of wandering the streets to get to safety.

The car came at me.

I felt him behind me.

I sprinted the last ten feet.

I turned the corner and ran down to the middle of the block.

The black sedan stayed on the street I'd come from, idling at the stop sign.

I saw the man looking at me.

Even from this distance, I saw his eyes and shivered. I'd had something similar happen to me before but now, I was more afraid than at any other time of my life.

Jared's body and those limbs and the disappearances at the camp had put me over the edge.

I have to move, I thought.

But the very idea of packing up my tent and all my meager belongings and finding such a good space as where I was now exhausted me. Most homeless were hassled by the police or driven out of neighborhoods by the people who got to live in actual homes. They didn't want to see us on the street. It was a reminder that they could be us if all their luck ran out.

I didn't have it in me. Especially now that Jared was gone.

I knew I was depressed and most likely in shock. I'd been here before and I had to be extra careful not to fall back into my old habits.

I had to find a way to get off the streets.

I'd heard that there was a housing project opening up on Riverside Drive for the homeless. They were talking about doing trailers, but the waitlist was super long. Maybe I could talk to someone down there and at least get myself on the list.

Those thoughts jumbled through my head as I dragged my bag of cans down Los Feliz Boulevard towards the river.

I couldn't see the black sedan anymore which was

calming my nerves somewhat. I wasn't happy to see the sun going down and by the time I reached my tent, it was dark.

I hadn't seen the sedan follow me, but so many cars streamed up and down that busy road if he'd passed me I wouldn't have noticed. The busy road felt safe.

I hid my cans in my tent and went looking for Donnie. He had mentioned he'd been followed by a car recently. It was early enough that he might not be blotto yet. I needed someone to acknowledge that it happened to them, too. I didn't want to be a lone target.

He wasn't at his tent. I heard a zip to my right and Matty poked his head out.

"Fancy seeing you out at night," he said.

"I was looking for Donnie," I said.

"Haven't seen him all day," he said.

"When was the last time you did see him?" I asked.

"Late last night," Matty said. "Can't be sure, though. I was pretty wasted by then."

I nodded and started backing up towards my tent.

"Want to party?" he asked.

I shook my head and got out of there before my cravings made it too hard for me to say no.

I zipped up the tent behind me and flopped down on my sleeping bag. I wondered if Donnie would be the next one to disappear. What if the man in the dark sedan had come to get him?

I could've told Matty about what happened but I could see that gleam in his eyes. His day was just beginning, and I didn't want any part of that. I turned on my flashlight and grabbed Jared's notebook to read. Maybe there was something in there that could give me some insight into what happened to him. I could maybe help the police and then they would have to help me. If I helped them, then that nice lady detective would have to help me get off the streets. Away from men following me in dark cars. Jared was looking into something and he must have found something bad. Something that got him killed.

I wasn't gonna be next.

6

DAY 2 – MARCH 7, 2019 - MORNING

Harri groaned as she took the elevator up to the eighth floor of the PAB building. She and Jake stayed up unpacking boxes until close to two in the morning while listening to the recording from Jerome Wexler on repeat over and over again.

It was hard to hear her sister's voice at the end, but each time they were able to pick out sounds here and there that Jake would jot down as something to research. And they had the entire kitchen finally unpacked and put away.

Her shift started at seven in the morning. She had two shots of espresso in her body already and was still exhausted. The good news was that now she had to leave her house so early to make it to work on time that she didn't hit too much traffic.

When she entered the RHD bullpen she saw Tom already at his desk, frowning at his computer screen.

"Little bit early to be looking like that," Harri said.

He turned to her with a scowl.

"You will never believe the email I just got," he said.

"Shock me," Harri said.

"The reason we couldn't find anything under Atkinson was that he does not exist. He was an undercover cop named Ethan Carle."

"Undercover?" she asked.

"He was with the gang units apparently and his handler is already on his way over to talk," he said.

"We could use conference room one. It was open when I walked by," Harri said.

"Detective Tom Bards," a voice said from behind Harri.

They both turned to see an Asian man in plain clothes standing in the doorway. He looked familiar to Harri.

"My name is Detective Charlie Hwang. I was Detective Ethan Carle's partner," he said.

"I was just telling my partner here that," Tom said.

Tom introduced Harri and led them all to the open conference room.

Tom and Harri sat down. Detective Hwang pulled a chair to the end of the table instead of sitting opposite them. Detective Hwang opened the manila folder in front of him.

"We made sure his ID was flagged in the system, so I was alerted immediately that you were searching for him. I hadn't realized his body had been recovered at first." He shook his head in disgust.

"You're both with the gang unit, right?" Harri asked.

"That's correct. With the new laws protecting our unhoused communities, the gangs have taken the opportunity to move into some of these encampments. They know we can't go in without a search warrant."

"I still can't believe that was made into law," Tom said.

"I'm in full agreement on the ridiculous place we've

been put in. It's all part of the new law put in place in the last election. We have the La Mirada Locos "LML" gang and the White Fence "WF" gangs battling it out over in the Northeast part of LA. They've taken over several of the encampments and are running drugs, guns, and sex workers out of the tents and RVs all over that part of the city."

"And Detective Carle was undercover trying to figure out exactly what?" Harri asked.

"We have information that one of the top lieutenants in LML had been smuggled across the border and was traveling through the different outposts to see how all of the various enterprises they had their hands on were going. He's remained hidden and Ethan suggested he could be using the encampments as a way to move around the city undetected. Ethan investigated at least three encampments in the last three weeks going from Skid Row to the LA River camps looking for any sign of him."

"Could he have been taken out by a gang then?" Harri asked.

"Maybe, but not likely. I read the coroner's report and saw his body had been harvested for tissue," he said. "Gangs don't play that kind of game."

"Never heard of gangs scamming like that?" Tom asked.

"I know some of the cartels have played around with stolen organs, but I've never heard anything about tissue," Detective Hwang said.

"We hadn't even heard of tissue donation," Harri admitted.

"Just because I haven't seen it doesn't mean they aren't doing it. Especially if there's money in it," Detective Hwang said.

"There's money in it. A body is worth about 100k in ligaments, bones, and skin. Other pieces too," Tom said and made a face.

Detective Hwang pursed his lips again. "They get rid of an undercover cop and also make money on his body," he said. "I could see the cartels being interested in that."

"When was the last time you talked to Detective Carle?" Harri asked.

"Part of his cover was that he was a recovering alcoholic. We used his AA meetings as a way to connect so he could keep me updated. I saw him last Sunday near the church on Kingswell and Commonwealth," Detective Hwang said.

"And how did he seem to you?" Harri asked.

"Off. He was jittery, excited. We'd finished background on all the players he'd given us and saw no sign of the lieutenant or his close associates. I wanted to bring him in but he wanted more time. Said he was working on something new and needed to stay out in the field," Detective Hwang said.

"Something different?" Harri asked, surprised.

"Carle said it was even bigger than the cartel guy. He told me he'd heard through the grapevine the cartel guy was already out of the country. He wouldn't go further into it though," Detective Hwang said.

A look crossed his face that made Harri pause. She got the distinct impression he wasn't telling them something.

"Did he mention anything about tissue donation? Could that have been what he was investigating?" Harri asked.

"He said it was early days. Wouldn't say anything

more. We were interrupted and he took off. That was the last I saw of him," Detective Hwang said.

He pursed his lips and let out a breath.

"Had you been partners long?" Tom asked.

"Four years," Detective Hwang said. "I should have pushed him harder to tell me what was going on."

"Did he give you any idea at all?" Tom asked.

"No. He said he was still piecing it all together," Detective Hwang said.

"And it had to do with the homeless community?" Harri asked.

Detective Hwang sighed heavily. "I just told you. He wouldn't talk about it. AT ALL." His eyes met Harri's.

Harri waited.

He wanted to tell them something. He dragged his eyes to Tom.

The room fell silent for a beat.

Tom acknowledged his discomfort. "It's not your fault. Partners get into disagreements all the time."

"He was killed after that meeting. If I'd pushed him harder for information, maybe he'd still be alive. Or at least we'd have some idea what he'd gotten himself into. He demanded I give him another week. Cover for him. Again," he said.

"Cover for him? Is that what the fight was about?" Tom asked.

"What makes you think we fought?"

"You didn't want to tell us about it," Tom said.

"It was more of a disagreement than anything else," Detective Hwang said.

"It's still not your fault," Tom said.

"Right, whatever," Detective Hwang grumbled.

"What did he ask you to cover for him?" Harri asked.

"That the lieutenant had probably fled the country

again. Carle wanted another week to investigate whatever he'd uncovered. He said it was so unbelievable he just needed another week to make sure he could convince our superiors."

"Why did you argue?"

"I wanted to know what he was working on, obviously. We were supposed to be partners. But he wouldn't tell me."

"Had he done that before?" Harri asked.

"You mean be a lone wolf?" Detective Hwang said. "It was a thing with him."

"And you didn't like that," Harri said.

"What partner does? I needed to know what I was sticking my neck out for. He promised me it was huge if he was right and I'd be the first to know."

"He didn't tell you anything else?" Harri asked.

"Just that he was meeting with someone and it would be the proof he needed to bring the case in," Detective Hwang said. "He wanted out of the gang unit. He probably thought this was his ticket. He'd wanted to be here, with you."

"What does that mean?" Tom asked.

"He wanted to get into RHD. He'd been looking into a transfer, but it looked all but impossible. I think he thought if he found a case it would be his way in. It had to be a case you all would take on."

"Did he tell you that?" Harri asked.

"Not in so many words," Detective Hwang said. "But he was interested in your kind of cases. He was done with the gangs."

"Did that piss you off?" Tom asked.

Detective Hwang shrugged. "I'm fine with the gangs. I just didn't like being kept in the dark. Especially if I was putting my ass on the line by not alerting our team that the cartel lieutenant had probably left the country. Which was the whole point of the operation. If Carle had said something, he might still be alive," Detective Hwang said. "I could have helped him. He made a stupid decision. Now he's dead."

"Any idea who he was meeting?" Harri asked.

Detective Hwang turned to her, disbelief crossing his face.

"I had to ask," Harri defended herself and decided to change the subject. "Do you have his home address?"

"He was in between apartments," he said. "That's why he volunteered for this assignment. He said he was in the right headspace to go homeless." Detective Hwang grimaced with that memory.

"Did Detective Carle have any family?" Harri asked.

"No. His parents are dead and he was an only child. No girlfriend or wife that I know of," Detective Hwang said.

"How long had he been in the gang unit?" Tom interjected.

Harri knew they could find that info through records but sometimes partners let more nuanced details slip.

"About seven years," Detective Hwang said, his fingers gripping the edge of the manila folder. His shoulders slumped in the memory. "He was a watcher. He knew everything that was going on in those encampments. He was an amazing detective. A real chameleon. I can't believe he's gone. You guys need anything else, I'm here to help you out."

"Did he give any indication of where he was headed to? Was he going back to his tent in the river encampment?"

Detective Hwang leaned back in his seat. After a moment, he shook his head no. "I left him standing in front of the church. I was pissed. The last thing I said to him was that he had until Wednesday. He said he'd call me sooner. That was it."

"What camp was he at before the one on the river?" Harri asked.

"The one at Sunset Boulevard and Vermont. That one is completely taken over by LML so I wouldn't go there alone. The actual homeless have been displaced into the side streets around there."

"Isn't that near a red line metro station?" Harri asked.

"Exactly. It's a total mess down there," he said.

"And the encampment before that?" Harri asked.

"McArthur Park. You can't miss it," Detective Hwang said.

"Is that one taken over by a gang, too?" Tom asked.

"It's mixed," Detective Hwang said. He looked at both of them to make his next point. "This thing he was chasing, it wasn't gang-related. He wouldn't do that to me. He would have told me if it was. It was something else. He wanted out of gangs, and this was going to be his ticket. I saw that gleam in his eye. I'd seen it before."

"Really? When?" Tom asked.

"A triple murder out in Highland Park. We were called in because it was at a known gang member's residence. Turned out to be unrelated and Carle was pissed when the case was transferred to RHD."

"Was that the Rondaleo case?" Harri asked.

She remembered that case. Two women in their early twenties were found shot in a small home. Another woman was found dead in a closet. It turned out to be a neighbor dispute.

"He wanted to investigate that case?" Harri asked.

"Yeah. He was pissed when it got pulled," Detective Hwang said.

"Was he a note-taker?" Harri asked.

"Absolutely. He carried his little black notebook everywhere. He'd had a mentor in Hollywood Division. A detective. He was teaching Carle how to work through the murder book. Old-school," he said.

"What's the detective's name?" Harri asked.

"Fernando Marcinello," Detective Hwang said.

Harri hadn't crossed paths with him.

"What about a bolt hole? Did he have one? In case he wanted to shower, clean up?" Tom asked.

"That's not how undercover works. At least, not for him. He was as authentic as possible," Detective Hwang said.

"Is there anything else you can tell us?" Tom asked.

"That's all I have," Detective Hwang said with a catch in his voice.

Harri knew he'd be blaming himself for the rest of his career. There was no way they would be able to alleviate his pain.

"Thank you for giving us what you did, Detective Hwang," Harri said.

Detective Hwang nodded, closed the manila folder, and walked out.

Tom and Harri stayed behind in the conference room.

"He's going to be thinking about that last encounter for a long time," Harri said after a good minute of silence.

"I don't know if I would have covered for a partner like that. But then I've never done undercover work, have you?"

Harri shook her head no.

"Our vic was a cop. Brings a whole new dimension to this case," Harri said. "The question now is was he killed because he was a cop."

"If he was angling for a case to get himself into RHD, then I'm guessing murder."

"The arms and leg then? The level of torture on those limbs indicates it would make that an RHD case," Harri said.

"But why would they be found with his body? Was it accidental because of the river flow from the storm?" Tom asked.

"Do we look into the gang angle?" Harri asked.

Tom nodded. "We should cover all our bases, but I'm thinking no. Detective Carle's request to his partner tells me it wasn't gang-related."

"Unless the gangs are getting into the tissue donation hustle?" Harri interjected.

"I'll make some calls about that," Tom said.

"It's those branded limbs Detective Carle was following. I don't believe in coincidences," Harri said. "He must have uncovered whatever it is while he was in the camp."

"I don't believe in coincidences either," Tom said.

"One way to find out. We should talk to Darlene again. We need to talk to anyone in that camp Detective Carle may have questioned," Harri said.

"Give me thirty minutes to make some calls. If we're going to the Vermont Sunset camp, I want backup," Tom said.

"I'll get coffee. Meet you downstairs," Harri said.

Tom left her in the conference room. Harri wasn't sure if she needed coffee. Her heart raced as the investigation twisted ahead of them.

The hunt had begun.

Nervous energy activated every part of her.

Their vic had uncovered something big and it probably got him killed. Which direction would it go? So far, they'd uncovered connections to gangs, undercover cops, tissue donation, and torture.

She agreed with Tom that the gang angle didn't make much sense in light of what Detective Hwang had told them. Harri guessed Ethan Carle's secret investigation had something to do with the limbs that washed near his body. The limbs all belonged to women. She couldn't imagine the pain and terror they must have endured in having their joints ripped apart.

If the two crimes were connected, then it must be centered at the homeless camps. That's where they would find the answers. Like Ethan Carle had.

Could he have given his notebook to Darlene to keep safe? Did he know he was walking into danger? Or had a trap been set for him?

7

DAY 2 - MORNING

S outhern California shimmered in the early morning sun beneath a bright blue sky. The Los Angeles River sparkled in the sunlight and the trees swayed gently in the light breeze. It was beautiful until the makeshift dwellings, tents, and garbage came into view.

Harri and Tom stepped through the chain-link fence to the right of the camp. The encampment extended under Los Feliz Boulevard and down the other side of the bike path. Harri looked around and frowned.

The police canvas from the day before listed thirty-two tents but now it looked like there were maybe fourteen total. The unhoused didn't want to deal with any police, apparently.

"This place emptied out fast," Harri remarked.

"I was afraid that would happen," Tom said. He wiped at his nose with a look of disgust.

Various food smells, sweat, cigarette smoke, and coffee mingled with the smell of urine, feces, and propane gas. It was quite the cocktail.

Harri looked down at the list of twenty-seven names she'd taken from the officers' canvas earlier. Most of the people were gone already.

"Should we start finding out who's left?" Harri asked as she frowned at the list.

After the initial sweep, they'd listed five people they'd be able to re-interview. Besides Darlene, there was Donnie Osgood, Matthew Raintree, a Rufus Dexter, and a Mark Johnson Junior.

Each of the names had their nicknames written by it: Donnie, Matty, Rufus, and Junior.

"Should we go down the line?" Harri asked.

"Let's start with this one," Tom said and pointed to the first ragged tent. It looked like it was just a small gust of wind away from blowing over.

"Knock, knock," Tom called out. "Good morning! LAPD. Rise and shine."

"We're ready for you, Matty," Harri said as she started to unzip the tent from the bottom. They could hear protestations coming from inside.

"Hey, start with someone else," a man's voice said. "I'm trying to sleep over here."

"C'mon Matty. It'll be over soon," Harri said in her sweetest voice.

"What are your names again?" Matty said from somewhere inside the tent.

"Detective Tom Bards and Detective Harri Harper," Harri said.

They heard movement from inside, but Matty didn't appear. His voice came through the thin fabric.

"Like I said before, I don't know nuthin'. I told them other cops already."

The strong stench of alcohol wafted out of the tent's opening.

"We only have a couple of questions," Harri said. "If you want us gone, just answer."

"Oh, is that all?" Matty grumbled.

A grizzled man with a gray beard and salt-and-pepper brown hair stuck his head out of the tent. His face was puffy and red, and his nose had the broken capillaries of a heavy drinker. He looked close to sixty but Harri knew his DMV license listed him as only fifty-one.

"What do you want to know?" Matty demanded.

"We're trying to piece together Jared's movements on Saturday and Sunday. Did you see him either day?"

"I saw him on both days. He was all in a rush on Sunday. Almost knocked me over," Matty said.

"Did you talk to him on Sunday?" Harri asked.

"Not on Sunday. Not after he almost knocked me down. I told him if he did it again, I'd have to kick his ass and he just runned off. On Saturday I did."

"What was the conversation about?" Tom asked.

"The weather, if you must know. We were all worried about the talk of rain. We talked tarps."

"Tarps?" Harri asked.

"Tarps. We were trying to figure out how to keep our mattresses dry. It rained for two whole days. My stuff is still wet," Matty said.

"Did Jared mention what he was going to do about the rain?" Harri asked.

"He didn't even care. Said he loved a rainy night. Damn fool probably never been out here when it's rained."

"Where is out here? Near the river?" Tom asked.

"Out here is outside. LA is great because it doesn't rain. But when it does, this city turns into a right vengeful bitch," Matty said and sighed.

"What time of day was this?" Harri asked.

Matty scratched himself. "I don't know. Early? Before lunch definitely. I'd only just woke up and was going for a leak."

"Did he mention where he was going that day?" Tom asked.

"No," Matty said. His face twisted in intense concentration. "You know what? He told me he was looking for work, but I don't think that was the weekend. Maybe Friday," he said and let out a loud belch.

Harri closed her eyes and worked hard not to gag in front of him.

"What kind of work?" Tom asked. He was taking the smell way better than she was.

"Day work. The only kind available to us," he said.

"Did you and Jared talk often?" Harri asked.

Matty shrugged. "Nah. Always asking too many questions. He was always with Darlene. Go ask her."

Harri nodded. "Oh, we will. Did you notice what kind of questions Jared asked?" Harri asked.

"Notice what? What you mean he asked questions? Course everybody asks questions. How else you supposed to have a conversation, right? How is your day? What you up to? Those are the kinds of questions you asking about?" Matty asked. "Cuz, yeah. He asked a lot of questions."

This guy has some attitude, Harri thought.

"Any questions that caught you off guard. That might have been more probing?" Tom asked.

"Probing?" Matty made a face.

"Did he ask about other people in your community?" Harri added.

"He was always asking about Darlene. Where she was? Had I seen her? Oh, and he asked about Big D and that other guy, Rich or whatever. Also, Marie's boyfriend, Arthur something," Matty said, finally sounding as if he was awake.

"Who's Big D?" Tom asked.

"He was a big guy that was at the end of the line." Matty motioned to the end of the row of tents. "He just got here and settled in. The next day he was gone."

"He didn't come back?"

Matty shook his head. "We never saw him again."

"Did he leave his belongings behind?" Harri asked. "How do you know he wasn't just out for the day?"

Matty frowned.

"People must come and go," Harri prompted.

"Nah, not like that. He was all excited about that tent so I can't see him leaving that behind. It was brand new." He nodded to himself.

"What happened to the tent?" Tom asked.

"Donnie took it over after a couple days because Big D was obviously not coming back."

"What happened to Big D's stuff?" Harri asked.

"You talk to Donnie about that. I had nothing to do with that. Anyway, Big D wasn't here long enough for me to know about his stuff."

Matty looked back and forth at them. "We done?"

"Almost," Harri said. "What about the other two you mentioned? Rich? Did he have a name?"

"That was his name. Rich something or other. Dunno his last name. And then there was Art. I know Marie from downtown. They was living behind Rodney. He disappeared too," Matty said.

For a drunk guy he was a fount of information, Harri thought.

Matty grunted and started to slink back into the tent.

"One last question, did Jared get into any fights that weekend? Anyone have a beef with him?" Tom asked.

Matty's eyes dropped to the ground.

"Nah, not that I saw."

He didn't sound convincing. Harri was sure he was lying. She snuck a peek at Tom. He'd noticed it, too. "You sure about that? You didn't get into it with him, did you?"

Matty looked up. He shook his head vigorously.

"We were all right, me and Jared."

"Have people been disappearing from the camp?" Harri asked.

"I don't know, man. People don't like the po-po showing up," Matty said. "Lots of folks left overnight. Knew you'd be back."

"Why'd you stay then?" Harri asked.

"Got too much stuff here," Matty said, nodding behind him.

"Were the disappearances concerning to anyone?" Tom asked.

"Concerning? Yeah, I guess maybe. Jared asked about people disappearing. But, I mean, come on. We're homeless. Everybody comes and goes and sits down and then leaves again. Probably why they call us the transient community," he said and cackled.

"Any women go missing recently?" Harri asked.

"I don't know nothing about no missing women. People come and go," Matty said. "Some people go to the hospital, some people go to the shelter, you know living out here isn't for everybody."

There is truth to that, Harri thought.

"What was Jared like when you saw him on Sunday?" Tom asked.

"Didn't talk to him on Sunday. He was rushing off to

somewhere. We talked a bit on Saturday about tarps. But he wasn't worried about the rain. He was all hopped up and excited. Thought he might be using again. Said he got some good news," Matty said.

"Did he tell you what the good news was?" Harri asked.

"I asked but he just shrugged and went on his merry way," Matty said.

"Where was he going?" Harri asked.

"Already said I do not know, Lady. Are we done? I really gotta take a leak."

"Yes. We're done," Tom said.

"Thank you so much, Matty," Harri said.

Matty grumbled and disappeared back into the tent, zipping it closed with a huff.

The two tents next to Matty's had no inhabitants inside. The fifth tent they checked was a bright red camping tent that had been reinforced with plywood on all sides to make it more of a standing hut. Sounds came from inside and Harri rapped hard on the makeshift door.

A younger-looking man came out. He was dressed in a dirty white shirt and jeans that were sliding down his skinny frame. His hair was buzzed short and Harri could see he was missing a few teeth when he smiled at them.

"Rufus Dexter?" Tom asked.

Harri had no idea how Tom matched the picture of the clean-cut young man in the DMV records they had to the gap-toothed man in front of them. She checked her notes. Rufus Dexter was listed as being 27. His DMV photo showed a blonde, blue-eyed guy smiling happily. The man standing before them looked like he was in his late 40s.

"We're here to ask you about Jared Atkinson," Harri stated.

"I heard you talking to Matty. I don't really have anything else to add except for he did go to the Riverside shelter that weekend. He told me how nice the trailers looked over there," Rufus said.

"Why don't you go to the trailers?" Harri asked.

"They got rules. Can't abide by rules," Rufus smiled.

Harri knew if he took housing from the city then he would be expected to submit to regular drug tests and staying clean while in counseling. Apparently, Rufus wasn't into being clean just yet.

"Did he ask you questions about Big D, Rich, and Art?" Tom asked.

"He didn't ask me those questions. But then I'm pretty new here, too. Only been living down by this river for about two weeks," Rufus said.

"And where were you living before?" Harri asked.

"Skid Row. The outer rim. Got a little bit too crazy for me there," Rufus said.

"Do you know of anyone that Jared Atkinson had beef with in the days leading up to his disappearance?" Tom asked.

"Now that you mention it," Rufus said dropping his voice down to a whisper. "Whitey. You know that woman named Darlene? Now, her and Jared were real close, but they fought that whole weekend. I overheard her saying she thought he was using again and went on and on about how bad that was. I couldn't hear what Jared said back to her but after that, he stomped out of her tent. Those two weren't doing so hot that weekend," Rufus said.

That's interesting, Harri thought. Why wouldn't

Matty want to tell them that Jared and Whitey were fighting that weekend?

"The fights were about him using? Was he a drug addict or alcoholic?" Tom asked.

"From what I understand they were both alcoholics," Rufus said. "Although I never saw either of them partying."

His eyes shifted to the right again. Harri had the distinct impression he was not telling them something.

"Is there anything else that happened during those fights?" Tom asked.

"Nah. It's not like they were at it constantly. Just little flares and then Jared would leave and she'd stay there fuming. I kept my distance when they were going at it because that girl has a gun for a tongue," Rufus said.

Harri noticed his eyes were glazing over a bit.

"When did you hear the first fight?" Tom asked.

"Uh, must've been Friday night. Couldn't find my dealer that night and had to go downtown again which is no fun," Rufus said.

"Did you hear what was said?" Harri asked.

"I heard Whitey asking him to talk to her. Then whatever Jared said, which I couldn't really hear, and then her yelling that he wasn't telling her everything," Rufus said.

"And then what happened?" Tom asked.

"Then there was a lot of whispering and after that, I heard the tent unzip and when I peeked my head out, Jared was stomping away back to his own tent."

"Did they get into it at all after that?" Harri asked.

"Yeah, the next morning. They always have their breakfast together super early. Used to. They used to always. I mean like I'd still be asleep and they'd wake me up with their talking. Anyway, that next morning I woke up to them raising their voices again, but I was too out of it to care what they were saying. Whitey yelled something and then I didn't really hear much again. She was looking for him all day after that," Rufus said.

"Did you see Jared again after that?" Tom asked.

Harri watched as the man's eyes went to the right again.

He had seen something, but he wasn't telling them.

"We're not here to twist you up. We're just trying to figure out what Jared was up to in the days leading up to his death," Harri prodded.

"I don't know nothing," Rufus said and Harri noticed sweat breaking out around his temple. He needed to get his fix. They weren't going to get anything else from him.

"Thanks, Rufus," Harri said.

He stumbled back inside his tent and Harri and Tom moved further down the lane away from the tents to speak without being overheard.

"Whitey didn't tell us about those fights," Harri whispered.

"No, she didn't. Neither did Matty and I wonder why," Tom said.

"Could he have been protecting Whitey?" Harri asked.

"That's a possibility," he said.

"Let's talk to her first and then go back to Matty and see if he'll confirm this story."

They struck out with Whitey. She was nowhere to be found and when they went to speak to Matty again, he'd already hit the bottle pretty hard in the time they were speaking with Rufus and was barely coherent. Harri tried the number Whitey had given them, but it was dead. Figures, she thought.

They decided to come back later in the afternoon and try again. They spoke to the other dwellers in the last remaining tents and were only able to get confirmation that there were no gangs in the small encampment.

The guy who'd taken over Big D's tent was nowhere to be seen. When Tom opened the tent, the stench was so strong Harri nearly vomited. All they'd managed to find out was that Jared was asking about three missing men who had disappeared in the last month. This had to be the case Jared was working on.

They walked back to the car discussing next steps.

"We need to figure out the names of Big D, and Rich. At least, we know that Art's girlfriend Marie lives behind Rodney and Hollywood. I think I know exactly where that encampment is," Tom said.

"Jared must have talked to her," Harri said.

"That's my thinking too," Tom said.

They got into the car and Harri felt the pull of the case. They were getting somewhere, and she didn't fight the rush of excitement in trying to figure out the puzzle. Three disappearances in a month were a lot, but these were also transient people who could be going in and out of hospitals, or shelters, or even leaving the city. Just because they disappeared and left their stuff behind didn't mean any harm had come to them.

"If Jared was looking for day work, that had to do with the case he was trying to suss out," Harri said.

Tom nodded thoughtfully.

"He didn't need the money and he was already convinced the cartel lieutenant had fled the country, so he had to have been following some lead there," Harri said.

Harri jotted her thoughts down in the notebook she

carried with her as Tom drove. She was happy they hadn't started the case of the branded limbs yet. That one wouldn't be as easy for her as this one. This one she had a handle on.

"I think you're onto something," he said.

"Me too," she said.

8

DAY 2 - AFTERNOON

Detective Harri Harper stepped out of the unmarked police cruiser a block away from Sunset Boulevard on Vermont Avenue. The block had manicured lawns in front of large, prewar apartment buildings. She was sure the rents for those apartments were high for the neighborhood.

"What's our plan if any of these people know Ethan Carle was really undercover as Jared Atkinson?" Harri asked.

"We'd need to pull them off the street immediately," Tom said. "The journos haven't caught wind our victim was an undercover detective. It would blow our investigation if anyone knew. What are you thinking?"

"I don't want to slip up. Every time I think of him now it's as Ethan Carle. No one out here knew him by that name. How about we agree to only use his cover name?" Harri asked.

"That's a solid concern. I agree. He worked too hard to blend into this community. We need to protect his real identity," Tom said.

Harri was happy he agreed with her. She felt grateful she was partnered with such an experienced detective who understood her and had her back.

"You said you know where this encampment is?" she asked, and Tom turned toward Sunset Boulevard.

"Follow me," he said.

The only sign of the encampment was garbage peeking out from the last apartment building. The block after the building was comprised of stores fronting Sunset Boulevard.

They walked over to the alley and the smell of urine assaulted their senses. Trash was piled all around the edges of the alleyway. Makeshift housing ran alongside the chain-link fence separating the alley from the apartment buildings on Vermont Avenue.

The dwellings were a mixture of tents, plywood huts, and cardboard homes. Numerous pieces of bikes were strewn around and she could see shopping carts near each one of the living units. She couldn't imagine how many unseen rats and cockroaches also made the camp their home.

She shuddered at the thought.

An elderly woman poked her head out of the nearest cardboard dwelling.

"You the cops? One of our neighborhood Karens call you again?" she asked with a huff. "We have a right to be here. Where are we supposed to go if you kick us out again?"

"We're not here to kick anyone out," Harri said calmly.

"We want to speak with a woman named Marie and her boyfriend Art," Tom said.

"What you want with her?" the woman asked.

Harri wanted to tell the woman it wasn't any of her business, but she didn't think that would help their cause. She noted the woman said 'her' and not 'them'. She could have information as to where Art had gone.

"What's your name?" Harri asked.

"Heather," the old woman said.

"And your last name?" Harri asked politely.

"Locklear."

Harri looked up at her. So, she was going to play that game.

"Oh, like the actress?"

"You have a problem with that?" Heather asked, glaring back at Harri.

"Not at all, Heather," Harri said. "Lovely name." She was trying to establish some rapport with the woman and could tell she was failing miserably so far.

Tom stood off to her right and she could tell that he was holding in a laugh. Thanks, Tom, she thought.

Harri continued.

"Have you seen this man here recently?" Harri asked and she pulled out the DMV photo of Jared a.k.a. Ethan Carle to show to Heather. The old woman peered at it and nodded curtly.

"Yeah, I seen him," she said.

"When?" Harri asked.

"Around dinner time on Friday. About six-thirty," she said, looking up into the sky.

"You're very accurate about that time," Harri observed.

"I'm on a tight schedule. Have to know when the restaurants around here dump their leftovers. If I'm late,

I don't eat. I got back Friday when he was asking around for Marie. Just like you're doing now."

Heather stuck her chin out in some sort of challenge. Harri shot a glance at Tom, but he shrugged back at her as if saying, this is your interview.

Harri sighed. She noticed four long white hairs coming off the woman's chin and couldn't tear her eyes away from them.

"What was he like when you spoke to him?"

"Whaddya mean what was he like?" Heather asked.

"Agitated? Calm?" Harri asked.

"Calm, I guess," Heather said.

"Was he friendly?" Harri asked.

"Way more than you. But you're a cop and he was one of us," Heather said.

If she only knew how wrong she was. Her statement proved how well Jared had blended in.

"Did he ask about anyone else?" Tom asked, finally getting into the conversation.

"Just Marie. And Art, but Art was gone by then."

"How long has Art been missing?" Harri asked.

Heather quirked an eyebrow at her. "I said he was gone, not missing."

Harri couldn't win with this woman.

"Gone then. How long has he been gone?" Harri asked.

"A week and a half," Heather said.

"Any idea where he went?" Tom asked.

Heather shook her head no.

"Which one of these is Marie's?" Tom asked.

"That one there," Heather pointed to a dwelling six spaces away. "See that cardboard sticking up over everyone else's place? Art built that for them," she said.

"What did you think of Art?" Harri asked.

"He was okay. Not a thief. Not a pig. He was trying to find work to get them into a place. Hard worker," she said.

"You don't think he could have been arrested? Or maybe ended up in the hospital somehow?" Harri asked.

"If he was arrested, how come you can't find him?" Heather said. "Anyway, he would have been back by now. He's gone gone. Sad if you ask me. Marie's all broken up about it."

She shook her head and turned toward the teetering cardboard contraption.

"Let me go get her. If you can find Art for her then talking to you won't have been a waste of my time," she said.

Harri wanted to laugh at the woman accusing her of wasting her time. Instead, she watched as she waddled down the alleyway to Marie and Art's cardboard home.

"Marie? Some cops out here wanna talk to you about Art."

She opened a cardboard flap and peeked her head inside.

"Oh no girl, you didn't," Heather wailed.

Tom took out his cell phone and dialed 911 as Harri rushed over.

"What's wrong?" Harri asked as she pushed past Heather.

An emaciated brown-haired woman lay on top of a dirty green blanket. In the dim light, Harri could see her bare left arm was lined with needle marks and a syringe hung from the latest puncture. White foam dripped from her mouth as she gurgled.

"She's overdosing," Harri called out. She could hear Tom giving dispatch directions to the encampment. She knelt near Marie and gently pushed her face side to side.

"Marie? Can you hear me, Marie?" Harri shouted. She put her hand on Marie's chest and felt it barely moving. Her skin was clammy and pale and even in the dim light, Harri could see it was turning blue.

Harri didn't think Marie had much time left. Fortunately, the paramedics were minutes away. Before Harri could start CPR, two paramedics pushed her aside. She backed out of the cardboard dwelling and watched as one of them gave Marie a shot of Narcan while the other took her vitals.

An EMT brought a stretcher into the small space and the team lifted her onto it. Everything happened so fast Harri only had enough time to ask where they were taking her.

Harri and Tom stood with Heather as the EMTs loaded a groaning Marie and a paramedic into the back of the ambulance.

"They're taking her to Hollywood General," Harri said. "One of us should stay with her. Should we split up to cover more ground?"

"We don't have any ground to cover." Tom sighed. "She's our best lead so far. We don't have any real names for any of these people. Not to mention hospitals have a nasty habit of discharging homeless patients without services referrals. We have to stay with her," he said.

"I hope we got here in time," Harri said.

"Me too," Tom said.

Harri and Tom drank bad hospital coffee while waiting for Marie to become lucid enough to speak. During those three hours, they discussed the case and compared notes as to who lied to them and why. Mainly, it was Whitey and Matty so far. They talked about how the three men who'd disappeared had all been reportedly looking for work. Was that a coincidence of their circumstances or the way they crossed paths with their killer?

The inconsistencies were building. They had enough partial information to keep pulling at the threads to see where the leads would take them, but not enough to have a good idea of what Jared had stumbled upon to get him killed. Harri hoped Marie would provide the next thread to follow.

They walked into the bright, clean room and Harri marveled at the difference surroundings made to the patient in the bed. Marie looked ill but like anyone else in a hospital. No doctor would know from looking at her that she was homeless or the paramedics had pulled her from inside what was essentially a gigantic box.

Before they could say anything, Marie turned to them with big brown, sorrowful eyes and said, "I wish you hadn't found me."

"We're glad we did," Harri said. "Are you well enough to speak with us?"

Marie shrugged.

"What does well enough even mean? I don't know what to do without Art," Marie said as tears ran down her cheeks.

"That's why we're here. Tell us about Art. What was his full name?"

"His name is Arthur Sharpe. We're from San Diego. He came up here because he's a musician and I followed him," she said.

"Had you known each other a long time?" Harri asked gently.

"Since high school," she said.

"And how old are you now?" Tom asked.

"I'm twenty-one. Art is twenty-three," Marie said.

"When did Art go missing?" Harri asked.

"Two weeks ago? Yeah, it was February 20th, I think. It was a tough week for us and he went to pick up some day work. He usually went to that Home Depot on Sunset. There's lots of jobs for day labor. For people's gardens and building contractors and stuff. He went and he never came back," Marie said. Her grief overflowed and sobs filled the room.

Harri and Tom waited several minutes as she pulled herself together again.

"There was a man who came around asking about Art?" Harri asked.

Marie nodded. "Jared. I don't remember his last name. I've been kind of a mess since Art disappeared."

"What did Jared want to talk to you about?" Tom asked.

"About the missing men. About Art," Marie said.

"Can you tell us about the conversation you had with him?" Harri asked.

"I told him about Art and how he'd gone to Home Depot. He asked me if I'd seen any white vans around our camp. I remember that because it was a ridiculous question. No white vans around the camp, but over by Home Depot? They're all white vans. Most construction workers drive white vans. He asked me if I knew Davis Hines. He called him Big D. Jared told me he was last seen at the Riverside Shelter and asked if me or Art had been at that shelter before Art disappeared."

"And had you been?" Harri asked.

Marie had given them another lead.

"No, we hadn't gone there. He also asked me if we'd been to the Los Feliz Library," Marie said. She picked up a glass of water from the bedside table and took a sip.

"Did another man go missing from the library?" Tom asked.

"Yeah. A guy named Rich. He went missing about a week before Art did. Jared said he'd last been seen at the library," Marie said.

"Did he mention anyone else?" Harri asked.

Marie shook her head no.

"Any women?" Tom asked.

She shook her head no and took another sip of water. She put the glass of water down on the bedside table and leaned into the pillows. Her eyes were bloodshot, and her skin was almost as pale as when Harri first found her. Harri pulled her eyes away from Marie's. She couldn't handle seeing the other woman's pain.

"Have you found Art?" Marie asked. "Is that why you came to see me?'

Harri and Tom glanced at each other.

"No. We found Jared's body in the river. We're retracing his steps to see how and why he might have been killed."

Marie sat up when she heard that.

"He was the only one helping me look for Art."

"We're looking for Art now too," Harri said.

Marie turned her face away from them and stared out the window.

Harri knew the interview was over. Maybe she shouldn't have mentioned finding Jared's body, but she didn't want the woman to find out in another way.

"Thank you for speaking to us, Marie," Tom said. "You've helped our investigation move forward and we'll do our best to bring Art back to you."

Marie nodded but didn't say anything.

Harri wondered if the next time they saw her she'd

still be living and breathing. She wasn't sure it would be a definite yes.

They left Marie in the hospital room.

Tom went to ask the nurse what the care plan was for Marie. He wanted to make sure she received a referral for services or was discharged to a women's shelter.

Harri waited for him to come back and jotted down what Marie said about the three missing men. Another thread pulled and more lines of inquiry to follow up on. They were moving forward and that was positive. The pieces were slowly coming into focus.

Jared left a faint trail for them to follow and she hoped it would keep on giving. Their next steps were the Riverside shelter and the Los Feliz library.

9

DAY 2 - AFTERNOON

The Riverside shelter was a three-minute drive from the homeless camp Jared occupied on the river. On the side nearest the river were about eighty trailers and RVs taking over the parking lot while on the other side of Riverside Drive was a huge warehouse tent that looked like it could sleep two hundred people on cots.

A man bearing a strong resemblance to the actor Gary Busey with a shock of yellow hair sticking out every which way, bright blue eyes, and a disconcerting grin on his face, greeted Harri and Tom as they walked through the door. He was taller than Tom and towered over Harri.

"What can I do for you, detectives?" he asked.

"We look that obvious?" Harri asked.

"Absolutely," the Gary Busey look-alike said. "My name is Eric Radford. I'm the director here. Assuming you aren't looking for a place to sleep?"

"Have you seen this man?" Tom asked. He showed Jared's DMV photo to Eric.

"His name is Jared Atkinson," Harri said.

"That the guy you found in the river?" Eric asked.

"Did you see him here at the shelter?" Tom asked, ignoring the other man's question.

"Yes. He didn't stay here, though. Just came. Hearing what happened to him was a real shame. He was a good man," Eric said.

"Did he stay here last weekend?" Harri asked.

"No, he never stayed here, like I said. He came by asking questions about some of the other residents."

"Do you remember who he was asking about?" Tom asked.

"Let me have a think." He paused for a moment and put his head down with his fist on his mouth, imitating the famous statue. This man was an odd duck, Harri thought.

"The name that immediately comes to mind is Marpessa Roberts. He said she was pregnant, I remember that. He said she was in her 20s, with long blonde hair and a big belly. I hadn't seen anyone like that. Would have remembered that because we haven't had any visibly pregnant women here. There's better places for pregnant women in the city. Always money for the unborn, right? It's after you're born that you're on your own," Eric said.

No one they'd interviewed so far had mentioned Jared was looking for a woman, much less a pregnant one.

"Did he mention why he was looking for Marpessa Roberts?" Harri asked.

"Said she was his sister," Eric nodded.

Harri and Tom had already confirmed the undercover cop going by the name of Jared Atkinson had no living relatives.

"Did you believe him?" Harri asked.

"Really not my place to question. Could have been his sister. Could've been a friend of his that he was worried about. Could have been his kid she was carrying. In this line of work, I don't pry, nor do I immediately think the residents are liars," he said.

Harri found it interesting he took such offense at that question. Tom took the initiative at the awkward pause to keep the interview flowing.

"Did he mention anyone else?" Tom asked.

"He mentioned two other names. Big D and Robert. No, Richard? I'm not sure. I wasn't paying close attention honestly," Eric admitted.

"Any reason, in particular, you weren't paying attention?" Tom asked.

"There was a lot going on. We were in the middle of intake. We open at six pm and there's typically a line," he said. "I sent him over to Irma. She's a volunteer."

"Is Irma working today?" Tom asked. He looked over Eric's shoulder at the vast space.

It was huge and filled with cots that each had foot-lockers at the end. There were no residents to be seen.

"The volunteers don't start until 4 o'clock. We're a night shelter only, so we open at 5 p.m. and everyone clears out by 8 a.m. Then we do general cleanup before the next night and do it all over again."

"How do the trailers work?" Tom asked. "As we drove in, we saw the trailers on the left side. Is that you, too?"

"It's part of the complex but a separate program. The trailers are a longer-term solution. People get placed in them and then come off a waiting list. This shelter here is for the night."

"Where do the residents go in the morning?" Harri asked.

"Back on the streets. A lot of people hunt for recycling. They panhandle on street corners and onramps to the freeways. You know, whatever people can do to make a little cash," Eric said.

"Had you ever seen Jared Atkinson before?" Harri asked.

"I don't think so, but we get a lot of people coming and going out of here. He was the first one to come asking for someone specific though," he said.

"You haven't had any people go missing from here?" Tom asked.

"How would we know? Our residents turn over nightly. Don't know how we'd notice anyone go missing. We have over 65,000 unhoused people in LA County. Too many people to keep track of."

That figure was astonishing to hear out loud, Harri thought.

"How can we contact Irma?" Tom asked.

"I can't give her information out to you," Eric said.

"We're the cops," Harri said.

"Are you?" Eric asked. "Haven't seen any badges or ID."

He had a point.

They both showed Eric their credentials. He studied them and then nodded.

"Can't give you her address, but her last name is Heller. I'm sure you can track that down, being detectives and all." He flashed them a big crazy grin.

"Thank you for your time, Eric," Harri said. She was ready to be done with this strange man.

Tom handed him a business card. "If you think of anything else, don't hesitate to call."

Eric nodded and saluted them.

Harri was able to pull up Irma Heller's address through the DMV dashboard. Thankfully, Irma lived close enough to the Riverside shelter they wouldn't have to drive far. Tom drove them over to the address on Hazel Kirk and they could see no one was home. Harri called the phone number attached to the DMV file and spoke to Irma. She was grocery shopping and they agreed to meet in front of her home in thirty minutes.

Tom grumbled about waiting for her, but Harri was energized by how far they'd advanced the investigation so far.

"Do you think the missing woman Jared was looking for is one of the torture victims?" Harri asked. She'd been mulling over Eric Radford's information that Jared was searching for a woman. That was a detail that Harri hadn't seen coming.

"I'm not sure we can connect the two cases yet. Nor should we. Maybe he had a lead on the missing woman and added her to the list," Tom said.

"I find it odd that only one of our witnesses mentioned a woman. I would think women would be more vulnerable out here."

"And the fact she was pregnant is troubling. Her name is rather unique. How many Marpessa Roberts could be out there?" Tom mused.

"I'll look through the databases for someone matching her description," Harri said.

"I think this is Irma Heller," Tom interrupted her and pointed at a woman carrying two bags of groceries. As she neared her home, Harri and Tom stepped out of the cruiser.

Irma Heller was a slim, dark-haired woman with an intense look on her face. She was dressed in yoga pants, a t-shirt, and sneakers, with her hair pulled up into a ponytail. Harri guessed she was in her late 40s.

"Are you the detectives that called me?" she asked, suspicion filtering into her voice.

Harri and Tom showed her their credentials. She peered at them and then placed her bags onto the sidewalk.

"Do you want to put those in the fridge?" Harri asked.

"I don't have anything perishable in there. Is this about the guy who washed up in the river?" she asked.

"Yes. His name was Jared Atkinson," Harri said and took out Jared's DMV license photo. "Do you recognize him?"

"Sure, I do. I spoke to him last Friday, I believe," Irma said.

"What about?" Tom asked.

"Davis Hines. He was known as Big D to his friends. Jared wanted to know if I knew him."

"Did you know Davis Hines?" Harri asked.

"He was a regular at the shelter. I wouldn't say we were close, but we chatted," Irma said.

"What else did you tell Jared?" Tom asked.

"He said Big D was missing and wanted to know where he was off to on the day he disappeared. When I told him, he lit up like a Christmas tree. Said I'd given him a puzzle piece."

Harri did her best to contain her excitement and kept her eye on Irma. "Where was Big D going that day?" Harri asked.

"Do you remember the exact day he disappeared?" Tom asked before Irma could answer Harri's question.

"About three weeks ago? It was on a Tuesday, I think," Irma said.

She turned to Harri. "Big D went downtown to CUCO, the California Unhoused Community Outreach center. It's a place where people can put themselves on a list to get work as a day laborer."

"Did Big D have a contact there?" Tom asked.

"Not that I know of. Jared asked the same question," Irma said.

"This was the puzzle piece you gave him?" Harri asked.

"I think so. He'd heard of CUCO, but wanted more information. I think the whole thing is a scam, personally, and I told him that," Irma said.

"Why do you say it's a scam?" Harri asked.

"It's a private nonprofit which isn't the problem. It has this whole job services division that essentially rents out homeless people for manual labor to general contractors. They work under the table. I think everybody's getting kickbacks over there."

"Explain that," Tom said.

Irma Heller sighed and looked over at her house. She picked up her grocery bags.

"I guess you might as well come inside," she said.

"Need help with those?" Tom asked.

"I got it," Irma said as she led them inside the small, Spanish-style house with roses out front and a Mercedes SUV in the driveway.

Harri wondered why Irma chose to walk to the grocery instead of driving, but inwardly shook her head. It didn't matter. Who was she to judge?

"Can I get either of you anything to drink?" Irma said as she placed her grocery bags on the kitchen counter.

Harri glanced around and observed the interior of the home was in either the original or restored condition. The white Shaker kitchen cabinets looked new, as did the stainless appliances. She guessed the home had been restored. Harri quickly clocked the car in the driveway, the home, and Irma's demeanor and wondered if she was a divorced woman with no kids volunteering because she didn't need to work but needed something to do.

"Do you live here with your husband?" Harri asked.

"No," Irma sighed and leaned against the counter. "He drank himself to death years ago. This was my mother's house. She died two years ago. What were we saying about Jared?"

"We were talking about CUCO and the day laborers," Tom volunteered.

"Right. Look, I wouldn't be surprised if Eric Radford gets some sort of compensation for sending people from the shelter down to CUCO for work. I think after those people sign up, the administrators who run the jobs office get a kickback from the contractors when they grab the people to work for the day. Most of those guys only get like $20 for a full day of labor. And they're happy with that. Could you imagine what an actual construction worker would be getting for twelve hours?" Irma asked.

"Wouldn't be twenty dollars for the day," Harri said.

"Exactly," Irma said.

"Did Eric Radford know that Davis Hines was going down to CUCO that day?" Tom asked.

"Of course, he did. Eric was the one who told me to tell him where to go. Davis has diabetes and has to find a way to regulate his blood sugar. He isn't bad enough to be on insulin yet. He's constantly needing to eat and without a home, or a fridge, or kitchen, or any of that it is just impossible for him. He wanted to work, so Eric sent him down to CUCO."

"Why do you think Eric didn't mention any of this to us?" Harri asked.

"I'm telling you, kickbacks," Irma said with a look of disgust on her face.

"But you've never seen money changing hands?" Tom asked.

"No," Irma shook her head. "But something is going on between Eric Radford and CUCO. That's the only place he sends anybody. This is Los Angeles. There are dozens of organizations working with the homeless, so why does Eric only send them there?"

"Anything else stand out in your conversation with Jared that day?" Harri asked.

"He told me he was going straight to CUCO after we spoke," Irma said.

"And this was also on Friday?" Harri asked.

"Yeah, as everybody was leaving. So close to maybe 8:15 that morning," Irma said.

"You have been so very helpful," Harri said.

"I really hope you catch Eric Radford at whatever illegal thing he's doing," Irma said. "That guy is a shady slimeball."

"Why do you volunteer there then?" Harri asked.

"I inherited more than just this house. My mother was a volunteer and after she died, I took her spot. But this is my last week. I found a church that distributes sack lunches to the homeless on weekdays and I'll be working there instead," she said.

"Good luck and thank you, Irma," Harri said.

"You won't tell Eric what I said, will you?" Irma asked. She suddenly appeared nervous. "I'll be seeing him all week."

"We won't if you don't," Harri smiled.

Irma returned a thin smile in relief. "Oh, I won't."

"One last question," Tom said. "Did you ever hear of a man named Rich? He hung around the Los Feliz library?"

"Not specifically, but the shelter is packed every night so I might've helped him," Irma said.

"We had to ask," Harri said. "Thanks again for your help."

Tom and Harri left Irma to her day.

They didn't speak to each other until they were safely in the car.

Tom was already tapping on his cell phone as he opened the car door. "I have the address of the CUCO building. It's downtown on Spring Street. About four blocks from the PAB," he said.

"It's disgusting how people find ways to make money off of other's despair," Harri said.

"Let's run background on Eric Radford and Irma Heller," Tom said. "And we have Big D's name finally. Two names identified. One more to go."

"Enough for a victim profile," Harri said.

"Seems the most important piece of their profile is they're homeless and desperate," Tom said.

"Right," Harri said. "Our killer doesn't care about race seeing as Davis Hines was black and Arthur Sharpe was white."

"The fact they disappeared on work searches can't be a coincidence," he said.

"The question Jared asked Marie suggests he had a line on one of these men getting into a white van," Harri theorized.

"Let's see who we can talk to at the Los Feliz library. I'm pretty sure they have cameras viewing the street. Maybe we'll get lucky running down our last guy, Rich."

"Then down to CUCO and onto the PAB? We should have enough time to run backgrounds on everyone we have so far," Harri said. "What about the tissue banks?"

Harri remembered they'd planned to hit some of the tissue banks on the list they'd compiled.

"I put in calls to six tissue banks in the area. I'm not sure how far we'll get without warrants but we also need to run background on all the owners. A scam like this needs someone at the top. Still trying to wrap my head around how the money exchange works for something you're not supposed to get money for," Tom said.

"The detectives in that mortician case could shed light on that," Harri said.

"You want to handle that?" Tom asked.

"I'm on it," Harri said.

"The Los Feliz library is only four or five blocks from here," Tom said.

Harri nodded and buckled up, jittery with adrenaline.

Jared had uncovered a doozy of a case. Her mind raced over the connections and implications of what they'd discovered so far. Homeless men looking for work. A feeder system into an organization that could identify the men healthy enough for the tissue procurement. Then the killer doing the deed and the cash flowing out. A person nobody would miss. A hundred thousand dollars was a lot of money for one body. How many people were profiting from a well-hidden death?

She loved this part of the job. She loved putting the pieces together and seeing where they fit. They'd been on the case less than forty-eight hours and they already had motive and plenty of opportunities. Now, they had to fill out their cast of characters.

10

DAY 2 - LATE AFTERNOON

As Tom predicted, the library was only minutes away. The community was like a village and Harri understood why so many homeless people chose the neighborhood. Between the shelter and the three churches within walking distance of each other, the people living on the streets had services they could use. The library was a welcoming place and Griffith Park and the Los Angeles River provided them with room to spread out. She knew Griffith Park didn't allow people to sleep overnight, but the river was close by.

They found the librarian soon after stepping through the double doors.

"Thank you for speaking with us," Harri said to Susan Fleming, the Head Librarian.

Susan was a large woman in her late 50s, and Harri guessed she was Filipino. She had a friendly smile and intelligent eyes. Harri didn't think Susan missed a thing in her library.

They sat in a small office behind the main desk. Susan

left her office door open which was driving Harri to distraction.

It was disconcerting for Harri to sense people moving back and forth behind her. All that police training kicked in and she wanted to have control of her surroundings. She had to fight the urge to constantly look behind her.

"Would you mind if we closed the door?" Harri asked.

"I would, in fact," Susan said. "I'm waiting for an important package from the central library and I don't want to miss it."

"I understand," Harri said, even though she didn't. She gulped down the lump in her throat and took out her notebook.

"We're here to ask you about a homeless man named Rich. Do you know a man by that name?" Tom asked.

"Another cop came around asking about him," Susan said. "You all must not be talking to each other."

This woman was sharp, Harri thought. How did she know Jared Atkinson was a cop?

"You remember the cop's name?" Tom asked.

"Ethan Carle. I took down his badge number if you need to see it," she said.

"He had his badge on him?" Harri asked with surprise. She probably shouldn't have said anything, but the information took her off guard. Jared Atkinson had been so scrupulous to hide his true identity during his undercover work that she was surprised he would out himself to a stranger like that.

"Did you take ours down as well?" Tom asked.

They'd shown her their credentials when they met her at the front desk.

"I have a photographic memory." Susan smiled. "So,

yes I do remember both of your badge numbers. No funny business, okay guys?"

Tom threw up his hands as if to say, nothing to hide here.

"Photographic memory?" Harri asked. "Is that since you were a child?"

Susan nodded. "Yes, my entire life."

"You ever run over to Vegas to count cards?" Tom joked.

Susan's hand pressed her chest. "I would never. That would be cheating."

Good to know, Harri thought.

"Did Jared, Ethan Carle, mention he was a cop when he first came in to speak with you about Rich?" Harri asked.

The fact that he'd shown his badge while undercover really threw Harri off. Could someone have overheard them talking and discovered Jared was undercover? That would put a whole new spin on their investigation.

She and Tom had been under the impression nobody knew and he'd been killed for sticking his nose in the wrong business as a homeless guy. If the killer knew he was a cop, their investigation had become way more complex.

"I'm not sure I should divulge that information," Susan said. "A library is a place of privacy and we Librarians honor that. For everyone."

"And we understand that." Harri nodded. "However, Jared Atkinson, or Ethan Carle as you knew him, was found dead in the river. It's been confirmed as a homicide. We're trying to retrace his steps in those last days before he met his killer."

"Oh, no," Susan murmured as she shook her head. "Oh, I'm very sorry to hear that about Ethan. He was a nice man, very polite. He seemed to really care about finding out what happened to Rich."

"Were you able to help him out with that at all?" Harri asked.

"I allowed him to view surveillance footage of the front of the library," Susan said. "Of course, I couldn't show him anything from inside the library because that would show what Rich was reading and checking out. Rich was a prolific reader and we enjoyed having him here."

"Would you have Rich's full name?" Tom asked.

"Oh, I don't think I can give you that information," she said. "At least not without Rich's permission or an official warrant signed by a judge, requesting that specific information."

"But Rich has been missing for weeks," Harri said.

"Missing?" Susan seemed doubtful. "The unhoused are transient. He could've gone to San Diego, or up to San Francisco, or anywhere really. I can't divulge that information without a warrant signed by a judge, or a court order."

The frustration Harri and Tom felt seemed to fill the room. Susan leaned forward and whispered to Harri.

"Would you like to see the surveillance footage I showed Detective Carle?"

"You still have it?" Harri asked excitedly.

"I saved the clip exactly as he asked me to. The original surveillance footage has been erased since then, but I do have the clip saved in three places, just as he asked."

"Can we see it?" Harri asked, the excitement oozing out of her voice.

If they had footage of the white van then they could have a license plate. A license plate would get them a name.

"Let me bring it up," Susan said. "I have it on my desktop, and a thumb drive, and it's also..." she pointed up.

"You hid it in the ceiling?" Tom asked.

"No." Susan's eyes twinkled. "It's in the cloud."

She typed for several moments and then swiveled the computer screen for them to view. A grainy video of the intersection of Franklin and Hillhurst came into low-resolution focus. Susan hit play.

Tom and Harri watched in breathless silence as a young, white male came out of the library holding a blue backpack.

A white van, looking a bit beat up, pulled up to the no-parking zone in front of the library.

"You recognize this man as Rich?" Tom asked.

"That is Rich." Susan nodded.

Rich walked over to the passenger side of the van and spoke to the driver. Harri and Tom both leaned in to get a better view of the driver, but the video was too grainy. Harri wondered if maybe the LAPD or SID video techs could clean up the footage for a better view.

The van drove away and both Harri and Tom groaned when they saw it had a clear plastic license plate holder that obscured the license plate. A scrambling mechanism in the plastic prevented the license plate from being recorded properly on traffic cameras.

"Can we have a copy of this to send to our video techs?" Tom asked.

"Of course. Should I email it to you?" she asked.

Tom gave her his email address and she sent the video off.

"Will you need the thumb drive, too?"

Tom nodded and she handed it to him.

"Don't worry, I won't charge you for that. It's from my personal office supplies."

"I appreciate that," Tom smiled.

"Anything else you can tell us about your meeting with Detective Carle?" Harri asked. Susan was a woman who noticed the details, Harri thought.

"His fingernails were clean. I don't see that very often with the unhoused individuals that come in to use the library services. I told him he should dirty up his hands if he wanted to keep himself undercover. Ethan Carle had a way about him when he spoke to you. He leaned in when he spoke. He wrote down everything I told him in a little black notebook. I could see he had lots of notes inside, and he explained he'd uncovered multiple disappearances within the unhoused population."

"Did he mention anything else about those disappearances?" Harri asked.

"No. He kept our conversation on Rich. He didn't know his last name either, by the way. I wouldn't tell him the kinds of books Rich took out, but I told him that Rich came in every single day when the library was open. He used our facilities to wash up. He had a favorite chair, and he would sit here for hours reading. We have a lot of unhoused individuals coming in to do that. Especially when it's hot out and they need air conditioning. We make sure to always have water out in the front hall so they can refill their water bottles."

"Did he ask any other questions about Rich?" Tom asked.

"He asked me when the last time was that I had seen Rich. We didn't speak that day, but it was an ordinary day. Nothing particular happened to make it stand out. I noticed within two days that Rich was no longer coming in. I hoped he'd found housing," she said and bit her lip, genuinely upset.

"Rich never had any episodes like some of the others do and he was such an intelligent man. It made me wonder how he got into his current circumstances."

"Do you have any idea where Rich was from?" Harri asked.

"He once mentioned being from back east. He said he came here for the sunshine and the movies," she said.

"Did you know if maybe he worked in the film industry?" Tom asked.

"Oh, I never ask. If people want to talk, that's up to them. I might ask how their day is going or something, but that's about it. It's not my business to pry," she said.

Susan stood up from her desk abruptly.

"It looks like my delivery is here and I don't know what else I can tell you."

"You've given us quite a bit," Tom said.

"I hope you find whoever hurt Ethan. He really cared about other people," she said. And with that, she left the office. They heard her soft voice at the desk saying hello. So much for libraries being quiet, Harri thought.

They walked out of the library to the parking lot.

Harri turned to Tom and said, "We need to find that notebook of his."

"If it hasn't been burned already," Tom said.

"You think we can get anything off that footage?" she asked.

"Not outside the obvious. We are now also looking for a white van. The kind of vehicle perfect for transporting bodies," he said.

"Wasn't there a serial killer here in the 70s that was picked up during a normal traffic stop? They checked in the van and found two bodies?" she asked.

"There was more than one," Tom said. "Windowless white vans are part of the serial killer starter kit."

"Now we know why he was asking about white vans," Harri said. "Too bad they're everywhere in this city."

"Let's see what involvement CUCO has in all of this. Since they're a non-profit, they'll have the paperwork we can find online and that should get us names," Tom said.

Harri nodded but groaned inwardly. She could see paperwork filling her vision. So many names to track down. Too many witnesses to question.

"Are we going to expand our team?" she asked. She'd be perfectly happy to have an officer do the grunt work.

Jared Atkinson's tortured body flashed through her mind and she had to shake it off. She didn't want to have a PTSD episode on the job, but the horror of what had happened to him stayed with her, even if it was after death. How many more bodies were out there like that?

"Where are the rest of the bodies?" she said aloud as Tom clicked open the car and got into the steaming hot interior. "There have to be more bodies. This can't be a one-off. It doesn't feel like it is."

Harri slid into the passenger seat as Tom started the car and the air conditioner.

"Here's what I'm thinking about that," he said. "If our killer had a line at a mortuary, then he would have access to their cremation oven. Now wouldn't that just be the perfect place to get rid of bodies?"

"Even more people involved in the scheme. Why wouldn't someone talk?" Harri asked.

"Money," Tom said. "We should start looking at mortuaries, especially with morticians who walk on the shady side of the street. Dr. Grimley said there was no guard on duty for the death industry, so I wouldn't be surprised if there's a facility being used to dispose of the remains once the tissue is harvested."

"I'll start making a list of those. Why don't you take the tissue banks and I'll take on the death industry," Harri said.

"Tissue banks scare you, hey?" he asked with a grin.

"You know how I am at the autopsies. I can't get Jared Atkinson's body out of my head. I think I'd rather talk to some funeral directors," she said.

"You got it," Tom said.

11

DAY 2 - NIGHT - DARLENE "WHITEY" WHITEMAN

I stood outside the largest RV on Franklin, a couple blocks down from Vermont, feeling nervous as a cat being out at night like this. It was past nine, but the girls don't start working the trailer until around ten.

I finally read through all of Jared's notes in the little black notebook he left behind. Jared was a cop. When I first figured that out, I had to put the notebook down. I couldn't read anymore because my eyes were filling up with tears. A cop. He wasn't like me at all. He had a life. He probably had a home somewhere and a family inside it. I knew he was keeping secrets from me. I never dreamed it could be something like this. Jared was an undercover cop looking for some gang member. Jared couldn't be his real name. Now, I didn't even know that much. He never had a problem with drugs or alcohol. His life never fell apart. He never woke up one day on the street because he had no place else to go. What about all those AA meetings? That was a lie, too.

He was never my friend, I thought again. He was never my friend. I thought back to the girls in high school who stopped talking to me after my brother caused a scene at school and got kicked out. They weren't really my friends. I thought of the people I knew at the insurance company where I worked and how they forgot all about me once I'd been let go. They weren't my friends, either. All the people I used to hang out with, my old neighbors, the people I used to go hiking with, none of them were my real friends. None. Not Jared, or whoever he really was, either. I had no friends.

The notes took a detour halfway through and Jared stopped writing about the gang member. He focused on the disappearances of Big D, Art, and Rich. Then he wrote about a woman called Marpessa Roberts, and someone named Rena. He wrote that both girls lived in the RVs parked along Franklin Avenue.

Everyone knew a guy named Miguel owned the RVs and parked them along a six-block stretch between Vermont and Normandy. I'd heard whispers that he lived in the neighborhood above Franklin in a big house and kept his girls in the RVs servicing clients.

Jared's notes didn't mention how he'd found out about the girls in the RVs or Marpessa Roberts. The last few pages were about his search for a girl named Rena and how she'd also gone missing Saturday afternoon. One day before Jared died.

I wished for probably the hundredth time I'd read the notebook sooner. I should've handed it to the cops. I only kept it from them so they wouldn't invade his privacy. That was back when I thought he was my friend and I should look out for him.

Now I was studying it as a guidebook to see if there were any clues as to what happened to him. I needed to know who was following me and why. Knowledge was power. That's what Grandpa always said.

It took me over an hour to walk from the river to this area of Los Feliz. My hip was acting up, so I was going slow. I went the long way, staying off Los Feliz, ducking through dark alleys, and hiding to look out every few blocks to make sure nobody was following me. I wasn't always this paranoid, but with Jared's death, the disappearances, and the car following me the day before, I was on full alert.

After I crossed Vermont and got a closer look, I was surprised by how junky the RVs looked. Why didn't the cops or the people living in the neighborhood complain about these eyesores and get them towed?

The first RV was a large white cruiser that looked as if it belonged in the 1980s or something. It had brown siding and plywood or cardboard covered all the windows so no one could see inside.

Several yards down, I could make out another RV, smaller than the first, with blue trim. Further down the block sat a squat rounded trailer, smaller than either of the first two. It looked like an old-timer from the 1960s. Plywood or cardboard covered all the windows.

Jared wrote the first RV was assigned to a girl called Gwen. Two girls lived in the second RV. His notes mentioned they worked together. The last RV had been Rena's.

I took a deep breath and knocked on Gwen's door. A girl looking no older than seventeen came out and asked what I wanted. I explained and asked if I could speak to her. Gwen said she had to throw on some clothes and to give her five minutes.

Which is why I was still hanging out around the back of the first RV, pretending I had a good reason to be there.

I finally saw the RV sway a bit closer to ten minutes

later. The little door opened, and Gwen stepped outside wearing leggings and a hoodie.

"Let's go for a walk," Gwen said. "I don't want anyone to see us talking. Especially Miguel."

"Sure thing. After you," I said.

We started on a leisurely walk as if we were two women out for a stroll through our pretty neighborhood. All we needed was one of those tiny dogs, I thought.

When we turned the corner and started up one of the side streets, I nodded and began to ask Gwen questions.

"I lived right next to Jared at the river camp. You know he was found dead, right?" I asked.

"I saw they'd pulled a body out of the river. He was supposed to meet with me that Monday, so I kind of figured it was him when I saw it on the news."

"He told me about how he was helping you search for Rena," I lied. I didn't want anyone to know yet that I had his black notebook. I might need it as leverage to get help from the cops.

"Rena's gone," Gwen said. "Nobody's seen or heard from her."

"Who's in the RV now?" I asked.

"Some new girl Miguel found down by the bus station. So many girls coming to Los Angeles and they're just ripe for the picking," Gwen said ruefully.

I heard the bitterness in her voice and wondered if that was her story, too. We all had stories of how we ended up on the street.

"Did you know Marpessa Roberts?" I asked.

"She was the girl in my place before me," Gwen said. "I don't know what happened to her, but Jared said she was missing, too. I guess that's why Miguel came looking for her replacement."

"Have there been other girls go missing before Rena?" I asked.

"Outside of Marpessa, no. I mean, as far as I know. I don't really know if she went missing or not. That was what Jared said, but couldn't she have just gone home?"

I doubted Marpessa Roberts had made it back to her real home. "Aren't you scared?" I asked.

"Yeah, but it's safer where I am now than where I came from. Are you?" Gwen asked.

"All the damn time," I admitted. It was the truth. I was scared all the damn time and it was exhausting.

"Can you tell me about Rena?" I asked.

"What do you want to know?"

"Was she as young as you?"

I looked at Gwen's flawless face, long hair, and perfect figure. She was pretty enough to be on television or in the movies. How did she end up hooking out of a junky RV on Franklin Avenue?

"I think she was fifteen or sixteen maybe," Gwen said.

"How old are you?" I asked.

"I'm eighteen," Gwen said. "Rena was young and looked even younger. The johns really like that."

I shuddered. Men were so gross. "When did Rena go missing?"

"That Saturday night. Actually, I don't think she's really missing. I think she had a secret john Miguel didn't know about. Rena talked to Jared Friday night and when he came back on Saturday, we found out she was gone. Miguel was so pissed. Said he had to cancel fifteen clients."

It was hard not to retch at the sound of that. Fifteen guys in one night? And the girl was only fifteen. I felt tears smarting in my eyes.

"How did Jared find you guys?" I asked.

"He came around asking about Marpessa. I don't know how he found out she was missing, but he was asking Jo and Lanie, and Rena about her. I didn't have much to say since I showed up after her."

"Did you ever wonder why he cared so much?" I asked.

"Because he's a cop, naturally," Gwen said. "My dad is a cop. So are all his friends. I can always spot a cop."

"Really? How?"

"I don't know," she said. "It's a look. A walk. The way they talk. You can just tell."

We rounded the corner and walked back toward the RVs.

"How come you're interested in all this?" Gwen asked.

"I need to find out," I said. "I need to know what's going on. A car followed me yesterday and I need to figure out for myself what Jared was up to. I feel like he dragged me into whatever he was working on and now I'm going to be next. I also want to know what happened to him."

"I get it. He was my friend, too. He made me feel safe," Gwen said.

"I know you don't have too much time left to talk. When was the last time you saw Rena?" I asked.

"Saturday morning. We had coffee. She took off after that and I didn't see her again. Jared came back around 9:30 that night, right before our shifts started and she was long gone."

"Did she leave any of her stuff behind?"

"I don't know. By the time I was done with my night shift and went looking through her place, all her stuff was gone. Miguel must have thrown it out. There was a new girl in there by Monday. Jared was doing everything he could to find out what happened to her. I know the first twenty-four hours after a disappearance are the most crucial. He left here looking, set on finding her. Maybe he did, and that's what got him killed." Gwen opened up her door and looked back at me. "You sure you want to be going down this path, too?" she asked.

I could tell Gwen was wise beyond her years.

"I'm not sure of anything, to be honest with you. I should probably leave the city, but I have maybe five dollars on me and where would I go? It's the only place I know. I'm stuck. Maybe if I figure out what Jared was up to, I can bring that to the police, and they'll protect me. Or I give them enough to find the bastard who did it." My voice cracked as I finished that last sentence. I sounded like a foolish old woman.

Gwen shook her head. "You're either the bravest person I know or the dumbest. Good luck because Jared didn't deserve to die like that."

Gwen disappeared into her place. The walk had taken us close to twenty minutes and as I stood there, I saw johns going into the second and third trailer.

I wouldn't get to talk to the other girls tonight. They'd be busy all night long. Now I knew why Jared was so preoccupied when I saw him Saturday night. I felt terrible all over again for giving him so much shit about missing dinner and about how he wasn't telling me what was going on.

Had Jared been trying to protect me, or the cases he was working on? I'd never know. I also didn't know how I'd be able to forgive myself for some of the things I'd said to him. Jared had been my closest friend in the three years I'd been on the streets and on his last weekend alive on this earth I'd come at him like an angry baby because he wasn't paying attention to me. It didn't matter if he was just pretending to be my friend because he was undercover. He'd treated me decently and with kindness. He'd made me feel just a little bit less like a piece of garbage.

My shoulders slumped from the shame of how I'd treated him before he'd died. Before he'd been murdered. I started the journey back to my tent when I felt prickles at the back of my neck.

I turned to see who was watching me and saw a man standing at the edge of the road Gwen and I'd just been on. He was short with stubby arms and stocky legs. He was cast in the blue glow of the neon sign above him, but I could tell he had dark hair and eyes and a scowl directed straight at me. I was about to give him the finger when I saw the gun he pointed at me.

I took a deep breath and turned around. I sprinted down Franklin Avenue toward Vermont. All I had to do was hit that corner. I zigged and zagged, knowing it was harder to shoot someone who wasn't running in a straight line.

I had no idea who the man was, but I hoped it was Miguel giving me a warning to stay away from his girls. I didn't know if I'd found out any new information, but the gun convinced me not to come back.

Maybe it was time to go to the police, turn in Jared's notebook, and ask them to protect me. It sounded like a way better plan than what I'd been doing. Who was I kidding? I wasn't brave. I was scared shitless and all alone on the streets.

The best I could do now was get back to my tent, make it through the night, and find a way to contact the woman detective first thing in the morning. That plan might actually keep me alive, I thought.

DAY 2 - NIGHT

By the time Harri and Tom got back downtown, the California Unhoused Community Outreach, CUCO, building was closed for the day. Instead, they went to the PAB and started the background checks on Davis Hines and Arthur Sharpe.

They found multiple drug-related arrests for both men. Art was a standout though, with a domestic battery charge filed against him by an ex-girlfriend named Marpessa Roberts. The arrest report listed an address for Marpessa Roberts on Vermont Avenue and also provided her Social Security number. Harri referenced that information in the DMV database to find Marpessa Roberts' driver's license.

Harri was sure the photo of the girl she was staring at matched who Jared was searching for information on at the Riverside shelter. Marpessa was the only missing female mentioned in the case so far.

So far.

She jumped out of her seat to tell Tom, but he wasn't at his desk. She'd become so engrossed in her work she hadn't noticed Tom leaving. She paused and looked around. Then she heard his voice coming from Lieutenant Richard Byrne's office. He must be giving the LT their debrief. She was glad he was doing it and not her.

Lieutenant Richard Byrne, her new boss, fought hard to keep her out of RHD for years. They had a well-known beef going back a long time. Richard was part of the old boys club that had no issues putting his hands were they didn't belong. Neither of them wanted to work with the other. RHD was the most prestigious murder division in the LAPD and Harri believed she'd earned her stripes to be considered for it. It was a non-starter until she worked with the venerable Detective Tom Bards on the Creek Killer case.

Tom had pushed for her to be transferred and become his partner. That finally broke down Richard's wall. Harri was always careful to stay professional with Richard at all times and avoided him the best she could. Whenever they needed to speak with Richard, Tom did the talking. The partners had discussed that strategy fully and agreed on it. She liked that everything was out in the open with Tom.

She walked by the LT's office to see if she could hear where the conversation was headed. She'd heard the top brass wanted to make an announcement that Jared Atkinson a.k.a. Ethan Carle was an undercover detective and part of the Gang Unit. Both Harri and Tom asked for more time.

As soon as she appeared in the doorway, Tom noticed and motioned for her to come inside.

"I was just bringing the LT up to date on our investigation," Tom said. Harri looked over at their unsmiling LT and saw the usual scowl on his face. Richard was never happy to see her. The feeling was mutual.

Harri reluctantly sat down in the only chair available in the office and told both men about Davis Hines' and Arthur Sharpe's various arrests.

"I did find a connection to one of our missing persons of interest. Jared had been asking for any information on Marpessa Roberts, a young woman reportedly pregnant at the time of her disappearance. I found a domestic battery charge against Arthur Sharpe filed by Marpessa Roberts about a year ago. I tracked down her ID and she matches the description Jared gave Eric Radford. She was his ex-girlfriend. I'm surprised the current girlfriend made no mention of her. I'm sure Jared must have asked Marie about her," Harri said.

"Why are you calling the dead cop Jared?" Lieutenant Byrne barked. "Thought his name was Ethan Carle."

"We agreed to refer to him by his undercover name so I don't slip up and give away info people shouldn't have," Tom interjected.

Harri's cheeks flushed. She was grateful once again to have Tom Bards as her partner.

"Do you have an address for her?" Lieutenant Byrne asked.

"The last listed address was on Vermont Avenue in East Hollywood. Since she was at the shelter, I'm assuming she no longer resides there. I'll send two officers on my team to canvass the apartment building for any information," Harri said.

They'd been assigned six uniformed police officers to help with the canvassing of potential suspects and witnesses.

"I was just telling the lieutenant about the white van and CUCO, and the potential connection to our three missing men and Jared Atkinson. There's precedent for predators using the promise of construction work to gain access to their victims," Tom said to Harri.

He turned back to Richard. "Arthur Sharpe also went missing while looking for work at a Home Depot on Sunset Boulevard. Day laborers there typically get work from building contractors. We both agree it's too much of a coincidence not to have something behind it."

"We've established the existence of a notebook Jared Atkinson was seen writing in by multiple witnesses. That's currently missing. The Los Feliz librarian was also shown his badge. We didn't find that in his leftover belongings," Harri said.

"Meaning we have an LAPD badge out in the wild," Richard stated. "That's just terrific."

Harri and Tom nodded.

"Where are you in the timeline?" Richard asked.

"We have Jared finding out about Davis Hines and CUCO from Irma Heller at the Riverside shelter first thing Friday morning. He visited the Los Feliz library that Friday morning, as well and watched the video of the homeless man, Rich getting into a white van. He spoke to Marie, Arthur Sharpe's new girlfriend at the Rodney encampment at around 6:30 that night and learned about the Home Depot. Witnesses at Jared's encampment say he was around there both Friday night and Saturday morning," Tom said.

"We also know he got into a fight with his closest friend, a Darlene "Whitey" Whiteman at the encampment on both Friday and Saturday nights. We need to conclude our interviews down there. I think we can pull more information out of some of the witnesses. One, in particular, might have more information about the nights in question," she said.

"Still have a lot of holes in his movements that weekend," Richard said.

"That's correct," Tom acknowledged.

"Our guess is he went to CUCO and tried to get day labor work through their connections like Davis Hines did. If I was undercover, I'd probably try to get into the mix and see the players," Harri said.

The lieutenant glanced over at Harri and narrowed his eyes. She maintained her composure and pretended not to notice his glare.

"We missed interviewing anyone at CUCO today because they were all closed up by the time we got down there," Tom said.

"I read the coroner's report. I have serious concerns as to what we're up against," Richard said.

"What kind of concerns?" Tom asked.

"Are the gangs getting into medical fraud now? How many serial offenders are we looking into? Where are the other bodies? Should we be announcing this to the public? How do we keep the journos and activists out of this? I'm getting pressure to make some sort of announcement and I've been putting them off. Once the media catches wind of this, it's going to be mayhem out there. I'm shocked they haven't caught onto it yet, to be honest," Richard said.

Harri was surprised he'd been so forthcoming. Richard was a political animal first and foremost, and he always made sure to keep himself ahead of any potential blowback. Harri wondered why he laid his thoughts so bare to them. What was his agenda?

"What are your next steps?" he asked.

"I have meetings scheduled with several tissue banks tomorrow after we check out CUCO," Tom said.

"And I've made a list of mortuaries to follow up on.

We're thinking this case has to involve the death industry," Harri said.

Richard pursed his lips. He looked constipated in Harri's eyes. She tried hard to keep her expression neutral.

"What movement is happening on the female limbs found near Detective Ethan Carle's body?" Richard asked.

"Without any sort of ID or a primary crime scene, we've put them on the back burner until the forensics on the limbs is done. In the Ethan Carle case, we have witnesses to talk to and uncovering the secret investigation he was working on," Tom said.

"I've tried to put off the higher-ups, but they forced my hand. A press conference has been scheduled for the day after tomorrow," Richard said.

"Will you be announcing that Jared Atkinson was an undercover cop?" Tom asked.

Richard smiled grimly. His expression confirmed the answer was a yes.

"Ethan Carle doesn't have any living relatives but there's been a word from the gang unit. They're insisting on full honors for their fallen colleague. The brass has agreed. A cop was murdered in our city, and that demands justice. I'm giving you five more uniforms to help with the canvassing and running down leads. What else do you need besides the extra bodies?" Richard asked.

"More time before the announcement but looks like we're not going to get that," Tom said.

"Correct. Forty-eight hours is all you have," he said.

"Thanks, LT," Tom said and got up. "We still have background checks to run before we leave for the night."

Harri stood up and followed Tom out the door without saying anything else.

When they were back at their desks, Harri finished giving Tom her updates. She didn't want to do that in front of Richard.

"I forgot to mention we need to interview Whitey again. She lied to us. Or rather it was a big omission about the fights she had with Jared both nights. I've tried calling Whitey on her cellphone but it's going to an automatic voicemail. She's either screening me or she's dumped the phone," Harri explained.

"And you mentioned wanting to speak with Rufus again?" Tom asked.

"He was holding something back from us. When we asked about the last time he saw Jared, he looked off to the side or down on the ground. He was under the influence but when we were questioning him, he had this unwavering gaze. But when we asked him that question, he looked away. My gut tells me he's keeping something back," she said.

"Do you think you could go down there and interview both of them before we meet with CUCO?" he asked.

"Sure thing."

"Richard also gave us a conference room to set up our chronology board. I've set Officer Cyndi Rodriguez to coordinate with all the new officers and give them their assignments. We'll fill up those forty-eight hours," Tom said.

He motioned for her to follow him to their new home. The small conference room was three doors down from the RHD bullpen. Several officers were putting up the chronology board.

Harri recognized Officer Cyndi Rodriguez and

Officer Tony Diaz at the large corkboard. A whiteboard was fixed to the wall next to it.

"Hi Cyndi, hi Tony," she called out to them.

"Hey Harri," Cyndi said. "Happy to be working with you again."

"Me, too. Welcome."

Tony nodded and went back to hanging up photos. Cyndi smiled and went over to the conference table stacked with paperwork.

The chronology board was a visual representation of Ethan Carle's aka Jared Atkinson's movements. Times, locations, and witnesses were already up on the board for parts of Friday and Saturday. Davis Hines' and Arthur Sharpe's photos were up underneath the label Secret Jared Investigation. Cards for Marpessa Roberts and no last name Rich were placed alongside Davis and Art's photos. Darlene "Whitey" Whiteman's DMV photo had been placed along the chronology timeline at the points she intersected with Jared. Harri added Marpessa Roberts' photo to the Secret Jared Investigation part.

The holes in the chronology were glaring and large. Chunks of Friday and Saturday were unaccounted for.

"We still have a lot of ground to cover," she remarked.

"I really believe when we go to CUCO, we'll get a larger piece of the puzzle for Friday and Saturday," he said.

"I hope you're right," Harri said.

"All these guys went looking for jobs as day laborers. I wouldn't be surprised if Jared did the same," Tom said.

"How many more people do we have on the team now?" she asked.

"Richard gave us six uniformed officers for

canvassing and routine interviews," Tom said. "We'll have five more by morning."

"Are you done canvassing the river encampment?" she asked.

"We finished today," Tony said.

"Would you be able to go and check out a residence for me?" Harri asked. "It's for Marpessa Roberts. I'll give you the information to add to the board. We need to see if she's still living at the address on the battery complaint I found. Maybe you could help me track down where she's living now?"

"Sure thing, Harri," Tony said. "Tonight, or tomorrow?"

"Tomorrow is fine. I'll email you the information."

Tony nodded.

"Thank you," Harri said.

She turned back to the board deep in thought. She'd been excited about how far they'd come in the investigation just hours ago and now looking at all the gaps they had, she felt they were still at the beginning. Her stomach grumbled in protest. She'd forgotten to eat. Again.

"I'm going to head out since I have an early morning at the river," Harri said.

"You're okay going there by yourself?" Tom asked.

Harri nodded.

"Are there officers still down there?" she asked Tony.

"No, we all packed up and left unless we should still have somebody stationed there?" he asked.

"SID took all of Jared's belongings, right?" she asked.

Tony looked confused. "You mean Detective Carle?

Harri nodded. "We are calling him Jared Atkinson to prevent slip ups and for less confusion."

"That's right. They took all of Detective, er, Jared

Atkinson's gear. The other residents there weren't too happy about that. One of them was already looking to move in, but we shut that down."

"I'll make sure the sun is out," she said with a grin to Tom.

Tom nodded and Harri took one last look at the sparse-looking board and left to grab her stuff and head home.

13

DAY 3 -MARCH 8, 2019 - EARLY MORNING HOURS

Harri Harper parked her car in the red zone at close to seven in the morning, just west of the entrance to the bike path and the Los Feliz river encampment. She was still exhausted even though she theoretically got a full night's sleep.

She'd crashed hard the moment she'd gotten home the night before and barely had a chance to catch up with Jake. She'd woken up before him and was out the door by six. Harri felt as if she hadn't slept a wink. She supposed that made sense since she'd dreamt of running through a dark forest all night long, her sister's disembodied voice calling out to her from somewhere in the darkness. Every hour, she'd gasp awake, relief flooding through her when she realized she was still in bed and that it was only a dream. Her extreme fatigue was even making her eyeballs hurt.

She walked against the early morning traffic to the bike path entrance. The morning was cold and gray with a marine layer that hung low over the city. Everything around her seemed dull and flat again.

Harri shivered in her lightweight blazer over her white button-down shirt. Her shoulder holster wasn't fitting properly because it kept catching somewhere near her left underarm. Everything was irritating her today.

She stepped through the chain-link fence and turned right toward Whitey's tent when something hit her full force from behind.

Before she could even cry out, an arm slithered around her neck in a chokehold, cutting off her voice and her air. Her body tensed and she panicked. Flashes of the director pulling her up by his makeshift noose raced through her mind.

She couldn't panic.

She had to think.

Against her best effort, her brain shut down as fear coursed through her body. Fear either made an individual get ready to fight or get ready to run. Unfortunately, with her PTSD from her encounter with the director, she froze instead.

No. She couldn't freeze.

She would die if she didn't do something and NOW.

Whoever was behind her, tightened their arm around her neck. Harri gasped for air as blackness crept in from the corners of her vision.

It was now or never.

Harri marshaled all the fear inside her and forced herself to move.

She dropped her chin down to put some space between the man's elbow and her neck.

With her right arm, Harri grabbed behind her and felt for fingers.

Her hand closed over two of his fingers and she yanked them back as hard as she could away from her neck.

The man squeaked in pain.

Gulping down air, she used her left arm to yank his other arm away from her, giving her enough room to slide her body down and away from his grasp.

She'd done it. She'd freed herself out of his grip and stood to face him.

The nearly nude white man whimpered in pain, clutching at his bent fingers. His blue eyes were ablaze and Harri recognized the fog of drugs. He had blood smeared near his nose, a rough-shaved head with scars, and tattoos filling his scrawny chest.

"I know who you are!" he screamed. "You can't get me!"

This man was in the middle of a full-on hallucination. Harri twisted away from him and got behind him. Sometimes in a drug-induced psychosis, individuals had super strength. Harri didn't want to find out if that was true. She needed to incapacitate him fast.

She yanked his arms back and dragged him to the ground, her knee in his back. He hit the ground with a thud and yelped out in pain. Harri pulled out the zip-ties she always carried with her and tied his arms behind his back.

He lay there moaning and screaming in front of her as she got back to her feet.

"You got some moves po-po," Rufus called out from across the way. He stood by the entrance of his tent, his eyes wide. He put his arms up in the air as a sign of surrender.

"Put your arms down, Rufus," Harri muttered.

"Gary been giving you some problems?" Rufus asked.

"Is this Gary?" Harri asked.

Her panic was subsiding but not fast enough. If she stuck her hands out, she was sure they would be shaking. She would not have a panic attack in front of Rufus.

Not today.

Not happening.

Harri shoved her fear down and took several deep breaths.

"Way too early in the morning for that," she said. Harri massaged her neck and hoped Gary hadn't damaged her throat muscles and vocal cords. They'd only been fully healed a month.

"You okay?" Rufus asked.

"He grabbed me from behind and tried to strangle me," Harri said, disbelief in her voice. "I'm a cop. Does he have a death wish?"

"Oh, girl. His brain is so gone," Rufus said. "He attacks somebody at least once a day."

"Why is he still out on the streets?" she asked.

"You tell me," he said. "I was sure he'd be finally put away after he was running naked against traffic on Los Feliz. But that wasn't enough and you released him back to us two days later. Ya'll be overcrowded," he said.

"Where is everybody?" Harri asked.

"Nobody's been back since you guys came," Rufus said, gesturing behind him. There were still only about eleven tents left.

"Why didn't anybody come out to check when he was screaming?" Harri asked.

"Why would anybody want to get in between him and whatever invisible thing he was fighting this time?" he asked.

Harri looked down and saw Gary had passed out and was snoring. She didn't want to leave him lying naked on the ground like that, but she didn't exactly want to call any cops to pick him up, either.

The man needed to be in a hospital on some serious meds. He'd attacked her, but he was also insane when he did it. She wasn't one of those cops who thought anyone who attacked one of them should be killed. Or jailed indefinitely.

Harri called dispatch and requested an ambulance to transport a psychotic man for evaluation.

"They just gonna release him back in a couple days," Rufus said.

"I can't leave him here like this," Harri said.

"I would," Rufus said. "What you doing here so early anyway?"

"Came by to talk to you actually," Harri said, her panic subsiding. She was breathing slowly, taking her time to speak each word. Her therapist had shown her that technique and it was helping her to calm down. Harri stood up straight and focused on the task at hand.

"You sure you doing okay?" Rufus asked.

"He was really strong. My neck hurts," Harri said, rubbing it.

"Want some ice for that?" Rufus asked. "I mean, I don't have any, but we could look around."

"I'll be fine," Harri said. "What you could do for me is tell me what you were keeping from us about Jared Atkinson."

Rufus folded his arms against his chest and cocked his head at her.

"How you know I didn't tell you everything?" he asked. "You read minds or something?"

"You have a tell. When I asked you when you last saw Jared, you looked away. That's your tell," Harri explained.

"Is that so?" Rufus smiled. "Well, good thing I don't play poker."

"I wouldn't start," Harri said with a grin.

Rufus nodded as he mulled her request over. Harri saw when he made his decision and stopped nodding. She stepped a foot closer to him.

"Jared snuck out of camp around eleven that night," Rufus said. "And he came back real late Saturday night, around three or four in the morning."

"Why were you up so late?" Harri asked.

"Drinking. Partying. The usual." Rufus shrugged.

"You were drunk that night?" Harri asked.

"I'm always drunk. Doesn't mean I'm lying, does it?" Rufus said sharply.

"No, no one said you're lying. And you're sure it was Jared?" Harri asked.

"I talked to him, didn't I?" Rufus said slyly. He hadn't mentioned that part.

"You saw him coming back at three in the morning?"

"About that time. I called out his name and he said hi. I asked if he enjoyed the girls on Franklin and he nodded slowly and went into his tent."

"Why didn't you tell us that before?" Harri asked.

"Didn't want Whitey to hear us talkin'," he said.

"Why not?"

"I told you. That girl's got a gun for a tongue and I don't need her shooting it off at me. She had a crush on him. I mean, she was all up in his business. There ain't no reason to be up in a man's business like that unless of course, you gettin' some," he said.

Harri didn't entirely buy that logic, but she let it slide. More importantly, who were the girls on Franklin?

"Tell me about the girls on Franklin?" Harri asked.

"There's trailers on Franklin, kind of between

Vermont and Normandie," he explained. "Miguel's got some tasty girls in those trailers. Cheap enough for us to even get some action."

"And that's where Jared said he was coming from?" Harri asked, confused.

"Well, he nodded, didn't he? Where else would he be at three in the morning? The guy didn't party like the rest of us. Plus, I have a buddy who hangs out in the 7-11 parking lot right over there. He seen Jared there going through the trailers. That's why I asked. He came off like a saint, all high and mighty, but lookee here. Jared Atkinson still needed to pay for it."

"Did he sneak off any other day?" Harri asked.

"Snuck off Friday night, too. Same way. Left around midnight and was back late."

"Did you talk to him on Friday night also?" she asked.

"Not that time. I was too drunk to carry on a conversation," Rufus admitted.

If he was so drunk, could she believe him about seeing Jared both nights? She jotted it down and hoped she'd be able to confirm it in some way.

They paused the conversation so Harri could explain what happened to Gary to the EMTs who'd just arrived. They tried to rouse the naked man and when he wasn't responsive but breathing, they got him on the stretcher and carried him out. The entire exchange didn't take longer than ten minutes but when Harri looked back to where Rufus was, he'd taken off already.

Harri had what she needed from him anyway. She walked over to Whitey's tent and called out to the woman.

"Whitey? Good morning. Are you home?"

When she didn't hear a sound coming from the tent, she unzipped it and peeked inside. The sleeping bag looked like it hadn't been slept in. All of her belongings were piled in a tidy way. Harri was tempted to do a quick search when she heard a sound coming from behind her.

Harri pulled her head out of Whitey's tent and faced Rufus again.

"What you doin' in Whitey's tent?" he asked, his voice no longer friendly.

"I've tried calling her numerous times at the number she gave us. She hasn't picked up and I'm worried about her. Have you seen her this morning?" she asked.

"Nah, I'm not even sure she came back last night," he said.

That didn't bode well for Whitey, Harri thought.

"Can I give you my number? I have to go meet my partner downtown but if you see Whitey can you call me? I'm worried she's gonna be another missing person."

"Sure thing," Rufus said with a frown on his face. "So, these missing people, it's a real thing then? They're not going to different shelters or setting up at another camp?"

"It doesn't look like it. Grow eyes on the back of your head and don't go anywhere with anyone you don't know or trust," Harri said.

"Give me your number. I'll call you if she turns up," Rufus promised.

Harri wrote her cell number down on one of her business cards and gave it to him. She told Rufus to take care of himself and headed back to her cruiser.

Harri wasn't sure if she'd make it to CUCO on time

or what excuse she could give Tom for why she was late. She didn't want to tell him about the attack, but she also couldn't lie to him. Why had she come down here on her own? She should have brought an officer with her. She'd remember that for next time. At least, she hoped she would.

14

DAY 3 - MORNING

Harri found it impossible to find parking near the California Unhoused Community Outreach headquarters. She'd called Tom to let him know she was running fifteen minutes late and explained what happened between her and Gary.

Tom apologized for not going with her that morning, but she waved away his guilt. She didn't want anyone on her team thinking she couldn't take care of herself. She was a Detective Division I and she could handle it.

The police psychologist had given her the go-ahead to return to duty and any cop would have been frazzled if they'd just been put in a headlock by a crazed drug addict. She thought she'd handled the situation amazingly, all things considered. Then her brain started whispering that she wasn't good enough for RHD. She knew it was bullshit, but at the same time, it wasn't as if she was exactly keeping her head down.

The circular thoughts continued as she drove around CUCO searching for a parking space. Always having to fight her own thoughts irritated her and once she parked, she was glad to get out of the car. Harri ran the two blocks to meet Tom in front of the entrance of CUCO.

The glass and metal headquarters for CUCO contrasted sharply with the area where the facility stood two blocks west of skid row. The headquarters building was modern and architecturally blank compared to the structures surrounding it. Harri looked up at it and she wondered if anybody worried about those windows being shattered every night.

"Sure you're okay?" Tom asked in concern.

"Stop it. I'm totally fine, Tom. I did the singing exercises the physical therapist showed me on the drive down here and everything seems normal," Harri said.

"Okay, then. We have another lead. I'm glad you went back there," Tom said as he opened the door.

"It's a good one too," she said. "Especially with Marpessa Roberts going missing like that. I'm wondering if she was one of the women in those trailers."

They stopped talking as they stepped up to the front desk. A petite woman with brown hair and eyes sat behind the massive desk. The name on her tag was Guadalupe.

Harri could see warrens of offices behind Guadalupe stretching down three long hallways. This nonprofit is well-funded, Harri thought.

They showed Guadalupe their credentials and she looked at them carefully.

"What can I help you with?" she asked in an accented voice.

"Have you seen this man?" Tom showed the picture of Jared Atkinson they'd been using with all the witnesses.

"I remember him. He came by last weekend," she said.

"Can you tell us what he was here for?" Harri asked.

"He was looking for day work just as a lot of the other men who come by," Guadalupe said.

"And how does one go about finding day work with your organization?" Harri asked.

"One fills out an intake form and then we put them on a waiting list. When companies request day labor, we go down the list and choose candidates who are the best match and give them a call," Guadalupe explained.

There was a formality to her tone and way of speaking. Harri noticed she kept her hands folded on her desk, the way schoolchildren do.

That was nice and simple, Harri thought. "Can we see the form?" she asked.

"No, you cannot," Guadalupe said.

"Why not?" Tom asked. "It's just a form."

There was an awkward moment of silence before Guadalupe stood up and said, "Excuse me."

Harri and Tom watched her disappear around a corner. They could hear Guadalupe's hushed voice in conversation with a louder man's voice.

"Well, what do they want?" the man's voice asked.

"I don't know," Guadalupe explained.

"Who sent them here?" the man's voice demanded.

"I don't know," Guadalupe said.

Harri and Tom looked at each other and waited while they heard the man slam a phone receiver into its cradle in irritation.

As the man rounded the corner to the reception desk, with Guadalupe right behind him, Harri heard him mutter, "always have to do everything myself."

When the man saw Harri and Tom, he straightened himself and smiled tightly.

"How can I help you?" he asked.

"I'm Detective Tom Bards. This is Detective Harriet Harper. We're with LAPD Robbery-Homicide Division," Tom said.

"And what do you want with us?" the man asked.

"We'd like to ask a few questions about a man who came by here last week."

"You have a warrant?" Guadalupe asked.

The man flashed her a look that made Guadalupe slink behind him.

Harri and Tom looked at each other. This was turning out to be an interesting interview.

"So, you're not going to give us a form without a warrant?" Harri asked.

"I don't think our attorneys would like that," the man said with another tight smile. "We've already been harassed by reporters, and we don't need the police scaring away the people we are here to help."

"What is your name?" Harri asked.

"Raymond Sklar," the man responded in obvious annoyance.

"And what is it you do here?" Harri asked.

"I am the CEO," Raymond Sklar said as if it was a burden to be speaking to someone so far beneath him.

"What reporters have been harassing you?" Tom asked.

"We know you're asking about the man who was found dead in the river. We can't have our organization involved in anything like that," Raymond Sklar said.

"How do you know Jared Atkinson was found dead in the river?" Harri asked.

Raymond Sklar looked pointedly at Guadalupe as if he was giving her permission to speak.

"A reporter was here before you came in. He showed me the same picture," she said.

"What was this reporter's name?" Tom asked. "Did they say what organization they worked for?"

"We don't have to answer that," Raymond Sklar said. "If you continue to harass us, you'll have to go through our attorneys."

"All right," Tom smiled. "What's the contact info for your attorney?"

"Guadalupe, I'll need you to spell your last name for me," Harri added.

Raymond Sklar scowled and went back to his office, leaving Guadalupe to write down the contact information for the CUCO attorneys.

The media was on their tail. The news must've gotten out that Jared was a cop and now the reporters were trying to put the story together. They had way less than forty-eight hours before the news was out that an undercover cop had been murdered.

They left Guadalupe sitting at the desk, nearly in tears. When they got outside, Tom took a right and walked toward Fifth Street. He turned the corner and stopped abruptly.

"What are we doing?" Harri asked.

"We're getting one of those damn forms," Tom said.

"Cool. How?" Harri asked.

"Ever stand outside a liquor store when you were a kid, waiting for someone legal age to buy beer for you?" Tom asked.

"No," Harri said.

"Oh, right." Tom rolled his eyes. "I forgot you were Little Miss Goody Two-Shoes."

"Say what you want, but one of us was an altar boy and it wasn't me," Harri said.

They waited on the corner another twenty minutes, watching the entrance of the outreach center. There were a lot of homeless men going in and out of that place.

"Are we waiting for someone of legal age?" Harri teased.

"Maybe," Tom said. "Keep your eyes peeled for a white van,"

"We should put a team on the entrance to surveil any vans picking up day laborers."

"Absolutely," Tom said.

A young man in his early twenties ambled toward them. His eyes were focused and clear and Tom nodded to Harri. This was their man.

"Hey, you going to CUCO?" Tom asked.

"Why are you asking?" the man asked.

"I wanted to get on the list for work, but the woman at the front desk doesn't like me. I might've gotten into a fight in front of the place and she's holding a grudge. Would you mind getting a form for me?" Tom asked.

The man looked him up and down.

"You look like a cop," he said.

"I am a cop." Tom sighed.

"Why didn't you just say so? You want me to get you a form?" the guy asked.

"I would love that," Tom said.

He started to go for his wallet and the man looked at him square in the face.

"I don't need your money, homey," he said.

"Thank you," Tom said awkwardly.

The man walked by them, shaking his head.

"Well, that didn't go as planned," Tom said.

"Let's see if he actually comes back with a form,"

Harri said.

They waited another fifteen minutes and to Harri's surprise, the young man came back. He handed them a form with an amused expression on his face.

"You cops are weird," he said as he walked away.

"I can't entirely disagree with that," Harri said as they scanned the form.

At first, it was mostly standard requesting name, date of birth, skills, and times available for work. But then there was a series of health questions that made them pause.

Why would a nonprofit company helping homeless people find work need their medical histories? On the back of the form, there were lists of diseases and medical conditions for the people to check off. The big ones were at the top: heart disease, certain cancers, diabetes, hepatitis. It was the perfect screening form for a tissue harvest.

"Are they allowed to ask all these questions?" Harri asked as she scanned down the page.

"I suppose they could get away with saying they needed it for insurance reasons," Tom guessed. "Like some liability insurance for the companies that came looking to get these day laborers. I don't even know if some of these people would answer truthfully, but it's weird how detailed this is. And look." He pointed to the bottom of the back of the page. "This asks them to release their medical information to them."

"I could see this place being in the pipeline for tissue harvesting," Harri said.

"Oh, for damn sure," Tom said. "I think we got what we needed for the time being. I'm heading off to my tissue bank interviews. Will you set up the team to watch this place? What else do you have on the docket this afternoon?" he asked.

"I was going to check out some mortuaries, but now I'm thinking I need to check out those trailers and talk to some of the women there, see what Jared was following."

"Let's meet back at the PAB at the end of day and fill out more of that board," Tom said.

Harri nodded, her mind already racing to the women in the trailers.

"The trailer women could be the victim pool for those limbs," she said.

"I was thinking the same," Tom said. "Where did you park?"

"Two blocks that way." Harri pointed back toward her car.

"I walked here from the PAB. If you were in my direction, I'd catch a ride but looks like it would be quicker to walk. I'll catch you later," he said.

"Good luck," Harri said.

She walked back to the car with a mind already on the questions she'd ask the girls. Her panic from the morning was long gone, replaced with nervous energy. The case was speeding up. The girls could be the key to what happened to Jared and she'd pulled that information out of Rufus. He'd folded pretty fast under questioning, but she didn't doubt he saw Jared coming back so late.

She did hope Rufus was right about where Jared was coming from, even if it was for the wrong reason. Harri was certain Jared wasn't having a good time with those girls unless following up on a lead could be considered a good time. He must have been as excited as she was now to hit that next clue. That next piece of the puzzle.

But was this piece what got Jared killed?

15

DAY 3

Harri called Officer Cyndi Rodriguez to coordinate the surveillance of CUCO and the task of taking down license plates of all white vans doing business with the organization. With that taken care of, Harri parked behind the first RV she saw on Franklin Avenue. Before she could even knock on the door, a short man came flying around the corner from one of the side streets.

"Hey! What do you think you're doing?" he shouted. "That's my property."

"I'm here to speak with your girls," Harri said coolly.

She pulled out her badge and held it up to his face. "What's your name?"

"I don't have to tell you that," the short man sneered.

Harri put her badge away and took a look at the man. He was about her height, which put him around five foot four, and stocky, with a brown, pockmarked complexion. His black hair was cut in a military-style buzz and his brown eyes were narrowed to slits.

"Okay." Harri sighed. "Look, I've had a hell of a

morning so far and I'm in no mood, so here's how this is going to go. You either answer all of my questions truthfully, and stand aside while I talk to these women, or I will call my partner down here so we can unleash a shitstorm together. He doesn't like to be left out."

"Go ahead," the man challenged. "Make my day."

Harri heard a faint giggle from inside the RV.

"Come out here, ladies," Harri called. "Now!"

The door to the first RV opened and a slim, dark-haired girl stepped out wearing a red bikini.

"Get back inside!" the man yelled.

"Shut up, Miguel!" the girl yelled back. "His name Is Miguel Watts," she said to Harri.

"Miguel." Harri shook her head. "You're not making good decisions today. What's it going to be? Am I having all these RVs impounded? Sometimes vehicles stay locked up in our yard for a long time while we search for evidence. How about your, um, workers here? Should I call my friends in Vice to come over and meet them? Or do you want to be a good little boy and work with me here?"

"I'm not talking to you out here on the street," Miguel said.

"Yes, you are." Harri pulled out the photo of Jared Atkinson. "I need to know everything you can tell me about this guy."

"Like what?" Miguel asked.

"Like when was the last time you saw him?" she asked.

"Saturday night," Miguel said.

"Why was he here? Was he a client?" Harri asked.

"Nah, he was a cop. Like you," he said.

That surprised Harri. "He told you that?"

"One of my girls, Rena May. She took off Saturday.

He came looking for her that night. Said he was a cop. No, former cop with an addiction. Said he could find her. I had no problem with that, so I told him where she liked to hang out."

"And where is that?"

"Little Rena liked her meth. Got it on Berendo. That was the last anybody saw her," Miguel said. "I've been waiting for her call." He took on the high pitch of a fake girl's voice. "Ay, Miguel. The po-po got me. Come bail me. Ay, Miguel. I OD'd. Come get me at the ER."

It was hard for Harri to hear how he talked about this girl.

"Knock it off," she told him. "Did Jared follow up on the dealer at Berendo?"

"That's what he said," Miguel shrugged.

"Did he ask about anyone named Marpessa Roberts?"

"The pregnant chick? Yeah, that bitch. If I'd known what a pain in my ass she was I never would've played her game."

"What does that mean?" Harri demanded.

"She came to me for protection. Wanted to pretend to be one of my girls so no one would mess with her. She never worked for me. It was all pretend. She paid me cash for Gwen's place," he nodded to the RV behind Harri.

"Who did she need protection from?" Harri asked.

"Her asshole baby daddy," Miguel said. "I thought it would be easy money, but it was drama, drama, drama. Her ex coming around. Cops coming around. I tried to show her how much money she could make with some of these freaks, being preggo, but she wouldn't do it. One day she went out for groceries and never came back. I lost money for two days before I brought Gwen in."

"Did she leave any belongings behind?" Harri asked.

"Nope." Miguel shook his head.

"Liar!" The dark-haired girl in the bikini shouted.

"Are you Gwen?" Harri asked.

The girl nodded and said, "Marpessa left some clothes behind and her stash of baby stuff. He threw it all away."

Harri sighed. "What did I tell you about lying to me, Miguel?"

"It was nothing," Miguel insisted. "Just fat girl clothes and baby stuff."

"Did anyone come looking for her after she went missing?" Harri asked.

"Your best friend, Jared," Miguel said.

"And no one before that?" Harri asked.

"Nope." Miguel shook his head.

"Did she tell you who the father of the baby was?" Harri asked.

"Oh, yeah." Miguel smirked. "She told me all about it over lemonade one time. I was gonna throw her a baby shower."

"I said knock it off," Harri warned him. "How long did your arrangement last?"

"Almost two months. I was sick of it. Was ready to toss her out when she disappeared."

That was a long time to live on the street like this while pregnant. Harri didn't think she would get anything more out of Miguel.

"I want to talk to each of the girls now," she said. "Alone."

"What's Jared done anyway?" he asked.

"He got murdered," Harri said.

Miguel Watts wasn't expecting that. He gasped and took a step back with wide eyes.

"Start with Gwen," he said.

He nodded to the girl, and she led Harri inside the RV.

She couldn't be older than maybe seventeen or eighteen, Harri thought.

Gwen had soft, brown ringlets that fell to her shoulders and big blue eyes with long lashes. She had light, creamy skin with a sprinkle of freckles along the bridge of her nose and cheeks. She was very cute in that girl-next-door way.

How many things had gone wrong for this girl to end up here? Harri thought.

Gwen led her to a dinette table to the right, behind the well-worn driver's seat. A large bed with rumpled sheets took up half the space in the back. A compact kitchenette was across from them. Everything was shabby and smelled faintly of mold and rose fragrance. Harri tried to imagine living in a place like this.

"Hi, Gwen. My name is Detective Harri Harper. I'd like to ask you some questions about Jared Atkinson. What is your full name?" Harri asked as she took her notebook.

"Why do you need that?" Gwen asked as she sat across from Harri.

"Listen, Gwen, you're not in trouble. Jared Atkinson was murdered. I'm investigating that and also what he was looking into."

Gwen looked at Harri with all the confidence of a high school mean girl. Finally, she puckered her lips and nodded. "You can call me Gwen Xavier," she said.

"When was the last time you saw Jared?"

"Around nine-thirty Saturday night. That's when we all realized Rena was missing," she said.

"Why did you think Rena was missing instead of escaping from Miguel?"

"Because she left stuff behind."

"What kind of stuff?" Harri asked. "Clothes? Personal things? Her phone?"

"No." Gwen shook her head. "Her purse and phone were gone. Jared checked all that. Her laptop was gone, too. She left all her designer clothes and some jewelry. Rena was a high-end booster when she wasn't tweaking. She cleaned up cute and could walk into any boutique on Rodeo and come out with half of it hidden on her person."

That was an interesting phrase for a young girl to use. Harri wondered how much exposure she'd had to the police.

"When did you last see Rena?"

"That morning. We had coffee together. Nothing unusual happened," she said.

"Do you know if Rena was seeing any clients on the side?" Harri asked.

Gwen shook her head and shrugged. "Maybe. Probably. You should know somebody else came around asking about Jared."

"Who was that?" Harri asked.

"A woman named Darlene Whiteman. She called herself Whitey. She said Jared told her about Rena disappearing."

"When did she come by?" Harri asked.

"Last night. She was scared. She told me somebody was following her," Gwen said.

Harri's stomach tightened. No wonder she couldn't find Whitey. Had someone gotten to her, or had she gone into hiding?

"Thank you for letting me know," she said.

Gwen nodded and looked back at Harri with that cool, in-control expression.

"Gwen, are you okay?" Harri asked, hearing the stupidity of the question as it came out of her mouth.

"What do you mean?" Gwen asked.

Harri glanced around and then back at the girl. "I mean, are you okay?"

Gwen smiled and shook her head. "Oh, honey. If you knew where I've been, you'd know I'm doing just fine."

Harri nodded and placed one of her business cards on the table. She left Gwen sitting at the dinette in her red bikini. Harri breathed deeply as soon as she was outside. She hadn't realized how badly the place smelled until she was out in fresh air again. She couldn't imagine a pregnant woman living there with her unborn child. This whole case was making her heart ache.

"Take me to your next girl," she said to Miguel, who was standing off to the side smoking a cigarette. They walked the two blocks in silence. The next RV was trashier and less well-kept than Gwen's, which Harri found hardly possible. It was a dirty white with peeling blue trim and duct tape covering holes in the siding.

"I don't know where Joey is, but Laney can talk to you. That last one has a new girl. She replaced Rena, so she doesn't know anything," Miguel said.

"Was that Rena's place?"

"Yeah," Miguel said.

"What did you do with her stuff?" Harri asked.

"Threw it out," Miguel said. "The clothes were too small for the other girls, and I needed the room."

"You need to stop lying to me, Miguel." Harri tried to hide her disgust at the man standing next to her.

"Fine." Miguel sighed. "I traded the stuff on the street. Some of the jewelry was good."

Without saying another word to him, Harri knocked on the door and took the small step up into the sad little RV.

The place had a similar layout to Gwen's. A large bed took up the back half, and the other half had an eating nook and a tiny kitchenette.

A pale blonde with pasty skin and stringy hair sat staring at Harri with dull, gray eyes. She looked like she was on something and Harri could hardly blame her.

"Hi Laney, my name is Detective Harri Harper," she said as she sat across from the young woman. "I'm here to talk about Jared Atkinson and Rena. Did you know Rena's last name?"

"No." Laney shook her head. "Rena May was her stage name. Miguel says Jared is dead."

"That's right. That's why I'm here to talk to you. When did you last see Jared?"

"He was here Saturday night. That's when we figured out Rena was gone. We had a big client coming. Jared was upset. He got into Rena's place before Miguel could get there."

Laney looked around and then dropped her voice to a whisper.

"Jared found the address book."

"He did?" Harri asked. At last, this was something.

"Don't tell Miguel," Laney whispered. "Rena was running side clients. She had one for that Saturday after she picked up her meth."

"Jared told you this or you saw it in her address book?" Harri asked.

"I saw Jared find it in her book. Dante. For three that day."

"You know how she met the man? Or her other clients?" Harri asked.

"She was on some app. On her phone. Kind of like all the other apps, but the guys know they got to pay," she said.

"And Miguel didn't know anything about this?" Harri asked.

Laney shook her head no. "He would have beat her. Hard."

"And when Jared went into her RV, he didn't find her phone or laptop?"

"All he found was her address book with Dante's name for Saturday. He asked me about it, but I never heard her talk about it."

"Where did she get her meth?" Harri asked.

"The gangs at the Berendo camp," Laney said. "They have the best meth around here."

Good to know, thought Harri. "And Jared knew about that?" she asked.

"Yeah." Laney nodded. "He said it was another piece."

"Another piece of what?" Harri asked.

Laney looked at her with that blank stare. "Pie?" she guessed.

No, not pie. It was another piece of Jared's puzzle.

"Did you know Marpessa Roberts?" Harri asked.

"The pregnant girl?" Laney asked.

"Yes, that one."

"She kept to herself. She didn't work like the rest of us. She had a deal with Miguel, but I don't know about that. She had a bad boyfriend. I saw him come around once, but Miguel chased him off."

"Was the baby his?" Harri asked.

"I don't know but he wanted her to get rid of it. He had a new girlfriend, and he didn't want a baby." Laney smiled. "He thought he was going to be a famous rock-

153

star and he didn't want her and the baby dragging him down. That's what I heard him yell at her."

Harri agreed with Laney that Art lacked perspective, but she guessed living on the streets required a certain amount of suspended self-awareness.

"How did she disappear?"

"We woke up one morning and she was gone. Her purse was gone, so we guessed she finally found a shelter," Laney said.

"Did you ever talk with the other girls about her?"

"No, not really," Laney shook her head. She couldn't meet Harri's eyes.

Harri tamped down the thoughts of what she'd like to do to Miguel. This girl was so lost.

"Can you think of anything else about that weekend? About Rena? Or Jared?"

"Are you going to find Rena?" Laney asked.

"If she can be found, I'll find her," Harri promised.

"Are you going to catch the guy who killed Jared?"

"Yes, I am." Harri nodded.

"Are you going to stop Miguel and the johns?"

"Have you had any johns who were violent?" Harri asked.

Laney looked at her with those sad dead eyes.

"Aren't they all violent?"

Harri was disturbed by her conversation with Laney and took a walk around the block to clear her head. The neighborhood was filled with single-family homes of a by-gone era and most of the yards featured flower gardens and manicured lawns.

It soothed her to see the Griffith Observatory directly

above in the hills and she remembered how her parents used to take her and Lauren there when they were kids. The view was magical, and she remembered how excited they'd been to be out so late at night. Their father had taken them to see Mars but the girls were even more enchanted by the view of the city sparkling beneath them than the telescope.

Her phone buzzed in her bag, and she saw it was Tom. She also saw two missed calls and a text from Jake saying "How's your day going? Love you!"

She smiled and answered the phone.

"Tom I was just about to call you," she started.

"We found the van. Abandoned on the side of the road down in Vernon. I'll text you the address. I think it should take me about an hour to get there. Where are you?" he asked.

He sounded out of breath and she could hear street noise in the background. It sounded like he was running to his car.

"I'm still in Los Feliz. It'll probably take me about an hour to get there, too. Who found the van?" she asked.

"Foreman from one of the warehouses down there called it in as abandoned. Said there was a dead dog smell coming from inside. Guess what the responding officer found in the back?"

"More dismembered body parts?"

"Tell the lady what she's won," Tom sounded like he was back in his car.

Harri picked up the pace to get back to her cruiser. "I have some leads myself and I filled another gap for where Jared was."

"Fantastic. I didn't get too far with the tissue banks. If we want any information from them, we're going to need a warrant, as expected. They really stonewalled me," he said.

Harri wasn't surprised by that. With these companies making so much money from harvested tissue, it was unsurprising they would do everything they could to protect their enterprise.

"See you in an hour," she said.

"Be careful driving," Tom said and hung up.

This was big.

If they'd found the same van seen on the footage from the library, there could be traces of Rich inside and they could use that to finally confirm his identity. Whatever body parts had been found inside could connect the two cases. If there was any trace of Jared Atkinson in the van, then everything would be coming together. Harri hoped the license plate and VIN would match on the van and lead them to the registered owner.

This was the physical evidence they needed to pinpoint suspects in this case. Her breath came out in short gasps as she arrived at the cruiser.

Harri tried to reign in her excitement. "Focus," she said out loud to herself. She needed coffee and something to eat. The reward for running around on an empty stomach and too little sleep was a headache. She pushed her hunger, fatigue, and thoughts of what she wanted to do to Miguel Watts aside. She needed to get down to Vernon in one piece. She typed the address Tom texted her into her phone to get the direction and peeled out of the parking spot.

16

DAY 3 - AFTERNOON - 4900 ATLANTIC BOULEVARD, VERNON CALIFORNIA

Harri found herself in a concrete industrial area off the 710 freeway south of downtown. The address was along the Los Angeles River, and it didn't take her long to find the crime scene. Four cruisers with flashing lights surrounded the white van, which was wedged between two pillars attached to a chain link fence. It looked like someone tried to drive the van from the river onto the road and it got stuck. It didn't help that two of the tires were completely flat. Tom stood between two detectives from Southern Division. She showed her badge to the officer manning the sign-in sheet just inside the crime-scene barricade.

Tom waved her over to where he was talking with a tall, slim black woman and a shorter, curvier woman who was writing in a notebook.

"This is Detective Nikki Reginald and Detective Mariella Ramos," Tom said motioning to each of the detectives. "Detectives, this is my partner, Detective Harriet Harper."

"You can call me Harri," she said.

"We got the call about the body part in a van," Detective Reginald explained.

"Were you first on scene?" Harri asked.

"No. A traffic officer was called to process towing the van. It had been abandoned for days," Detective Ramos said, reading from her notebook.

"We were just getting to that part with Detective Bards," Detective Reginald said. "One of the workers at that factory." She pointed at the building behind them, "walked by here the last two days and noticed the van hadn't moved. This morning he noticed the smell and called the abandoned vehicle hotline to report an abandoned vehicle. When the officer arrived, he opened the back and found the arm."

"Can we see the arm?" Harri asked.

She didn't see anyone from SID. Had they been called? She wasn't sure they would get Dr. Grimley for only an arm. It's not like she'd be able to pronounce the time of death.

"It's over this way," Detective Reginald said.

She led Tom and Harri to the back of the van and Harri covered her nose with her hand. Putrefaction had started days ago, and the arm was a mottled purple and engorged with bloat. It looked like it could explode at any moment. Harri could barely make out the brand all over the arm but it was there.

"And the officer found it like this exactly?" Tom asked.

"Yes. He said he only touched the back handles of the van," Detective Ramos added.

"To my untrained eyes, the cut at the shoulder looks similar to the other arms," Harri said to Tom.

"Looks the same to me. I'm pretty sure this is the van our other limbs came out of. Well, well what do we have here," Tom said.

"What am I missing?" Harri asked.

He pointed deeper into the darkness of the van and Harri squinted to see a piece of shiny plastic sheeting connected to the metal leg of the driver's seat. It looked like a potential match to the plastic wrapped around Jared Atkinson's body.

Harri turned to him. "Could Jared Atkinson's body have been inside this van, too?" Harri tried not to sound giddy with excitement. "The plastic around his head was torn. Could that have happened when whatever happened to this van?"

"Maybe," Tom said in a soothing tone. "We won't know for sure until we have the lab test the sample but I'm thinking the same."

"The two cases are connected after all," Harri said with a grin.

All four detectives stared silently into the interior of the van.

The case had shifted again.

"Wait," Harri said. "What did happen to this van?"

"Wrecked and abandoned," Detective Ramos said. "The driver was probably unlicensed, uninsured, drunk, here illegally, something."

"How did it get all the way down here?"

"The river. The storm," Tom said. "Maybe the rain surge carried it all the way."

"Where exactly was your other crime scene?" Detective Reginald asked.

"One of the river islands just below Los Feliz Boulevard," Tom said.

"That's a long way," she said.

They'd been working under the assumption the branded limbs and Jared Atkinson's body had found their way into the river at different places but on the same night.

Could Jared Atkinson have stumbled upon two cases that were connected? The modus operandi of Jared's murder and the dismembered branded limbs were so different it was reasonable to assume they were dealing with two killers. Yet, somehow, all the remains had made it into the same van.

"Could this be evidence of another illegal enterprise entirely?" Harri thought out loud.

"What do you mean?" Tom asked.

"I'm not sure. Think this through with me," Harri said. "Jared's body and the limbs are so different. Two different modus operandi, right? So, say we do have two different killers. Two different kinds of victims, different MO. What do the killers have in common?"

"Besides being vicious murderers that must be stopped?" Detective Reginald asked.

"Right," Harri continued. "Besides being sickos preying on innocents. The tissue harvesters and the person dismembering people have the same problem as every other killer in the world: Body disposal. Every murderer has to figure out what to do with the body. What if this van is part of a black-market service that takes care of body disposal? Any kind of body. No questions asked. For a price, of course," Harri theorized.

"Are you suggesting murderers are outsourcing the disposal of their victims?" Detective Ramos sounded skeptical.

"That's murder 101," Tom said. "Habeus corpus. Show me the body. Murder is hard to prove, even harder without the body. How many killers have gone free because there was only circumstantial evidence and no body?"

"Wow," Detective Reginald said. "Okay, so following your logic here. This van is transporting bodies, but something went wrong with the body disposal this time. What?"

"The rainstorm," Harri said simply. "Can't ever count on the weather. These could be two completely separate killers that used this service. Jared Atkinson's body and the dismembered limbs were together in the van because they were in transit on the way to being disposed of somehow. The two cases don't necessarily have to be connected outside of the body disposal."

All four detectives stood silent again as they looked into the back of the van and considered Harri's new theory.

"For what it's worth, I can't think of any better explanation at this time," Detective Reginald said. "It was a bundled transport. For efficiency."

"Exactly. It doesn't make sense for the remains to be in the same van unless they were all in transit together to be disposed of," Harri said.

"So, what exactly are we looking at here?" Detective Ramos asked.

"A murder courier," Tom said, rubbing his face. "Someone found a niche in the murder market."

Harri turned at the sound of voices in the distance and saw two vans from the coroner's team had arrived.

"The driver's DNA and fingerprints better be in there," Tom said.

Dr. Grimley did, in fact, decide to come down and view the arm. She was flanked by three of her most experienced SID technicians. Harri recognized Paul Gibson and another SID technician from the Creek Killer gravesite last year, although she didn't remember his name. Everyone said their hellos and Dr. Grimley took a look at the arm.

"This arm definitely belongs with the others. I was finally able to determine the potential method for removing the arms from the torso. He used extremely sharp shears to cut through the skin and then cut whatever tendons and ligaments were left connecting the bones. That's what made these ragged cuts right here," she said as she pointed to the edge of the skin where the armpit should be.

"Hey, Brian. Will it be possible to get fingerprints from this interior? I have a feeling it was underwater for a period of time," Tom asked one of the SID forensic techs.

"Depends on how long it was submerged. We can develop latent prints by using cyanoacrylate. Even after ten days of submergence and saltwater, techs were able to lift latent prints," Brian said.

"I'm sure your lab is slammed but is there any way that we can rush this?" Harri asked.

"We'll do our best, as always," Dr. Grimley said.

"We could be looking at two more missing women, one missing since just last night. We could potentially find them alive," Harri said.

She knew she was being optimistic about Rena because they had no idea where that killer was holding the victims or for how long before the actual murder.

"Can we tell from the condition of the arms and leg how long the women were kept captive before their deaths?" Harri asked.

"It's hard to say with only their limbs," Dr. Grimley said. "To pull them apart like that, it could take a machine minutes, hours, or days. I didn't see any other signs of torture outside of the abrasions where they were bound and, of course, the branding."

"Who is the other woman?" Tom asked.

"Whitey. Darlene Whiteman ended up going to talk to the trailer girls last night after dark and no one has seen her since."

"How did she know about the trailer girls if she didn't know Jared was a cop?" Tom asked.

"She told one of the girls that Jared had told her he was looking for Marpessa Roberts and also Rena May," Harri explained.

Tom was about to say something more, but Detective Ramos interrupted them.

"What's our best guess for how this van got out of the river and onto the street?" Detective Ramos asked.

"I don't know this area very well but in other parts of the river, there are access points. The film companies shoot commercials around the downtown area and manage to get equipment trucks down there," Harri said.

"We should talk to that factory worker," Tom said.

Detective Ramos gestured to an Asian man in his late forties wearing a backpack and mechanic's coveralls.

"His name is Lee Chan. He works at that distribution center," Detective Ramos said.

Tom and Harri joined Lee and nodded to the officer standing with him.

"Thank you for calling in about the van," Harri said.

He nodded but didn't say a word. His eyes kept shooting over to the back of the open van and then down to the ground.

"It must have been traumatic seeing that arm in there," Harri said.

"I've never seen anything like that before," Lee Chan said.

"When did you first see the van down here?" Tom asked.

"I started my shift Monday morning after the big rain," he started. "I took my lunch break around one. I usually run along the river before I eat. When I started on my run, the van was already there. It was wet and damaged but there was nobody inside," he said.

"And did it move since Monday afternoon?" Harri asked.

"No," Lee Chan shook his head. "I realized it was dumped yesterday and was going to call you guys but then I got busy. But today when I was running by, and it stank...I thought maybe somebody was inside and needed help."

He shook his head and laughed ruefully. "Stupid, I know."

"And then you opened the back," Tom prodded.

"I saw the arm and ran back to work. I called the cops the moment I got away from that smell," he said. "I'll never forget that smell as long as I live."

"Thank you, Mr. Chan. You gave the officer your contact information so we can reach you for an official statement?" Tom asked.

"Yeah, he has all my information. I work over there if you need me. I'm there Monday through Friday," he said.

"Thank you for that," Harri said and nodded to the officer that Lee could go.

Harri and Tom stood to the side and watched as the van was loaded onto the flatbed tow truck that had arrived.

"We could have the driver's DNA in there. Hopefully, a lot more," Tom said.

"The van appeared here Monday afternoon. If the water carried it, even for just a few miles, how did it get out of the water?" Harri asked.

"That's a damn good question," Tom said.

"What if someone else saw it first and thought it was perfect for salvage? What if that person, or persons, got it out of the riverbed and then saw what was in the back and fled?" Harri asked.

"Abandoned twice?" Tom nodded. "Yeah, I could see that scenario. Maybe even more DNA and fingerprints for us. I doubt the driver would have survived the fall into the river. Not with the way it flooded Sunday night," he added.

"So how did this van get into the river?" she asked. "And where?"

"Had to have wrecked somewhere near Los Feliz, or upstream from there or its washes Sunday night," Tom said.

"We don't have another body, so did the driver survive?" she asked. "I didn't hear of any rescues out on the river Sunday night."

"Maybe he jumped?" Tom suggested. "He lost control of the van but managed to get himself out before it went into the river?"

"Then why didn't he come back for the van?" Harri asked.

"Or we have a floater somewhere. He must have known what he was transporting. If he did survive, he must be out there somewhere praying everything got washed into the ocean never to be found again," Tom said.

"Bad luck for him," Harri said.

"We have to wait and see what the evidence tells us," Tom said. "Hopefully, we'll find DNA or fingerprints for the driver and our guy, Rich."

If they were lucky enough to find prints or DNA inside and they could connect the van picking up Rich from the library, they might have a shot at finding Rena and Whitey.

17

DAY 3 - NIGHT

Darlene "Whitey" Whiteman hadn't been seen since the night before, so Harri and Tom decided to stop at the river camp before heading home. They were racing against the clock, but Harri was exhausted from the day that started with being attacked at river camp that morning.

Harri beat Tom to the encampment. After she checked in with Jake, she sang and did her vocal exercises the entire way back from where the white van had been found. She didn't care how crazy she may have looked to any other drivers who saw her. After all, she'd been attacked only that morning, although it felt like ages ago to her now.

Her fear was gone. Or it could be masked by the excitement of finding the van and potentially having hard evidence finally. Harri took a few deep breaths to center herself and then stepped out of the car as Tom pulled up in the parking space behind her.

"We made good time," she said.

"I have no idea how we missed the afternoon traffic,"

Tom said. "How do you feel about being back here?"

"It's fine. I'm fine. It was more of a little altercation between me and an extremely psychotic, drugged-out unhoused person," she said.

"I'm really surprised that you didn't arrest him and put it on the record," Tom said.

"He was psychotic, completely out of his mind. His getting stuck in jail would serve no purpose whatsoever," Harri said. "I don't need anyone questioning why I came here alone. And also, I am totally fine."

"I'll trust you on that, Harri," Tom said.

There was something in his tone that Harri didn't like. He was twenty years her senior and had an incredible amount of experience under his belt. He was a mentor, as well as a partner. She needed him to see her as his equal and not be worried about her. After all, she'd saved his life on their last case.

"It's beautiful here in the evening," Harri said, changing the subject.

They walked to the chain-link fence and the entrance to the bike path.

"Yeah, I suppose it is," Tom said but he seemed to be deep in thought.

Harri didn't say anything else until they got onto the bike path and saw Rufus sitting in front of Whitey's tent.

"That's not a good sign," Harri said.

"About time you guys got here," Rufus said.

"I didn't get any calls from you," Harri admonished him.

"Oh, girl. I lost your card right after you left. Figured you'd be by again doing your investigation and stuff."

"She hasn't come back yet?" Harri asked.

"Nope. Been sitting here all day watching her place and keeping an eye on my own stuff."

"When was the last time you saw her?" Tom asked.

"Last night about nine. Couldn't believe she was out of her tent after dark. Offered her some booze to be friendly, but she snapped off at me about her sobriety and said she was off to see the trailer girls," Rufus said.

"And you didn't see her after that?" Tom asked.

"I was pretty drunk by then but not all the way. I checked inside to see if she'd maybe slipped in but no, sir. She's gone."

"I'm going to check inside," Harri said and gave him a pointed look.

Rufus nodded and moved his plastic chair out of the way.

"You're the po-po, go on ahead."

Harri unzipped Whitey's tent and pulled out her flashlight. She clicked it on and crawled inside to see that the place was surprisingly neat. To the right was a foam mattress with a clean sleeping bag rolled up on top of it. There was a stack of about seven books next to the mattress.

Harri went through them all and saw they were science-fiction, mostly Kurt Vonnegut. She rustled through the food basket next to the book stack but saw nothing there but granola bars and three cans of sparkling water. Next to that was a large backpack and Harri felt a pang of guilt, but then pushed it away. She still hoped Whitey had gone into hiding, but that seemed even less likely now that Harri saw her backpack. She stuck her hand into the bag and felt around but all she found were clothes and small bottles of shampoo, conditioner, and body wash.

"Harri," Tom called. "We gotta go!" Something in his tone told her it was urgent.

Harri nearly knocked Rufus over coming out of

Whitey's tent.

"Hey," Rufus protested. "That's police brutality."

Harri ignored him as she rushed to Tom's side.

"We have to get over to the library," Tom said.

"Why? What's happening?"

"Tell you in the car. Leave yours here," Tom said as he walked away.

Harri pulled another one of her business cards out and quickly wrote her cell number on the back. She handed it to Rufus.

"Call me if you see or hear anything about Whitey," she said. "Don't lose it this time."

"Righty-o, lady po-po," Rufus said.

Instead of telling her what was going on, Tom handed Harri his cell phone as he buckled himself in and started the car. Harri buckled in and read out loud a set of texts as Tom sped to the Los Feliz library.

"Hello Detective Tom Bards. This is Susan Fleming. We met yesterday at the Los Feliz library. I provided you with footage of a white van. I hate to disturb you as I know you must be incredibly busy with your police work. However, I discovered something in the book returns from last night that I believe you need to see immediately. Please come to the library immediately. I have cleared all the patrons out of the library and locked the door. Please come now."

"We are on our way. Keep the door locked if you feel unsafe."

"What do you think she found?" Harri asked.

"Don't know, but whatever it is scared the hell out of her," Tom said as he sped through a light just turning red.

"She must be terrified if she kicked people out of the library before closing time," Harri said.

Tom parked sideways in the first empty spot in the

parking lot. He and Harri rushed to the front door of the library. It was locked. Harri knocked on the door as Tom texted Susan to let her know they were outside.

Harri peered through the glass door and saw a sliver of Susan Fleming's face as she peeked around the corner. Harri waved and Susan hurried to unlock the door.

"Oh, I'm so glad you're here," Susan said. "Come inside. Hurry!"

Tom and Harri stepped inside, and Susan locked the door again.

"Are you all right?" Tom asked.

"Oh, yes. I'm perfectly well, thank you," Susan said as she led them into her office.

Tom and Harri sat across from the Head Librarian.

"What do you have for us?" Harri asked.

"I found it in the night drop. I am so sorry I didn't process the book returns until just now, but there weren't that many, and no one has requested any books that are out, so I…"

"Susan," Tom said calmly. "What did you find?"

Susan didn't say anything more. She reached into her desk drawer and pulled out a black notebook. Harri knew immediately that it had to be Jared Atkinson's notebook. She closed her eyes and inwardly did a happy dance.

Tom took the notebook from Susan and fanned the pages to see if there was anything loose inside. There wasn't. He handed the notebook to Harri and stepped outside the office to make a call. Susan smiled politely and followed Tom out of the office.

Harri flipped open to the first page and started reading, hardly believing her eyes. It was Jared Atkinson's notebook. Harri quickly scanned to the pages he'd most recently written. His entire investigation was there.

They'd finally be able to complete the timeline. She flipped to the last entry and saw it had been written Saturday night. Jared wrote that Rena was missing, just like Marpessa Roberts. He'd detailed how he'd staked out the Berendo camp and confirmed Rena bought meth there the afternoon she'd disappeared. He'd also been shooed away by a woman who was her own personal neighborhood watch. She flipped back a couple of pages to see what Jared had done earlier in the week before he vanished and saw the entries for CUCO.

"You all right in there?" Tom asked her.

"Yup," Harri answered as she continued reading.

Tom returned to the office and sat down next to her. "I'm going to follow Susan Fleming home. I don't want uniforms over here. That'll just tip someone off that we found something," he said.

"Okay," Harri said. "I'll get myself back to my car and take this downtown for processing. I want to scan it in."

"How's the story?" Tom asked.

"Maybe Whitey had Jared's notebook this whole time. She was the closest friend he had. I don't know what she was thinking, but it's all in here, Tom. His entire investigation," she said.

"Why didn't she give it to us?" Tom shook his head.

"She kind of did," Harri said. "I think Whitey dropped it in the book return last night after she went to see the trailer girls."

"If you're right, then that means she at least got this far," Tom said.

"Could she be in hiding?" Harri asked.

"No," Tom said. "No. Where would she go? Why would she leave her backpack behind? That doesn't make sense."

"Yeah," Harri mused. "But what if she was heading back, figured out she was being followed or something, and dropped the notebook here to keep it safe? She comes to the library all the time. She's smart enough to see that Susan Fleming would find it and call us."

"That makes sense, but then why didn't they come and ransack her place?" he asked.

"Because Rufus was sitting there the whole time. I guess they could have killed him but that would've brought even more heat down on the camp," Harri said.

"But if Whitey was out and about, they might've grabbed her thinking she had it on her. If I had such a valuable piece of information, I'd be keeping it with me at all times," Tom said.

Harri started quietly reading out loud Jared's movements on Saturday.

He'd gone to CUCO, filled out the application, and given Guadalupe his burner phone number. Then he hung around with four other men waiting to be called. Around eleven that morning, a white van pulled up. The man driving was named Patrick Smith of Smith Construction.

Jared then described how he and another man, Keith Walker, were driven to a home being torn down and were assigned to carry heavy construction materials from the site into a dumpster. He worked there all afternoon and at the end of the shift Patrick took down both of their phone numbers with the promise of more work.

Jared had starred this entry writing that Patrick Smith said they didn't always have to go through CUCO to get work from him. They could call him directly. Jared also noted that CUCO took kickbacks from Smith Construction and other construction companies in the area.

Jared wrote that he hadn't found any leads on

Marpessa Roberts and he went to check on the trailer girls and discovered that Rena had gone missing.

Jared wrote that he'd traded information with Miguel and found out that Rena got her drugs from the Berendo camp, which is what Harri had already learned from Laney.

Jared wrote that he'd staked out the Berendo camp, watching the drug deals go down for hours before he was shooed away by a local homeowner. He'd then entered the camp and pretended he needed meth and talked to Rena's drug dealer.

The dealer told him that Rena had been there earlier that day and had been bragging that she'd scored a wealthy john who was going to get her out of that trailer. In the last entry, Jared wrote that he'd returned to camp at nearly four Sunday morning.

"Patrick Smith of Smith Construction," Tom said. "He had a white van, and he was the last person from CUCO to see Jared. I'm not sure we'll be able to track down this Keith Walker but we should be able to pull papers on Patrick Smith."

"Jared must have left his notebook behind when he got up Sunday morning, so we still have that day to account for," she said.

"Change of plans," Tom said. "We aren't sleeping tonight. I'll drop you at your car, then Susan Fleming at her residence and meet you at the PAB."

"We should also put an APB out for Darlene Whiteman."

"Let's hope those SID techs get something from that van tonight too," Tom said.

"If Darlene Whiteman has been taken, we have to move fast," Harri said. "This notebook could be the way to find her."

DAY 3 – NIGHT - WHITEY

I woke up groaning in complete darkness. My head was thick with fog, and I fought against whatever crap that man had injected into my neck. The last thing I remembered was walking down Los Feliz Boulevard just past Griffith Park.

I was exhausted and scared of every little shadow. I kept looking behind me when really, I should have been looking in front of me.

I wasn't fast enough when the man came from behind a cement wall and ambushed me. I didn't even have a chance to scream before I felt a prick in my neck and then darkness. And now I was here. Wherever here was.

A soft cry came from somewhere to the left of me. Was that what had finally woken me up? It sounded like a young girl, but I couldn't see her because it was pitch black. My eyes strained for any little bit of light but there was nothing.

"Hello?" I said.

The girl gasped and then whispered, "Hi."

"My name is Darlene. People call me Whitey," I whispered into the darkness.

"My name is Marena. Everybody calls me Rena though," the girl said.

"You're the missing trailer girl," I said too loudly. I'd found her. Then the realization of our situation struck me and my heart sank. I'd been caught by the same man who had taken Rena. The same man who'd probably killed Jared Atkinson.

"How long have you been here for Rena?" I asked.

"Feels like forever," Rena said. "Dante was supposed to be my ticket out of that hellhole."

"Is Dante the one who put us in here?" Whitey asked.

"Yes," Rena moaned.

"Do you know his last name?"

"He went by Dante on the app. I met him on Sugar-Daddies. He told me he actually wanted a girlfriend and I fell for it like an idiot," she said.

"But aren't you only fifteen?" I asked.

"I'll be sixteen in a month and I've been out on my own since I was thirteen. I know how to survive, lady," she grumbled in the darkness.

"How did you get here then?" I shot back.

"I fell for his sweet-talking," Rena said with a sniff.

"Has he come back since he put you here?" I asked.

The girl started to cry again, so I knew the answer to that question.

"Do you remember when I arrived?" I asked.

"I don't know. It's been a while. I thought you were dead at first. You wouldn't move even if I hit or kicked you. But if I stayed real quiet, I could hear you breathing. He drugged you. Just like he drugged me in the car."

"What does he want with us?" I asked.

"I don't know," Rena whimpered. "He started talking about going into purgatory and hell. That we needed to atone for our sins. Well, me at least. He was talking about my sins. He didn't say anything about you. He dumped you on the ground and left without saying another word. He took the light away again," she said.

"You said he picked you up in a car? What direction was he driving in? Do you remember?" I asked.

"Um, west?" Rena sounded like she was guessing. "He said he lived somewhere near that big university near Brentwood. He told me he had a really nice home in the hills there," Rena said and I could hear some sort of pride in her voice.

Is that how he'd gotten her into his car? Dangling the rich life to a girl who was turning tricks out of a beat-up trailer on Franklin Avenue?

I shivered. We were both in bad trouble. I thought about the arms the cops found down by the river with Jared's body. I didn't want to think that's what we were headed for.

We had to find a way to escape out of here.

"How many entrances are there to this place?" I asked.

"What?" Rena asked.

"Did you see how many ways in or out of here?" I asked.

"It's so dark, I have no idea," Rena said.

I tried to stand up, but my head swam and I fell back to the floor with a grunt. All right then. Maybe I couldn't stand yet, but I could crawl.

I felt my way to where the floor touched the wall. I felt the smoothness and guessed the floor and wall were made out of concrete. That was not encouraging, but I pushed thoughts of dungeons out of my mind. The texture was smooth and not like rough concrete blocks I'd seen in other basements.

I guessed we had to be in a basement because of the lack of light and the way the sound bounced around. It was like being in a grave.

No. I couldn't think about things like that. The only way the girl and I were getting out of this place alive was if I kept my wits about me. I crawled along feeling the wall with my fingers ahead of me until I came to where the wall turned at a 90° angle.

I counted each crawl to figure out the general measurements of the room we were in. Everything ached and my head swam, but I kept on crawling and counting until I felt the outline of the door.

"What are you doing?" asked Rena.

"Trying to figure something out," I said.

It felt like a regular door that was about two crawls wide. I moved on and finished the perimeter. I didn't find any other openings.

"Okay, there's only one door," I said as I sat back and rested. "He must be getting air in here somehow, though. There must be a vent but it's probably on the ceiling. I can't stand up because my head is swimming, but could you try?"

"Okay," Rena said. "What do you want me to do?"

"Just stand up and hold your hands up above your head and see if you can feel anything."

I heard scuffling somewhere to the left of me. Then I heard soft footsteps as Rena moved around the room.

"I feel it. I feel the vent. It's right here," Rena exclaimed.

"Can you feel air coming through?" I asked.

"Yeah, I feel air. But how does that help us?" she asked.

"That means this room isn't completely soundproof," I said.

"But he's probably the only one who can hear us," Rena cried. "We're never going to get out of here."

"Don't panic, girl," I said. "The fastest way to get yourself killed in situations is to panic. These freaks love getting off on your fear. Just take a deep breath and swallow it all down inside. There's two of us now and neither of us are tied up. Maybe there's a way for us to overpower him."

I knew I was being overly optimistic but I sure as hell hadn't come this far to only get this far. I didn't want to die in a big black hole next to a crying fifteen-year-old girl. There had to be a way out of this mess.

"Rena, tell me what you know about this guy and start from the beginning," I demanded.

"I don't know that much," she said.

"You said his name is Dante and he talked about hell. Was this guy smart-looking?"

I remembered reading about some poem from the Middle Ages called Dante's Inferno. I didn't pay much attention in English class but that had stuck with me because they'd done the section with this crazy-ass painter named Bosch who had all these pictures of people being flayed, impaled, and killed in horrifying ways. Supposedly it went along with that poem.

"As I said, I met him on this app called SugarDaddies," Rena said. "He said he was some rich art dealer and that he lived on the West Side and was looking for a relationship with a young girl he could teach the ways of the world. We talked for like two weeks and he seemed really smart and nice. He was telling me about all these cool places he could take me to. I've never been anywhere except here and my shit hometown in Nevada. I really wanted out of that trailer."

"Was the first time you met him in the car?"

"Yeah," Rena said. "I picked up some stuff from my dealer. I only do meth when I have to do older guys because gross. He picked me up in this really nice car. I think it was like a Mercedes, but like something a rich grandpa would drive. I was expecting a fast sports car but I guess it was okay. Dante is good-looking for an older guy. Maybe in his thirties or forties? He's obviously way older than me but a lot more handsome than the guys Miguel makes me do."

"So, he picked you up, and then what happened?" I asked.

"I went to grab lip gloss from my bag and he stuck something in my neck. Next thing I know I'm down in this dark hole and he only comes once a day to bring me water and bread. He talks about some weird river and crossing it and like atoning for my sins and then he leaves again. It's really weird and scary." Rena sniffed.

Rena's fear made her sound childlike and that terrified me. Hearing her talk about the creep was freaking me out. Freaks were the worst. I took my own advice and swallowed down my fear so I could ask more questions.

"Okay, so he's a weirdo. He sounds young enough to still be strong. He'll probably have a lot of upper body strength, but there's still two of us and only one of him. When I was crawling around I didn't feel anything else in the room. Does he bring your food on a tray?" I asked.

"No, he brings me a plastic cup and then just a little loaf of bread," Rena said.

"What does he do with the cup after it's empty?" I asked.

"He takes everything away."

"Does he stay and watch you eat?" I asked.

"No, he closes the door, and then as soon as I'm done

eating, he'll open it again and grab the cup from me," Rena said.

That wasn't good news. There was no way for him to know she was done unless he had cameras in here. Probably had microphones, too.

I dropped my voice to a whisper. "Rena, come closer so we can whisper together."

Rena scootched over until she bumped into me.

"Sorry," Rena whispered back.

"He must have a camera in here watching us. That will make it harder to ambush him. Can you hear anything before the door opens?"

"Um, kind of like footsteps, I guess. I heard some shuffling the last time the door opened," Rena said.

"That gives a few seconds to set up then," I whispered back.

"Is he watching us right now?" Rena asked.

"I'm pretty sure he is," I said.

This was a huge wrinkle in my plan, but I still thought two women could overpower one guy somehow. We just had to figure out how.

My mind thought of all the plots in the books I'd read. How had the heroes escaped? There was always something. I just had to think. I breathed in and sighed. Jared had easily overpowered Psycho Gary that one time, but I wasn't strong like Jared. I wondered what Jared would think of me right now.

He'd think I was a damn fool for not giving his notebook to that lady detective first thing. Well, at least I'd stashed it in a safe place before this freak Dante grabbed me. I had to think. I had to think like Jared. I owed him that. Maybe if a cop could pretend to be homeless then a homeless woman could pretend to be a cop.

19

DAY 4 - MARCH 9, 2019 - SATURDAY

Harri yawned and took a sip of what felt like her first coffee. She'd had so much coffee throughout the night the caffeine wasn't making a dent anymore. Harri and Tom had pulled an all-nighter working through Jared's notebook. They were finally able to confirm the chronology of his movements up to Sunday morning with the last entry in the notebook.

They ran background checks on every name found in the notebook and outside of the more garden-variety aggravated assaults and drug charges, one name stuck out.

Patrick Smith of Smith Construction was the man who picked up Jared that Saturday to work as day labor. Their search for Patrick Smith came up empty, just like with Jared Atkinson. For a moment, Harri wondered if Patrick Smith could be another undercover cop. She quickly dismissed the thought.

Patrick Smith did not exist in any database they could find, and his company, Smith Construction was owned by what appeared to be a shell company. As they dug deeper, it appeared that Smith Construction was the lowest level in a totem pole of shell corporations, which meant each level up was even more secret to prying eyes than the one below it. Smith Corporation was owned by a shell company, which was owned by another shell company, and so on. Each shell company had only a registered agent and obviously hired directors.

Harri and Tom concluded that Patrick Smith was most likely Jared Atkinson's killer. Harri wondered if Patrick Smith had uncovered Jared Atkinson's real identity, or if Jared had become a nuisance or liability somehow. Now, they had to discover who Patrick Smith really was. They planned to go back to CUCO with the warrant Raymond Sklar had demanded. A judge signed the warrant for their records pertaining to Smith Construction only an hour ago.

CUCO wouldn't be open for another few hours so Harri decided to reach out again to Detective Lenny Fioranello in Hoboken, New Jersey. He was the main detective in the groundbreaking case on tissue harvesting Dr. Grimley had told them about.

She waited until 9 a.m. Jersey time and as soon 6 a.m. chimed on her watch, she called the number his lieutenant had given her.

Detective Fioranello picked on the first ring.

"Lenny speaking," a man's voice with a strong Jersey accent answered.

"My name is Detective Harri Harper calling from the Los Angeles Police Department. I was given your name by your lieutenant to speak to you about your Matthew Michael's funeral home case," she said.

"Oh yeah. My lieutenant told me about you. What would you like to know?" he asked.

"We're currently working a case where the body appears to have been harvested for tissue. We're not having an easy time navigating the nuances of the death industry."

"Ah. Tissue banks stonewalling?"

"Exactly," Harri answered. "We're not entirely sure how the money flows to the various people along the chain."

"I can give you a quick rundown. It's actually brilliant," Lenny said.

"Really?" Harri understood how Detective Fioranello could admire an aspect of crime. It wasn't the illegality or immorality that was admirable, but sometimes the ingenuity was incredible.

"Well, before you do that, let me just see if I'm getting it right. Was Matthew Michael the owner of the funeral home?" Harri asked.

"Yes, he was," Lenny confirmed.

"Okay," Harri continued as she scribbled a flowchart in her notes. "As I understand it, his scheme was harvesting tissue from the corpses his funeral home was hired to bury."

"Correct," Lenny said. "Actually, he preferred bodies that were slated for cremation. Less of a hassle for him that way."

"Interesting," Harri said. "And, of course, he did whatever he was doing without knowledge or consent of the family or next of kin."

"Correct," Lenny said. "We couldn't get him on regulatory violations because it was too slow and out here funeral homes are under the supervision of two separate agencies. What he went down for was fraud. He was lying to his funeral home clients, and he lied to the organizations he sold the tissue to. He altered a ton of documents, sometimes completely falsifying the cause of death."

"Why was that even necessary?" Harri asked.

"Had to cover up anything that would disqualify the tissue," Lenny explained.

"What would cause disqualification?" Harri asked.

"Any type of cancer, sepsis, hepatitis, HIV, IV drug use, and the like," he said.

Harri paused and thought over what Lenny had just said.

"So, disqualifying tissue was illegally removed from a corpse and then sold to some doctor or whoever had use for it, and then what?" asked Harri.

"And then a twenty-year-old college student being treated for minor burns to her back from a car accident dies from a Doxorubicin overdose because her skin graft tissue came from one of Matthew Michael's corpses that had just died during chemotherapy," Lenny said bitterly.

"Damn." That's horrifying. Harri could tell he was still angry about the injustice surrounding the case.

"How did you follow the money?" Harri asked.

"Fee-based kickbacks," Lenny explained. "The procurement and distribution of the tissue can run anywhere between $80,000-$200,000. Per cadaver. Each step has its own fee, which is essentially a kickback. There are several steps along the way. They have to find a body and clean it, which they call processing. The next step they call procurement. That's when they actually strip the tissue off the body. After that is distribution. This is where the tissue banks get involved. They sort the tissue, label it, and control inventory. The banks can store tissue for two to three weeks, but we found some storing tissue for longer than that. The distribution company handles sales and delivery to hospitals, clinics, and doctor's offices. Some of the tissue banks also take care of their own distribution," Lenny said.

Harri was quiet for a little too long and Lenny picked up on that.

"More than you ever wanted to know, right?"

"Right," Harri agreed. "And each step generates a fee?"

"Correct," Lenny said. "Everyone gets their slice of birthday cake."

"Are these companies running as for-profit or nonprofit?" Harri asked.

"A lot of them now are being run as for-profit businesses. And the money flows downward."

"How does that work?" Harri asked.

"Everything is based on fees. Say the funeral home needs to use a special room for the procurement, they'll charge the tissue bank. If they need to transport the body, they add another fee. The fees could be for identifying a candidate, which is when they find a body suitable for harvest. Cleaning fees. Fees for equipment and supplies. They could charge all kinds of fees for the Procurement Specialist.

"A Specialist? What's that?" Harri asked.

"The people who actually scrape the skin, remove the bones, and cut out the ligaments. All these people get kickbacks from the tissue bank. Now, the tissue bank gets paid by the distribution company. These are for-profit companies. Both the tissue banks and distribution companies are supposedly regulated by the FDA," Lenny said.

"But they aren't?" Harri guessed.

"It's a bunch of self-regulation by a lobbying group for the industry. Allegedly."

Harri finally understood how the money flowed and

why it would be profitable for someone to get into the tissue-harvesting business.

"Where does the actual tissue procurement happen?" Harri asked.

"In our case, the funeral home had a special room set up and sterilized to do the procurement. They charged a $1000 to use it and another $1000 to sterilize it after," Lenny said.

"They didn't need a separate lab to do the removal?" Harri asked.

"No. The room just needs to be sterilized. That's all. The procurement team has a bag of tools they use. It's pretty straightforward."

"Our coroner mentioned there have been contamination scares in recent years. Do you think this is a widespread problem in the industry?" she asked.

"I think we only scratched the surface, to be honest. My guy only got eight years because it was fraud," he said. "We don't even have a law on the books to charge them for this kind of thing," Lenny said with disgust in his voice.

"Which part of the process makes the most money?" Harri asked. "It doesn't feel like a funeral home would be getting the largest portion of that $200,000 per cadaver."

"In our case, it was the tissue bank profiting the most. It depends on how much skin, bones, and ligaments they were able to get out of one body. And then the funeral home was next in line for the most kickbacks," Lenny said.

"Did any of your guys have medical training?" Harri asked.

"None. The actual harvesting is pretty brutal. The procurement team does need some training in using the various tools for harvest, but it's on-the-job education and you don't need any medical training to cut out tendons, or scrape skin, or pull out veins. Just a strong stomach."

"In our case, we think someone is killing homeless people to harvest their tissue. We were originally looking at the death industry, but we'll have to look at the tissue banks since they're the ones making the most," she said.

"It's a billion-dollar business. Every day more and more doctors need tissue. I think the funeral home could be just as much of a moneymaker as a tissue bank," he said.

Harri couldn't think of anything more to ask.

"Thank you so much for the explanation. I really appreciate it," Harri said.

"Not a problem," he said. "Do me a solid, though."

"Sure, what do you need?" Harri asked.

"Catch this son of a bitch," Lenny said.

"Oh, I will," Harri promised.

She got off the phone with Detective Lenny Fioranello and briefed Tom on everything she'd just learned.

"We have to crack those tissue banks. This whole operation must have an established pipeline. The question is how many people involved in the process know the victims are being murdered for the tissue?"

"All the money flowing down the chain could give them a reason to turn a blind eye and not ask questions. Whatever their share in two hundred grand per body is could be enough to keep people quiet.

Tom looked down at his notes.

"There are five accredited tissue banks within fifty miles of Los Angeles. Two of them are multinational corporations. This feels to me like a smaller, homegrown operation. What do you think?" Tom asked.

"I agree. This feels smaller. More rogue," Harri said.

"One of these bigger companies could have a corrupt general manager, but the bigger the company, the more compliance and internal politics to deal with," Tom said. "I found three smaller companies that aren't attached to these huge corporations." He circled the names of BiometSource, CryoSynth, and Cellmedtech.

"The bigger question is how can we get them to talk," Harri said.

"We have to find the connections. Let's cross-reference business licenses between all the companies that own Smith Construction with these smaller tissue banks. Hopefully, someone was greedy and stupid and put the tissue bank under one of these shell companies."

"Tissue banks operate out of brick-and-mortar buildings with work addresses. Someone owns that property or at least has a rental agreement," Harri said.

"Exactly," Tom said.

Tom's phone rang and he picked it up immediately. He listened for several minutes before saying, "Thank you for putting this on the fast track." Tom hung up and turned to Harri.

"That was SID Forensics. They found two latent prints in the van. They ran them through the system and came up with two different hits. One fingerprint came from the stick shift and belongs to a Juan Bindo. He had an aggravated assault outside of a nightclub where he worked as a bouncer. They have an address for him in Glendale Rancho. The other print is a gang banger by the name of Sean Daniels out of Compton. He's probably the kid who found the van and then bailed when he found what was in the back."

"He wouldn't be the gang connection Jared Atkinson was originally looking for?" Harri asked.

"If he's out of Compton, then he's probably not associated with the Mexican cartels," Tom observed. "Juan Bindo sounds like the better bet. He lives in the rancho and that's damn close to where we found the remains."

"What if he works for one of our companies? Maybe the funeral home or one of the tissue banks?" Harri asked. She shuffled through her notes. "If he's driving the van, I bet you he's in the first part of the harvest process. He might work for the funeral home."

"Or he could be the transporter for the murder courier body disposal theory we talked about. He gets a call from the funeral home, he gets another call from the limb killer and then takes them all to be disposed of," Tom said.

"Cremated," Harri said. "The detective I spoke to said cremation was his guy's preferred method, over burial."

"Makes sense," Tom nodded. "A lot less to deal with. No evidence. Just turn the incinerator on and there you go."

"But why wouldn't the funeral home do the cremation at its own location? They have incinerators on site."

"Good point," Tom said.

"Let's go find Juan Bindo and see how he fits in to all this," Harri suggested.

"Yeah, let's get something to eat on the way," Tom said.

"Juan Bindo might lead us to a funeral home," Harri said. "And the funeral home might lead us to one of the tissue banks."

Even though she was dead tired, the chance to get closer to who was behind this made her body buzz.

20

DAY 4 - EARLY MORNING

Harri and Tom made it to Juan Bindo's address by 7 a.m. They'd pulled up his DMV records to see what he looked like and then looked over an online map of his street to decide the best place to stake out his apartment building.

The Glendale Rancho was a unique district on the other side of Griffith Park. It was in the city of Glendale, just over the border from Burbank, and was one of the neighborhoods that felt more like a village. Major film studio lots edged the neighborhood, which was known as an equestrian pocket. The historic LA Equestrian Center was what drew most people to the area. Glendale Rancho sat right on Riverside Drive and that whole stretch of road catered to the equestrian crowd with horse stables, horse feed stores, and horses grazing in the front yards of small ranch homes.

They pulled up behind a pickup truck half a block away and parked with a clear view of Juan's front door.

"Let's hope he's not an early bird," Harri said.

"Nobody's up, not even the horses," Tom said.

They'd grabbed coffee and doughnuts on the way over in the hopes that even more sugar and caffeine would fuel them through the rest of the morning. Harri hadn't eaten since Jake had stopped by the PAB with tacos for her and Tom around ten the night before. She was grateful Tom pretended to be on a call so she could have some time alone with Jake. She felt like she hadn't seen him in days, even though it really hadn't been that long. She knew Jake understood what it was like to be chasing a case, but she also felt as if she was sometimes too much to handle. She shook her head. No. She knew Jake didn't feel that way. That was her PTSD talking.

"What?" Tom asked, noticing her shaking her head.

"Something is bothering me, and I can't wrap my head around the angles," Harri said.

"Let's talk it out," Tom said. "We've got time." He gestured to the sleepy street in front of them.

"When I was talking to the detective from New Jersey he told me that in his case the funeral director had set up a special room for the procurement of the tissue. He said it worked great for the funeral home because they could charge two more fees for it," Harri said.

"Why two?" Tom asked.

"A fee to use the room and then a fee to sterilize the room," Harri explained.

"Ah," Tom nodded. "The old get 'em coming and going."

"The way these kickbacks work is a fee for everything, every step in the tissue harvesting process. So, if we are dealing with a funeral home like in the other case, then it would make sense for them to have a special room too, right?" Harri asked.

"I see what you're getting stuck on," he said. "Why was anyone transporting a body and those limbs? If the funeral home has its own room and an incinerator, then there's no reason why Jared's body should be in that van. All they had to do was wheel him over to the cremation room and stick him in the oven. Why was his body in that van? And the limbs don't add up, either. Why weren't they harvested? There were some usable bones and tissue there."

"Remember how Dr. Grimley said the ligaments and tendons were stretched and torn," he said. "Maybe they couldn't use those."

"But they could use the bones," Harri pointed out. "Where were these body parts taken from and where were they being taken to?" she asked.

"Why was Jared's body wrapped in plastic? Was that done for transport? Can't put plastic in the cremation furnace oven thing. It would just melt and make a mess, right? If he wasn't being cremated at the same place they harvested his tissue, then what's the explanation?" Tom asked.

"Maybe they couldn't use the cremation oven," Harri said.

"Exactly. What if something happened to the oven? What if they did harvest all his tissue and then they wheeled him in to cremate him and the oven wasn't working?" Tom said.

"They had to cremate him as soon as possible. It's a funeral home. They could have stored a body until they got the cremation oven working again. But not Jared's body because that wasn't a legitimate death and disposal, it was a murder disposal," Harri said.

"Jared's body and the limbs had to be disposed of. The cremation oven was broken. So he decides to transport the body and the limbs somewhere else to dispose of them," Tom theorized. "The only reason this whole thing came to light was that we found Jared's body and then his notebook. This is a disaster for that whole organization," Tom said as he bit into a doughnut.

"So, what do we think about Juan Bindo? Just a transporter? Maybe he's the murder courier, but no one at the funeral home knows?" Harri asked.

"They have to know," Tom said.

"Okay, maybe they know. Maybe Juan takes orders from someone?" Harri theorized.

"No way," Tom shook his head. "He had to know what he was transporting and that it was illegal as hell."

"So where was he taking them for disposal?" Harri wondered.

"And on a rainy night?" Tom asked.

"Nobody wants those remains around," Harri said. How many people were in on this scheme, she wondered. The more people who knew, the more chances they would get caught. And they hadn't been caught yet.

"What if there was infighting?" Harri asked.

"Infighting between the co-conspirators?" Tom asked.

"Criminals tend to be hotheaded and don't play well with others. What if there was some sort of argument and our guy took the bodies as leverage? Or insurance he'd be kept in play? Still get paid or whatever. His co-conspirators couldn't kill him because he had the goods on them?" Harri suggested.

"That's an interesting theory," Tom said.

Harri could tell her partner was losing steam. His eyes would slowly close and then he'd catch himself and shake it off. They both needed naps. They'd work better on some sleep.

"Why don't you take a power nap and I'll watch the door? I'll wake you up in fifteen and then I can sneak a nap. We have to get some sleep or we won't be firing on all cylinders," she said.

Each time she thought of sleep, she also thought of Whitey's tidy bedroll in her tent. It was so humble, but it was Whitey's home. She pushed thoughts of Whitey being tortured away. Why hadn't Whitey given them Jared's notebook when she found it? Because she didn't trust cops, Harri thought.

Harri wanted to break down Juan Bindo's door, but she knew that wouldn't get them the information they needed. He would clam up. They'd get stuck explaining their actions and writing a report. All their evidence was circumstantial. The fingerprint put Juan Bindo in the van, but could they prove he was in the van at the same time as the branded arm that was still in the back when the van was recovered? They could bring him in for questioning, but they didn't have time to sweat him for twenty-four hours. She agreed with Tom that he was probably a bit player in this operation. The information they needed was who the other co-conspirators were.

"A nap sounds great," Tom said. "Start the clock."

Harri nodded and watched as he closed his eyes and reclined his seat.

She took another sip of coffee and a big bite of doughnut. The sugar and caffeine needed to keep her eyes open and her blood pumping.

Harri sat like that for another half hour with no one on the street but a horse and rider. She watched as the young girl in equestrian gear pressed a button at the horse level to get the light to change for the crosswalk. Harri had no idea that was even a thing.

As the morning wore on, the neighborhood woke up. She saw four more horses coming out of their stables or garages and into the front yards of the homes. Their owners fed them breakfast and watered them.

A group of tourists rode horses toward one of the trails leading into Griffith Park. She watched as a man hitched a team of horses to an old-fashioned Conestoga wagon and drove them down the middle of Riverside Drive. Her eyes fell closed and she knew then she needed to wake Tom up. It was closer to 8:15 a.m. now and they had a big day ahead of them. They had the search warrant for CUCO and their records on Smith Construction. The team still needed to sift through lists of companies to find the connection between a tissue bank, a funeral home, and the construction company.

The front door opened to Juan Bindo's apartment and Harri sat up straighter.

"Tom, Tom! Wake up, it's him," she hissed.

Tom's eyes flew open, and he sat forward as he moved his seat back in position.

"Is he on the move?" he asked.

"He is. And he looks rough," Harri said as she peered closer. Juan had bruises on his face and his left arm was in a sling. Harri detected a slight limp in his walk.

"Looks like someone might've been in an accident," Harri said.

"Means he was probably driving when the van wrecked," Tom said.

"Do we arrest him now or do we follow him?" Harri asked.

"We know where he lives so we can always come back and pick him up. Let's see where he goes first," Tom said.

They watched as Juan got into an older Chevy pickup and pulled out into the road. Tom counted four clicks out loud before he followed him.

Harri didn't know how long they had before Juan noticed them following him. The city was taking its time to open and there weren't that many cars on the street. Tom kept a good distance between them even though there were so few cars on the road, and followed as Juan took a left onto Sonora Avenue. They tailed him as he drove east, going deeper into Glendale.

Tom took a right on Glenoaks Boulevard as Juan did and slowed their pace. Juan pulled up to a red brick building. Tom found a parking spot at a meter with a view of the building and they watched Juan Bindo walk inside.

"We caught them," Harri said excitedly.

They both sat and stared at the white-on-blue signage on the beautifully green lawn surrounded by bright red petunias. It said Green Acres Funeral Home.

"We're only a couple miles from the LA River now," Harri remarked.

"It would be a short drive to get there," Tom said as he pulled out his phone and dialed the number on the sign for Green Acres Funeral Home. The call went to an automated voice mail system stating they opened at 10 a.m. and to visit their website.

"All right then," Tom said. He found their website on his phone and scrolled through to their list of locations.

"And here we have it," he said.

"Have you solved our inconsistency?" Harri asked.

"Well, Detective Harper," Tom said. "We are at their Glenoaks location, but they also have a location on Glendale Boulevard, near Forest lawn. The fastest way to get there would be hopping on the I-5 and getting off at Los Feliz and then over to Glendale Boulevard."

"But that's too close. The van wouldn't have been able to fall into the river at Los Feliz Boulevard because the water would have got it stuck on the little island. It's too close to the scene," she said.

"Yeah, you're right. What about this? Juan didn't want to go on the freeways with bodies in the van for some reason. What if he went down the back way and crashed into the Verdugo Wash off San Fernando Road? He could cross the smaller roads to get to Glendale Boulevard. If he went into the Verdugo Wash, the van could have swept into the LA River and then stopped closer to where it was found, losing Jared's body and most of the limbs on the way. That seems more probable."

"That's possible," Harri admitted, but she was still unsure.

"Now that we have a line on Juan Bindo, let's check out the Verdugo Wash and see if there's any signs of an accident."

"Okay, let's see. Maybe we'll even get lucky with cameras," she said.

"Let's not get our hopes up too much. San Fernando Road is industrial over that whole area. Some places are so spread out that even if there were cameras, they might not catch anything."

"A girl can hope," she said with a smile.

21

DAY 4 - SATURDAY EARLY AFTERNOON

Tom mapped out routes between the Green Acres Funeral Home on Glenoaks and the second location on Glendale Boulevard. The map app on his phone showed four different ways of getting there but only one way was along the LA River.

"We're going down to San Fernando Road," Tom said from the passenger seat. Harri had switched places with him so that he could navigate.

"That's the industrial patch," Harri said as she pulled into traffic.

"Which makes perfect sense when you're trying to get somewhere in a rainstorm without being noticed by cops because you're a murder courier," Tom said.

"But San Fernando Road doesn't run alongside the LA River the entire time, does it?" Harri asked as she took a right on Highland Avenue and drove down to San Fernando Road.

"No, it doesn't. But it does cross over the Verdugo Wash and I'm thinking that's where he went in," Tom said.

"I'm taking a left or right on San Fernando Road?" Harri asked as they hit the light.

"It's a left and the wash is about six blocks down. It's right after the power plant," he said.

"We might get lucky with cameras then," Harri said.

"The train tracks run alongside the entire length of San Fernando Road," Tom said.

"Do they have cameras on the tracks?" she asked.

"On some lanes," he said.

The light turned green and Harri took a left onto San Fernando Road. She kept their speed low, close to twenty-five miles an hour, and she was thankful there were two lanes on each side of the road so other cars could speed past her.

She didn't care.

They drove along for five blocks and as they passed Grange Street, Tom pointed to a line of broken trees. There were deep grooves in the dirt and damage to the bush that was right in front of an opening leading into the Verdugo Wash.

"There. That's where the van went in," he said.

Harri parked on the shoulder of the road and they both got out of the car.

"We'll have to get a traffic investigation team out here," Harri said.

"Looks to me like he lost control of the van. Maybe he was looking down at his phone," Tom looked around, surveying the scene. "Yeah," he continued. "He was probably looking at the directions or a text. Look, he barely missed that telephone pole. He hopped the curb over here." Tom pointed to black skid marks on the side of the curb.

"He took out that little tree there and then maybe

only had enough time to brake. He slid into that electrical pole. If it was during the rainstorm, he could've hydroplaned and totally lost control. The van could've tumbled over itself right into the wash," Tom said.

"There used to be a chain-link fence here," Harri said as she pointed to the ragged fence curled up to her right.

"That's not going to stop a van going over the edge like that," Tom said.

Harri looked along the ground to see if there was any evidence the van had been there four days ago, but the rain washed a lot away. Harri didn't see any evidence of the van or Juan Bindo having been there. All she saw was hard-packed dirt and stones.

"No, it's not," Harri said.

Harri and Tom both stared down into the Verdugo Wash, which was now a trickle. The wash was a type of release valve for water flowing out from the overwhelmed drains and into the river. The Verdugo Wash was nearly empty, but the night of the rainstorm it must have been a roaring, turbulent waterway.

Tom called in the Traffic Accidents Investigation team and gave them the location while Harri looked around to see if any cameras were visible. The power plant was out because it was too far away, and she didn't see any cameras on the poles that lined the train tracks along San Fernando Road.

There were traffic lights in front of them, but no visible cameras were attached. Across the street was a window tinting garage and a two-story office building. Harri didn't see any visible cameras on either of those buildings. Maybe the traffic investigation team would find something more concrete than skid marks and broken branches.

Tom got off the phone and said that the team would be there in the next half-hour.

"I'm thinking they might be our best bet," Harri said. "I'm not seeing any cameras on the poles, traffic lights, or those two buildings."

"That tinting place has a light over the front door canopy. See it?" he asked.

Harri nodded.

"Maybe there's a camera on that light too," he said.

The window tinting business had a vinyl banner on the fence in front advertising their rates and phone number.

Tom dialed the number. Harri heard someone pick up on the other end. Tom explained what they were looking for and gave her a thumbs up. He listened a moment more and said they'd be right there. He hung up and turned to Harri.

"There's a camera in that light and they do have footage from Sunday night," Tom said.

Harri did a happy dance on the side of the road.

"Should we leave the car here or park it in their lot?" she asked.

"Let's leave it here so the traffic team can find the site if we're not back from seeing the footage when they get here," he said.

Harri locked the car with her key fob, and they dodged traffic to cross San Fernando Road to the window-tinting place. As they reached the front gate, it slid open to let them in. They walked through a small parking lot to the front door where a tall, Hispanic man stood and grinned at them.

"I'm glad I can help," he said as he waved them inside. "My name is Neal Flores."

"I'm Detective Tom Bards and this is Detective Harri Harper."

They both showed him their credentials.

"Thank you for helping our investigation," Harri said.

"You're looking at a car that went over into the Verdugo Wash?" he asked.

"Yes, a van. It wasn't reported and we found the van near the river," Tom said.

"I've only seen the wash flood once but boy it was scary. I thought I was going to lose this whole building that night."

"Don't want to be near the river when it rains here," Tom said in agreement. "Does the camera have a full view of the street going all the way to the train tracks?"

"I think so," Neal said. "We had a bunch of break-ins a few years ago and my wife made me install the camera because sometimes we work late. It's all industrial over here and I don't know what the thieves thought they could get from a window-tinting shop, but it is what it is. Punks," he said.

Neal led them to a small office and sat in front of an ancient-looking PC. He logged into the security system and pulled up the camera footage.

"You said Sunday, right?" he said.

"Yeah, it was during the rainstorm," Tom said. "You wouldn't have by chance been working that night?"

"No, we're closed on Sundays," Neal said. "Here you go."

He'd opened a file with several folders and found the one labeled Sunday night's date. He clicked on it and there were twenty-four video clips.

"May I?" Tom asked.

Neal nodded and got up. Tom leaned in and clicked on the first one.

"Are you going to watch every single one?" Neal asked.

"I'm afraid we don't have a time for the accident," Harri explained.

"If you don't mind us sitting here and viewing all these videos, you can go on with your work if you want," Tom said.

"Thank you. I have a lot to get done," Neal said.

He wandered away and Harri pulled up a chair from along the back wall and sat next to Tom. He started clicking through the video clips.

"That night was rainy," Harri said as they watched the rain start pouring down on the screen. "I'm worried it will be hard to see that side of the road during the downpour."

Tom kept clicking and hit the jackpot on the 17th video clip. They watched as a white van veered into view from the right and swiped the electrical pole. The van then jumped the curb, and the driver's door popped open. A figure flung out as the van hit the next pole, careened through the bushes, and disappeared.

The driver lay on the side of the road clutching his arm. The video was grainy, and the rain came down hard at that moment making it difficult to see the figure clearly. They couldn't exactly see his face, but his body type matched that of Juan's and when he got up, his walk gave him away.

"That's Juan Bindo. He was driving our van," Harri said.

"Let's make a copy of this," Tom said. His phone buzzed and he read a text coming in.

"The traffic investigation team is here. They parked

behind the cruiser," Tom explained. They left the office and asked Neal to email that video and the one after it to Tom's LAPD address. Neal sat back down at his computer and did just that. When they saw the email leave Neal's email box, they thanked him again for his help and told him he might need to come in to make a statement. Tom asked him to preserve the camera and the entire folder of footage for Sunday night.

"Understood," Neal said. "Happy to help however I can."

They took their leave of the window tinting business and Mr. Neal Flores and walked back out into the sunny day. The cavalry had arrived and parked on the other side of the street behind the cruiser.

Tom and Harri ran across San Fernando Road again and Tom went to speak directly to the head detective, a man named Matteo Cruz.

"Matteo, meet my new partner Detective Harri Harper," Tom said.

"Nice to meet you, Harri," Matteo said. "Tom's one of the best."

"He sure is," Harri said.

Tom waved them off and explained to Matteo their theory of how the white van had ended up in the LA River.

Matteo listened and nodded. "From my initial inspection, I can imagine that. You say you have a video?" he asked.

"Yes. It's grainy and is obviously from only one side but you can get an idea of what happened," Tom said. "I'm sending it to you right now."

Tom opened the email on his phone and forwarded the file to Matteo's address. "You think you need us here?" Tom asked.

"I don't think so. I can leave the report on your desk when we're done," he said.

"Call me if you find anything that might've come out of the van," Tom said.

"Sure thing," Matteo said.

"You don't want to stay for the investigation?" Harri asked in surprise.

"I just got wind that Richard Byrne is having his presser in front of the PAB in half an hour. If we hurry, we can see it live," he said.

"And why do we want to do that?" Harri asked dryly even though she knew it would be good to see what Richard said.

"I want to get downtown to get the arrest warrant going on Juan Bindo. We have a small window before he figures out we're looking at him and takes off on us," he said.

"That makes more sense," Harri said.

"Want to drive?" Tom asked.

"Why don't you drive this time," Harri said.

Tom laughed and got into the driver's seat.

Harri soon regretted asking Tom to drive. He was an aggressive driver, especially compared to Harri and she felt carsick. They did, however, make it downtown in time to see Lieutenant Richard Byrne in front of at least twelve different camera crews talking about Jared Atkinson's case. They were walking up the main path toward the front door of the PAB when Lieutenant Richard Byrne announced that Jared Atkinson was an undercover detective named Ethan Carle. The press corps went crazy with questions and Harri and Tom got out of there as quickly as they could in case any of them recognized them as the detectives in charge.

"Our investigation just got a lot more complicated," Tom said.

"I doubt any homeless people will want to talk to us now," she said.

"They still want to find Whitey," Tom said.

"Let's hope that's enough incentive," Harri said.

Her mind was already racing forward. They needed to find out who owned Green Acres Funeral Home.

22

DAY 4 - SATURDAY - LATER AFTERNOON

W hen they reached the RHD bullpen, they split up. Tom took over the paperwork for the arrest warrant. He knew a Judge who would take his calls on a Sunday. Harri got to business researching the Green Acres Funeral Home. She'd even put a call in to Harvey Berger, the forensic accountant who had consulted on the Creek Killer case. He'd been a friend of her former partner in Cold Case, Detective Rob Lakin. Harvey called Harri right back and took fifteen minutes to explain shell companies to her.

Harri's head was spinning by the time he was done, and he'd only given her a quick overview.

"Did you watch the documentary on the Panama Papers?" Harvey asked.

"Harvey, you know I don't have time for that kind of thing," Harri laughed.

"Well, if you had, then you'd know more than I can tell you over the phone. Suffice to say shell corporations were designed to secure funding for startups. Once you know the rules, you know how to get around them, and that's what's going on here," Harvey said.

"How can I find out more?" Harri asked.

"You can't," Harvey said. "You need to know how to look, and you need to have the tools and the friends to help you."

Harri had always appreciated Harvey Berger's blunt honesty. "I can't pay you," Harri said simply.

"I'll do it for the glory and the story," Harvey said. "Let me look around and see what I can find out. I'll call you back in a few hours."

Harri went back to the conference room that served as their case command center and completed her notes on the case. Where could Whitey be? Was she in hiding? Had she been taken? Where was Rena? Was there any chance both women were still alive?

She stepped across the hall into an empty conference room and called Jake.

"Hello stranger," he said.

"Hi." Harri smiled into the phone. "It's good to hear your voice."

"Thanks for calling me back," Jake said. "I just wanted to make sure you'd had a bite to eat and a nap."

"Yes, on the bite," Harri admitted.

"Maybe you can take a nap now instead of chatting with your dreamy boyfriend?"

"Yeah, I should probably. I'm really running on fumes here."

"As much as I love our chats, I think you should get some sleep," Jake said.

"I know. I just wanted to hear your voice and say hi and tell you that I love you."

"I love you, too," Jake said. "Now get some sleep and call me later."

Harri hung up and turned the lights down in the conference room. She leaned forward in the chair and rested her head in her arms folded on the conference table. She fell fast asleep almost as soon as she closed her eyes.

The dream was the same. She was running through the dark woods on the island. She could hear the pounding of her footsteps as she ran. She could hear the thumping of her heart as if it came from all around her. "My name is Lauren Harper." Lauren! Where are you? Where are you? Her sister's voice kept repeating the phrase and Harri ran toward the sound of her sister, but it was all around her.

"Come find me." Jerome Wexler's voice mocked her as she crashed through the forest, wildly pushing tree branches out of her way. She had to find Lauren. She had to save her. Then Harri was at the water's edge of the island. She heard nothing in the dark silence except her own heart pumping loudly. Across the water, at the shore of the mainland, she saw Lauren standing next to Jared Atkinson.

"Lauren!" Harri screamed her sister's name. Lauren smiled and waved. She pointed at Jared Atkinson. Jared waved at Harri and then pointed at his left ankle. The brand of the owl shown red on his ankle. Then he pointed up at the tree next to them. An owl screeched from behind Harri. She turned to see the owl's talons coming at her face. Harri covered her face and was about to scream when her vision was flooded with light.

Harri startled awake to see Officer Cyndi Rodriguez standing in the doorway.

"Oh, Harri," Cyndi sighed in relief. "Sorry to wake you. Tom's looking for you."

Harri wiped her mouth with the back of her hand and shook the nightmare from her mind. She smiled at Cyndi and followed her out of the room.

She saw two missed calls from Harvey Berger and then a text saying he understood how busy she was and to check her email. When she did, Harri saw that he'd emailed her an attachment containing a summary of all the information he'd been able to find so far on Green Acres Funeral Home and its connected associations. Harri printed the attachment and sat back at her desk to read the summary.

"Got anything good?" Tom asked.

"Sorry I disappeared on you," Harri said. "I put my head down for a moment and I drifted off."

"You needed the sleep," Tom said as he looked over her shoulder at the summary.

"Who are Jedediah and Patrick Sumner?" he asked.

Harri hated when Tom looked over her shoulder.

"Oh, you're about to find out," she teased him.

By the time dinnertime arrived, Harri had gathered even more information on the Sumner brothers and when Tom showed up at her elbow with warrants and a big smile, she decided to call a meeting with the team.

"The entire team needs to hear this," she said.

"New information or leads to run down?" he asked.

"Both, you're gonna love it. You got the arrest warrant?" she asked.

Tom nodded. "I got arrest and search of home, vehicle, and workplace. We should bring him in tonight I think," he said. "Before he tries to squirrel away."

"Okay, let's do that," Harri said. "I'll make my updates as quickly as I can and then we can delegate assignments."

"Tony just got back with the goods from CUCO," Tom said.

Tom had assigned Officer Tony Diaz to serve the search warrant to CUCO for the Smith Construction paperwork. He'd returned with two banker's boxes of documents to sift through. It took another ten minutes to get the team together in the case command center.

"Are those the CUCO files?" Tom asked.

Tony nodded.

"They give you any crap about it?" Tom asked, remembering their run-in with the CEO.

"Nope. The lady handed them right over," Tony said.

Harri wondered how many documents had been destroyed before the warrant was served. She pushed the thought from her mind and focused on the task at hand. She stood in front of the whiteboard depicting the chronology for the last known movements of Jared Atkinson.

"Hi everyone. First of all, I want to thank everyone for all the hustle and hard work you're putting in. Tom and I both think we've assembled an amazing team on these cases, and we appreciate the help. I want to update all of you on new information and next steps. We finally found some of our missing links. We have a funeral home that is also connected to Smith Construction and Cellmedtech Tissue Bank."

Harri handed a stack of the summary Harvey Berger had emailed her to Officer Cyndi Rodriguez who passed them around to the team.

"We also have a warrant for Juan Bindo," Harri continued. She pointed to Juan's picture on the corkboard.

"Our subject works at the Green Acres Funeral Home and was driving the van recovered with a missing branded limb in the back. It's still being processed, but we're confident this is the same van that at some time last Sunday night was transporting Jared Atkinson's aka

Ethan Carle's body and the first branded limbs recovered," Tom said.

"Who are these Sumner brothers?" asked Officer Tony Diaz.

"They're our next focus after we bring in Juan Bindo," Harri explained. "Patrick Sumner is Patrick Smith, from Smith Construction. His older brother is Jedediah Sumner, the owner of a shell corporation several levels away from the company that owns Green Acres Funeral Home."

"He doesn't directly own Green Acres?" Officer Cyndi Rodriguez asked.

"No," Harri shook her head. "Believe me, I know it's confusing. A series of shell companies owns all three holdings. However, the forensic accountant I talked to did find credible information tying Jedediah Sumner to the funeral home and therefore, the two other entities, Smith Construction and Cellmedtech Tissue Bank."

"Is he our main suspect now?" Officer Tony Diaz asked.

There were four other officers in the command center with them, but Harri didn't know them by name. Cyndi had been coordinating the new additions to their team and because Harri and Tom had been out in the field so much, she hadn't had an opportunity to introduce herself to the rest of the team.

"Both of the Sumner brothers are," Harri said. "Jedediah has a younger brother named Patrick. It looks like they may be co-conspirators. Patrick Sumner was indicted back east, seventeen years ago in Connecticut where he worked as a dentist. He was caught abusing OxyContin after he messed up a patient's teeth and jaw. They sued and it was discovered that Patrick Sumner had been under the influence while he performed procedures on numerous patients. He lost his license and then it looks like he became a procurement specialist at a tissue bank in New Jersey. And then he disappeared off the radar. I was unable to find a Patrick Sumner after 2005. Because of the Smith Construction connection, I looked up Patrick Smith and he's a match to Patrick Sumner. DMV photos from New Jersey match DMV photos here in California. They are one and the same."

"What other evidence do we have these guys are involved?"

The officer who asked the question was older than the rest of the team. Harri had seen him around but had never worked with him.

"I don't think we've met before. What's your name?" Harri asked.

"Donald Chow," he said.

"Everything is circumstantial at this point. We know that Juan Bindo was working for them. According to their website, they have five employees listed: Jedediah Sumner is a Funeral Director, Eleanor Dowd is a Funeral Services Assistant, Mason Walcott is the Embalming Specialist, and Alexander Marchand is the Cremation Specialist. Juan Bindo was the Removal Technician, meaning he was the one who went to residences and care facilities to pick up the deceased and transport them to the funeral home."

"So, he's essentially a driver," Cyndi finished.

Tom nodded and came to the front of the room to stand next to Harri.

"Tissue harvesting is not the same as organ harvesting," Tom said. "You don't need any special skills, but you do need training. A lot of funeral homes that also sideline into tissue donation have a separate room used by the procurement specialist to harvest the body. Now, seeing as Patrick Smith was a procurement specialist in New Jersey, the working theory is that he's the one actually harvesting the bodies and most likely killing them since he's also the one picking up homeless men from CUCO to work at Smith Construction."

"With these kinds of schemes everybody gets kickbacks because tissue donation is supposed to be not-for-profit," Harri explained. "We also have to assume that CUCO is collecting fees, which are more kickbacks. When we met the CEO of CUCO, he was unpleasant and uncooperative, so we're assuming for now that he's the one getting the kickbacks. His name is Raymond Sklar, but we haven't had a chance to research him yet."

"I can do that," Officer Cyndi Rodriguez volunteered.

"Perfect. It would be great if we found enough information that we could subpoena his bank records if that's at all possible," Harri said.

"Seeing as it's a nonprofit organization they have certain public tax filing commitments to keep their status," Tom explained. "So, we might be able to look at financials through that lens."

"Okay, here's the fun part," Harri said. "Everyone please refer to the handout. According to the forensic accountant's research, Willoughby White Corporation owns Beauchamp Investment Holdings, LLC which owns Beran & Butterfly, LLC which is the company that owns Green Acres. Got it?"

Harri ignored the sounds of murmuring and flipping pages and continued.

"Okay, now Sandstone & Bradley, LLC owns Smith Construction and also JJSM, LLC. JJSM owns all of these companies mentioned so far, in addition to Cellmedtech Tissue Bank. The mailing address for JJSM and Beauchamp Investment Holdings is the same, but we're assuming it's an attorney or proxy director, so we're probably not going to get anything from that. Now the interesting thing is, the *WHOIS* web registration lookup on the Green Acres Funeral Home website uses the same email address as JJSM and Beauchamp Investment Holdings. Who wants to see what they can get out of the lawyers?" Tom asked.

Donald Chow and an officer named Gerald Moore volunteered for that task.

"What's our overall theory of the case right now?" Officer Tony Diaz asked.

"You want to explain it?" Harri asked Tom.

"From the evidence we have gathered so far," Tom started. "Detective Ethan Carle went undercover to see about a Mexican drug lord using homeless encampments to remain undetected as he checked out his Los Angeles operations. During his investigation, Detective Carle discovered that multiple homeless people had disappeared without a trace. They hadn't been admitted to medical or psychiatric hospitals, or incarcerated, or gone back home. He began to investigate, which led him to CUCO and how they hired their day laborers. Going from the chronology of events as listed on the board, he worked as a day laborer on Saturday for Patrick Smith. At that time, Patrick Smith took his cell number and said to give him a call if he wanted more work. Detective Carle then uncovered missing women who were working out of trailers on Franklin Avenue. These investigations hadn't crossed paths yet.

Tom stopped and took a sip of water before continuing.

"We now know that Patrick Smith is Patrick Sumner. The circumstantial part of this is that Ethan Carle's body was then found on an island in the LA River at the same time as several women's limbs were found with a specific brand. We located the van down near Vernon with yet another branded limb inside, and pieces of plastic that appears to match what Ethan Carle's remains had been wrapped in. We now have a suspect who was driving the van when it went off the road. That man's name is Juan Bindo and he works at the Green Acres Funeral Home where Patrick Smith's brother, Jedediah Sumner, is the Funeral Director. All locations of Green Acres Funeral Home offer onsite cremation services."

"So, you're thinking Detective Carle uncovered the scheme of luring homeless men to do day labor off the books where they were then killed and harvested for the tissue?" Officer Tony Diaz summarized.

"In a nutshell." Tom nodded.

"Then their bodies were cremated?" Donald Chow asked.

"Also correct. We think the reason why none of these people had been found before was because they were cremated at a Green Acres Funeral Home. Now, we don't know what happened on the night of Sunday, March 3rd that caused the branded limbs and Ethan Carle's body to be in that van. There was a rainstorm and it's possible the Green Acres on Glenoaks lost power or the furnace there wasn't working for some reason. We still don't know why Juan Bindo risked transporting Ethan Carle's remains and the limbs while it was raining, but he must have had one hell of an incentive."

Harri pointed to a map on the board. "Green Acres has another location on Glendale Boulevard and what we're theorizing is that he was taking back roads to transport the bodies from one funeral home to the next," Harri added. "From a nonworking cremation furnace, to where one was working."

"So, who killed Ethan Carle?" Officer Tony Diaz asked.

"Our primary suspect for that is Patrick Smith," Harri said. "Dr. Grimley found a small needle puncture at the base of his neck. We believe Detective Carle was injected with something that stopped his heart almost immediately. Their goal is to have the person die without harming the body and then harvest the tissue, and it has to be done quickly."

"What about those limbs and that weird brand. Has anyone done a search for that image yet?" Cyndi Rodriguez asked.

"We haven't done the research yet on the brand. The fact they were in the same van obviously connects them to Ethan Carle, the missing trailer girls, and the Sumner brothers. But the MO is so completely different, and the reason for killing doesn't appear to be the same. So we believe the limbs were a simple disposal job. Maybe they have a contract with the actual killer who murders these women and they're paid to get rid of the bodies," Tom said.

"So now, we need to build a case," Harri said.

"And that's through Juan Bindo?" Gerald Moore asked.

"What we really need is Juan Bindo to inform on his employers. He's our low-hanging fruit. Tom was able to secure an arrest warrant and also search warrants for his home, vehicle, and workplace. We'll bring him and, at the very least, charge him for fleeing the scene of an accident so we can hold him for as long as possible and interview him."

"What if he doesn't talk?" Officer Donald Chow asked.

"If he doesn't talk, then we move onto the next employee. We have three chances to break someone into telling us how terrible their bosses are," Tom said.

"What if all these people are getting kickbacks?" Officer Tony Diaz asked.

"We should assume all of them are being compensated in some way, but all of their danger thresholds will be different and that's what we'll use to get them to talk," Tom said.

There were no other updates for the team. Tom had already briefed everyone on the Verdugo Wash site and to alert them when the report came in from Detective Matteo Cruz.

"Hope he's not a runner," Officer Tony Diaz said as Tom and Harri prepared to leave.

"I'm still hoping we have the element of surprise," Tom said.

"After that press conference, who knows," Officer Tony Diaz said.

They'd been briefed on what Richard Byrne was going to say about the investigation and knew he would be holding back most of the facts they had so far. The big bombshell was that Ethan Carle was an undercover cop and Harri didn't see how that would scare Juan Bindo into talking. They left the team to get started on their new tasks and assignments.

Tom looked over at Harri and frowned. "What are you worried about?"

"Thinking about Whitey and those limbs," Harri said.

"Yeah. We're running out of time," Tom said.

"I hope those limbs are somehow connected to Green

Acres because if Juan doesn't talk I'm afraid we'll lose Whitey," Harri said.

"Don't think like that. Let's bring him in and make him beg to talk," Tom said.

Harri just nodded.

23

DAY 4 - 7PM

The arrest of Juan Bindo was uneventful. Harri and Tom had requested four additional units as backup and when Juan opened the door to his apartment and saw them all outside, he offered himself up to be taken in immediately and without incident. Harri was happy the arrest went smoothly because she couldn't shake the feeling that time was running out for finding Whitey.

They took Juan Bindo to Hollywood Division and put him in an interrogation room. They left him there, handcuffed to the table with an officer standing guard. They watched him behind the two-way glass to see how he would react for several moments. He was stoic. Usually they'd leave him stewing in there as a tactic for him to crack under pressure. They didn't have the luxury of time. They entered the room again.

Harri announced their arrival to the recording along with their names, date, and time. She and Tom sat down across from Juan with the metal table between them and began the interview.

"Please state your name for the record," Harri said.

"Juan Bindo," Juan said.

"What were you doing on Sunday night, March 3, 2019?" Tom asked.

"I was at home," Juan said.

That was his first lie and we weren't ten seconds into this.

"Where do you work?" Tom asked.

"You know where I work," Juan said, boredom dripping from every word.

"Please state it for the record," Harri said.

"I work as a removal technician for Green Acres Funeral Home," Juan said.

"What does a removal technician do?" Tom asked.

Juan yanked his arm against the handcuff. "This is hurting my arm."

"Could you please answer the question?" Harri asked.

"I drive to where the bodies are, pick them up, and bring them back to Green Acres," he said.

"Were you transporting a body on the night of March 4, 2019?" Tom asked.

"I told you I was home that night," Juan said.

"What happened to your arm? And your face?" Harri asked.

"That's none of your business," Juan said.

"We have video, Juan," Tom said, going in for the kill.

"Is that so? Then I'm not answering any more questions. I want a lawyer," Juan said.

Damn, Harri thought. The interview had gone nowhere fast.

"Are you not willing to answer any more questions?" Tom asked.

"I am not. I want my phone call and to speak to a lawyer," he said.

They had no choice but to do as he wished. Harri announced their departure and they left Juan sitting handcuffed to the table.

"That was fast," Harri said. She was sure he'd flip because he was an underling. Underlings tended to cooperate with authorities about their bosses. They'd been very wrong about that.

"Wanna try scaring him by throwing him into general population?" Tom asked.

"I don't think that'll do anything, do you?" Harri asked as she stared at Juan through the two-way glass. His main emotion at the moment seemed to be boredom.

"He did time on the assault charge, didn't he?" Tom asked.

"No, he got some sort of community service," Harri said. "Why?"

"He didn't look fazed at all about being arrested," Tom said.

"Maybe he knows he'll be taken care of," Harri said. "The tissue harvesting business is worth millions of dollars with just twenty bodies a month," she said.

"That could pay for a good lawyer," Tom said.

"Let's book him and send him to County. Then see who bails him out," she said.

Tom nodded and left to get the booking started. Harri stared at Juan, willing for him to talk. He turned his head and looked at the mirror in the room. Did he know she was looking at him through the two-way glass? She needed him to talk, but she knew that wasn't going to happen.

After they made sure Juan Bindo was on his way to County jail to be held until his bail hearing, Harri and Tom went back to the PAB to update the team. Everyone was just as disappointed as they were when they told them Juan had lawyered up.

"What was he booked into County on?" Officer Cyndi Rodriguez asked.

"We charged him for the murder of Ethan Carle," Tom said. "Carle's DNA and the plastic sheeting in the van before going into the wash were enough for that. None of us think he actually killed him and he called our bluff."

"So, now we hit the rest of them, right?" asked Officer Tony Diaz.

"Yes, we should start with Eleanor Dowd," Harri said.

"Why her? Because she's a woman?" Cyndi asked.

"Not so much that, but she's the Funeral Services Assistant which looks like she handles administration and the PR. She's been with the company awhile, so she'll have something to tell us. What have you been able to uncover from the warrant for CUCO?" Harri asked.

"Was the owner there?" Tom asked.

"No, only the receptionist, Guadalupe. She was the only one who helped," Cyndi said.

"I saw the two banker's boxes when we walked in. Is that everything they had on Smith Construction?" Harri asked.

"Yes. We watched her take the Smith Construction files from the file cabinet and put them into those boxes. We did a quick search to make sure she'd given us everything. We couldn't find anything else labeled Smith Construction," Tony explained.

"Have you gone through all of it?" Tom asked.

"We got through most of it this afternoon," Cyndi said.

"Most of it is lists of names of workers Smith Construction uses every week," Tony Diaz said.

"How many people are they using?" Harri asked.

"About twenty to thirty people a week. The same names keep coming up," Cyndi said.

"Any of our missing guys?"

"Davis Hines and Arthur Sharpe are on there, as well as Rufus Dexter. Now, Rufus has a separate file, and it seems he gets paid $20 for each person he refers to CUCO to sign up as day labor. Looks like he's been a recruiter for the last two years," Tony said.

"Nice he didn't mention that," Harri said to Tom. "He's part of the assembly line."

"Does he know what he's a part of?" Tom asked.

"He seemed genuinely broken up over Whitey being missing," Harri said.

"I could see why he would say CUCO is a good way to make money. It must be better than panhandling off the freeways," Cyndi said.

"We'll go back and ask him about it," Harri said.

"If he'll even talk to us at this point," Tom said.

Harri had momentarily forgotten about Lieutenant Richard Byrne's announcement to the press that Jared Atkinson was an undercover cop named Ethan Carle. They still had no idea what the fallout from that news would be for the rest of their case.

"Anything else that stuck out for you in those files?" Harri asked.

"We don't know how much CUCO was paid by Smith Construction for each of these men," Tony said. "If Rufus is getting a $20 referral fee, then CUCO has to be getting pretty good kickbacks from Smith Construction for providing the laborers."

"There were no invoices or documentation about money exchanging hands?" Harri asked.

"No contracts, no quarterly statements. None of that kind of paperwork at all," Tony said.

"The other thing that stuck out for me is that each of the men who signed up for CUCO's day labor program filled out that form. Most of them only put down a name and a phone number that's probably a pay-by-minute cell phone. They didn't have identification, or next of kin, or any of the other info an HR department would collect. They also had each of the men sign an insurance liability waiver, which seems odd. What insurance company would honor it without verification of ID? I can understand why CUCO would keep the liability waiver, but why the health chart?" Cyndi said.

"The guy who got the form for us wasn't homeless," Tom said. "He was just someone looking for a day gig. He probably had legit identification and all the other personal information you're talking about, Rodriguez."

"So, why weren't they sweating the homeless guys?"

"Oh, god," Cyndi looked like she was going to be sick. "It didn't matter if the homeless guys gave them sketchy information because they knew even if they got hurt or something, no one would care. No one would miss them or sue the company for worker's compensation or anything like that."

"Because one way or another, the homeless guys that were in decent enough health were going to Green Acres eventually," Officer Tony Diaz said in disgust.

Harri couldn't ignore her excitement at the team figuring out another part of the puzzle, but the thought of Rena and Whitey flashed through her mind.

"Thank you both," Harri said to them.

"Outstanding work," Tom agreed.

Tony and Cyndi looked as exhausted as Harri felt. Everyone on the team had been grinding away without sleep for too long.

"Oh, one other thing," Tony said. "We got word from forensics that were looking over the van."

"Tell me they were able to find an owner," Tom said.

"It's bad news. The VIN plates were all scratched or removed. Whoever did it knew all the places to look for a VIN. They got every single one."

"How many places does a VIN exist?" Harri asked.

"Depends on the make and model. Window, wheel shaft in front of the engine block, in front of the car frame, in the rear wheel wall, driver-side door jamb, driver-side doorposts, and underneath the spare tire. If you can believe it, they managed to get 'em all. They scoured it," Tony said.

"Did they find any more of Juan Bindo's finger-prints?" Tom asked.

"Yes. That's some good news. His fingerprints were on the wheel, partial on the car lock button, and the gearshift. They also got a definite match on the plastic piece in the van to the plastic that was wrapped around Ethan Carle. And the best news, they did find Ethan Carle's DNA inside the van. So, it's confirmed. We're able to place both Ethan Carle aka. Jared Atkinson, and all of the recovered limbs in the van. We can't confirm they were there at the same time, but because of the storm wash out, it's safe to assume that they were," Tony said.

"Which places Juan in the van during the storm, with the limbs and the body. That should help set his bail higher than the price of a latte," Cyndi observed.

"Better be higher than the price of my house," Harri muttered.

"Let's see how he feels after a long night in County jail," Tom suggested. "Haven't heard any counsel has shown up for him."

"Still don't have a clue where Whitey or Rena might be," Harri said.

"We have three more Green Acres employees to interview," Tom said.

"Will that be tonight? Do they know Juan Bindo's been picked up?

"We interview them all tonight. I don't care how late it gets. Once they get to work tomorrow they'll know if they don't already," Tom said. "Whoever's a part of this will start destroying evidence."

"We have the element of surprise going for us since it's Sunday night. Intake and booking take time. He might not even get a phone call until tomorrow morning," Harri said.

"Are we not sleeping again tonight?" Cyndi asked.

"We can't do that again. Let's have a skeleton crew tonight and we can do shifts. Everybody's off seven hours in between," Tom said. "Except for you and me, Harri. We'll catnap in the room across the hall. After we interview Eleanor Dowd and Alexander Marchand, of course."

"Who do you want to talk to first?" Harri asked.

"Eleanor. Mason Walcott lives in Burbank so he's not too far from her. Alexander Marchand lives on this side of the hill in East Hollywood. We can take him last and hopefully we don't have to wake him up."

24

DAY 4 - NIGHT

Harri called Jake before they left the PAB. He was unhappy she wouldn't be getting any sleep again that night. He told her he had news about the Wexler investigation but that it could wait. She made him promise he wouldn't do anything without her and he laughed. He was more concerned about her being behind the wheel with so little sleep in the last 48 hours. They said their I love yous and hung up.

The drive to Eleanor Dowd's home in Burbank was a quiet one. Harri drove while Tom napped. She let him sleep an extra five minutes when they arrived at the small house off of Magnolia Boulevard.

Eleanor Dowd was not happy to have someone ringing her doorbell after dark. It took them several minutes to convince her to let them inside. Now, they sat on an uncomfortable, but stylish mid-century modern sofa in her living room as she sat across from them on a matching chair.

"I don't understand what this is about. It's almost 9

p.m. Something happened to Abigail?" she asked as she tucked her bare feet under her legs.

Eleanor Dowd had an old-fashioned name, but she looked like a modern woman of a certain age. Harri had come to recognize the well-preserved look of women somewhere past their mid-forties who'd likely come to Los Angeles with stars in their eyes. Eleanor had the look of a Homecoming Queen who'd maybe spent some time in the beauty pageant circuit. She was trim, busty, and wearing a full face of makeup even though all she had on was a matching purple velour sweatsuit from Victoria's Secret.

"No, it's nothing like that," Harri assured her. "We're here on a murder investigation."

"Murder?" Eleanor asked in astonishment. "Who the hell's been murdered?"

"It's no one in your family," Harri said. "We're more interested in your workplace."

Eleanor looked at the two of them in surprise. "At Green Acres?" she asked.

"Yes, let's start with this question," Tom said. "Tell us about—"

Eleanor popped up from her chair and went to the bar cart on the opposite wall. "If we're talking about murder, I need a drink," she said as she poured amber liquid from a decanter into a crystal rock glass. She turned back toward them and offered the decanter. They both shook their heads. Eleanor nodded and sat back down with her drink in hand.

"What were you saying, handsome?" she asked Tom.

"Tell us about the procurement room at Green Acres," Tom said.

Eleanor's beautiful face twisted into an expression of

disgust. "I can't believe I work in a place that does that to a human body," she said.

"You don't believe in tissue donation?" Harri asked.

"I guess, in theory," Eleanor sighed. "Honestly, before I worked at Green Acres, I never even thought about it. I had the box checked on the back of my license and that's all there was to it. After Patrick started working with us about a year ago, I was walking by the room and I saw him crack open somebody's leg to get the bone out. I have never been more repulsed in my life. It was revolting."

"So, you know Patrick?" Harri asked.

"Is he the one that's dead?" Eleanor asked.

"No. Sorry to disappoint," Tom said.

"We're having a hard time tracking him down," Harri said.

"Not surprising. He's a shady guy," Eleanor said. "I know he's Jed's brother, but I mean, he is a very shady guy. I try not to have any interaction with him whatsoever."

"He ever bother you?" Tom asked. "Make unwanted advances?"

"Oh, no." Eleanor shook her head. "I shut that down the very first time we met. I'm not having any me-too moments with that creep."

"What exactly do you do at Green Acres?" Harri asked.

"I'm the Funeral Services Assistant. I do most of the PR and I work with families when they first come in. I explain the procedures because most people don't know how the funeral service process works. Most of them are grief-stricken and need some handholding, so between me and Jed we take care of the customers."

"You're kind of like the face of the business along

with Jedediah?" Harri asked.

"Yes, you could say that," Eleanor said as she sipped her drink.

"You said Jedediah and Patrick are brothers?" Harri asked, curious how the men handled their different last names.

"Hard to believe, but that's what Jed told me. I'd only worked with Jed about a year before Patrick came. Green Acres wasn't the busiest funeral home. The death industry is a hot market and Green Acres is a lower middle-tier funeral home. We have easy payment plans. Then Patrick showed up and everything started changing," she said.

"How do you mean?" Harri asked.

"Well," Eleanor sighed. "Patrick owns a construction company."

Amongst other things, Harri thought.

"He started making all these changes, which I guess were good for business. Like he remodeled the viewing room, which was outdated. We were under construction for about a month with that. He also created the procurement room and that's how the program got started. Patrick had been a procurement specialist on the East Coast and convinced Jed."

"And that part of the business is booming?" Harri asked.

"Oh, yeah," Eleanor nodded. "They do at least one body a day," she added with a slight shudder and took another sip of her drink.

"You have that many dead bodies coming through?" Tom asked.

"Four million people live in Los Angeles, Detective. People die every day," she said.

"Do you know how the tissue procurement works?"

Harri asked.

"I don't want any part of that," Eleanor said. "When I saw what they did to those bodies, I told Jed to keep me out of it."

"What about the people who work there? Do you know Mason Walcott well?"

"He's the embalmer," Eleanor said with a nod.

"What about Alexander Marchand?" Harri asked.

"He does the cremations. Kind of a Jack of All Trades," Eleanor said. "Kind of a weirdo, too. I'm glad he doesn't ever engage with the customers. He stares."

"He's a creeper?" Harri asked.

"I wouldn't say he's a creeper, but you know, people who work in the death industry are… unique. Alexander is comfortable in his uniqueness, you know? He can be OCD, which can be annoying, but it's the staring," she said.

"What about Mason Walcott?" Tom asked.

"Mason is a sweetheart," Eleanor said.

"Your sweetheart?" Tom asked.

"Oh, no," Eleanor shook her head and laughed. "God, no. He's just the sweetest man, and so is his wife."

"He has a family?" Harri asked.

"They have twin boys. I think they're like eight at this point," she said.

"Was Mason helping with the procurement?" Harri asked.

"Oh, I don't know about that. You'd have to ask him. I don't know why he would. He didn't get along with Patrick, either. Neither did Alexander. Patrick is an off-putting guy," she said.

"In what way?" Harri asked.

"Well, he thinks very highly of himself, for one thing. He can be loud. Demanding. Always talking about all the money he's making and how amazing he is and how many companies he has. He's good at tooting his own horn, you know? Some people might call him charismatic, but I think he's just a narcissist," she said.

"How many companies does he own?" asked Harri.

"Oh, I don't know. Who even cares?" Eleanor rolled her eyes and took another sip.

"What did Jedediah think about his brother?" Tom asked.

"Jed is the oldest and I feel like he takes responsibility for Patrick. He's always protecting him."

"Protecting him from what?" Harri asked.

"Oh, I don't know. I stay out of it. Just overheard Jed complaining once. Listen, I have no problem answering questions, but I'm confused. Who got murdered?" Eleanor asked.

"We're investigating the murder of Jared Atkinson who, at the time of his death, was posing as a homeless man," Harri said.

She hoped Eleanor hadn't caught the news yet.

"Posing?" Eleanor asked. "Oh, the undercover cop! I thought he was found in the river?"

"He was, but there's evidence that his tissue had been harvested," Tom admitted.

Eleanor's mouth formed into an O and her hand drifted to cover it.

"You don't think Patrick killed him and then took all his tissue?" she whispered.

"Why would you say Patrick?" Harri asked.

"He's the only one capable of murder in that family," Eleanor said.

"And not Jedidiah?" Tom pushed.

"I don't believe it. Jed is a sweetheart," Eleanor said.

"That's what we're investigating right now."

"Do you know if there were any problems with the cremation incinerator over the last weekend? Specifically on that Sunday during the rainstorm?" Harri asked.

"How did you know that our cremator was down?" Eleanor asked.

Harri's heart skipped a beat at Eleanor's question. They had been right after all.

Harri resisted the urge to look at Tom, and had to pretend to write in her notepad to keep from showing her excitement.

"Was the cremator down in the Glendale location as well?" Tom asked, picking up the thread without missing a beat.

"No, that's why we've been moving all the bodies from Glenoaks. There's a part that broke. I think in the wheel mechanism and for some reason, it's been on backorder. We've had a lot of services moved to the Glendale location. It's not that far away," she said.

So, their theory of why Juan Bindo was driving out on a rainy night with a corpse and a bunch of limbs in the back of his van proved to be correct. Hot damn.

"May we ask what you were doing on Sunday night?" Tom asked.

"I was here doing a Netflix and white wine chill with my friend Sarah," Eleanor said.

"May we have Sarah's last name and number?" Harri asked.

"Do you really need that?" Eleanor asked.

"We need to confirm where you were Sunday to dismiss you as a suspect," Harri said.

Harri's use of the word suspect triggered an internal alarm within Eleanor Dowd.

"Should I be looking for another job?" she asked.

"We aren't at liberty to say anything else about our

investigation at this time," Tom said.

Eleanor looked at Tom and then Harri, studying them to see if perhaps their faces would give her an answer.

"Your body language is telling me I should be looking for another job," she said.

"Do you know where Patrick Smith lives?" Harri asked, trying to redirect Eleanor.

"I don't know. Not far from Jed, who's in Studio City. I heard them talking once about getting dinner. Patrick said he'd walk to Jed's because it was only a block away. That's all I know about Patrick's life, and it's all I want to know," she said.

"Who takes care of the records for Green Acres?" Harri asked.

This question confused Eleanor. "What kind of records are you talking about?"

"Is there a business manager or a finance guy that does the books and keeps records of the money coming in from the funerals and the tissue procurement?" Tom asked.

"Oh, now I see the kind of investigation you're running. You want to know how much money Jed is making on the tissue procurement."

"Something like that," Harri said.

"I don't do the books. Jed does all that. He might have an accountant, but I've never seen anyone around the office. It's always Jed and Patrick doing the books on Friday nights," she said.

"Every Friday night?" Tom asked in surprise.

"Ever since Patrick came," Eleanor said.

"You do enough business weekly for that to be done every Friday night?" Tom asked.

"How would I know?" Eleanor shrugged and took another sip of her drink. "We do two to three funerals a week. We're lower middle-tier, like I said. The tissue procurement happens at least once a day and they have contracts coming from other funeral homes, too. Not every funeral home has a procurement room."

"And all those files are kept..." Tom trailed off, hoping Eleanor would finish for him.

"In Jed's office. On his computer and in the file cabinets," she said.

Eleanor had provided a wealth of information.

"All right, we're going to end here and let you get back to your evening," Tom said as he stood. "Thank you so very much for being candid with us," Tom said.

Harri and Eleanor also stood and followed Tom to the door.

"I wish you could tell me more about what's going on," Eleanor said as she escorted them out. "I wouldn't be surprised if Patrick got the whole place in a jam."

"Have a good night, Ms. Dowd," Tom said.

Eleanor nodded. "Good night, Detectives."

She shut the door and then Harri turned to Tom with a smile.

"Did you catch any lies in that one?" she asked.

"No, she put her likes and dislikes right out on the table," Tom said as they walked back to the car.

"I hope Mason will be as forthcoming," Tom said.

"You think she'll call anyone to warn them?"

"No, I don't think so. If she calls anyone tonight, it'll be about a new job," Tom said.

Harri nodded and smiled as Tom started the car. It was his turn to drive and her turn to nap. The fatigue crept through her body. She leaned back in the passenger seat and closed her eyes. She wouldn't have a nightmare. She would rest and get to the next interview refreshed.

Hang on, Whitey, she thought.

DAY 4 - NIGHT

Mason Walcott lived in an area ten minutes from Eleanor Dowd's home. The neighborhood was well-kept with neat, green lawns, artfully placed lights illuminating the landscaping of the single-family homes. It looked like a perfect picture of suburbia, Harri thought.

She checked the time and frowned.

"It's nine-thirty. Think it's too late to bother a family man on a Sunday night?" Harri asked.

"Let's be quick," Tom said.

"We shouldn't go to Alexander Marchand's later than ten-thirty, I think," Harri said.

"We need to interview Marchand tonight," Tom said.

"Let's get this started then. I hope this goes as easy as Eleanor," she said.

"He's got twin boys. Should mean he's efficient with his time," he said.

"Speaking from experience?" Harri teased.

"What do you think?" Tom asked.

Harri gave him a tired grin and went to knock on the door.

"Who's out there?" a man's voice demanded.

Harri noticed the kind of doorbell that was connected to a camera and alarm system.

"LAPD," Tom said as he looked around for the camera.

"What?" the man's voice asked. "What did you say?"

Harri could hear what sounded like screaming children in the background. She pulled out her badge and held it in front of the doorbell.

"Los Angeles Police Department," Tom said.

"Coming!" the man's voice called from the other side of the door. Footsteps drew closer and the door opened to a short man with dark hair and tired eyes wearing pajamas.

"Police? Who are you? Why are you here?" Mason asked.

"My name is Detective Tom Bards, and this is Detective Harri Harper," Tom said.

"What is this about? Is Marlene okay?" he asked.

"We're not here about anyone in your family. Who is Marlene?" Harri asked.

"My wife. She's a Pharmacist at Providence. She's working the night shift," he said.

"This is about Green Acres, Mr. Walcott," Tom said.

Mason Walcott crossed his arms at his chest and stepped back.

"Can't you come see me there tomorrow? It's almost ten o'clock and I'm still trying to get my kids to sleep," he said.

"That one of them there?" Tom pointed behind Mason to where a little boy in Spiderman pajamas watched them from the hall.

Mason turned and yelled, "Frankie! Get back in bed."

"I want to see the policeman," Frankie protested.

Mason turned back to Tom and Harri in defeat. "Come on in, please close the door behind you."

As they did so, another little boy perfectly matching Frankie, but wearing Captain America pajamas joined his twin in the hallway.

"Are you a policeman?" the twin asked.

"We both are," Harri said and smiled at the boys.

"Do you ride a motorcycle?" Frankie asked.

"No," Harri said. "Aren't you supposed to be in bed?"

"Johnny had to go to the bathroom," Frankie explained.

"I drank all the lemonade and then I had to pee," Johnny said.

Mason sighed and rolled his eyes. "Okay boys, back to bed."

"Can I see your badge?" Johnny asked Harri.

"Can I see your gun?" Frankie asked Tom.

"No, you may not," Tom said sternly. "Guns are not toys, and the two of you are supposed to be in bed. Now, if your father agrees, Detective Harper will let you see her badge, but then you have to go straight to bed without getting up again until morning."

The boys looked at Mason who nodded. "Do you promise?"

"We promise," the twins said together.

"You know, it's against the law to lie to the police," Tom said. "If you promise, you have to do it."

The boys nodded and then rushed to Harri's side. She pulled out her badge and showed it to them. They both marveled at it, whispering how they would become cops when they grew up.

"All right, boys," Mason said. "Back to bed."

The twins squealed in excitement, shouting goodbyes and goodnights as they ran down the hall to their bedroom. Once the door to the bedroom closed, Mason turned to the detectives.

"Let's go in the den where little ears can't hear," he said as he led them to the right.

The den was a comfortable space strewn with superhero toys. Harri was careful not to step on anything as she made her way to sit next to Tom on the overstuffed sofa. Mason plopped down on the loveseat next to them and sighed.

"Thanks for that," he said. "Whenever Marlene works the night shift, I have a hell of a time getting the boys to stay in bed."

"I've had nights like that," Tom said.

"We apologize for bothering you so late, but we're trying to piece everything together as quickly as possible," Harri said.

"What is this about?" Mason asked.

"We're deeply sorry to be disturbing you this late, Mr. Walcott," Tom said. "We wouldn't be here if it wasn't urgent. A woman is missing and we need to find her before something bad happens to her."

"Bad, what do you mean bad?" Mason sounded panicked. "Oh, god. It's not Eleanor, is it?" he asked.

"No, this isn't about Eleanor," Harri said. "Let me go back. A body was found with evidence of harvested tissue."

"Harvested tissue? Like in tissue donation? I'm an embalmer," he said.

"Yes, we know," Harri said. "We've spoken to Eleanor, and she mentioned how much tissue procurement business Green Acres is doing."

"Yes," Mason agreed with a nod. "I guess we do at least one a day."

"Mr. Walcott, we need your help," Tom said. "Give us ten minutes and we'll be on our way."

"What do you want to know?" Mason sighed wearily.

"What is your part of that business?" Harri asked.

"What do you mean?" Mason asked.

"The tissue procurement part of the Green Acres Funeral Home," Harri said.

"We understand that Green Acres has a procurement room created specifically for tissue harvesting," Tom said.

"What do you know about tissue harvesting?" Mason asked.

"Probably not as much as you," Harri said.

"Yeah, it's a nasty business, but it's necessary," Mason said.

Harri thought he sounded a little defensive.

"This country doesn't like dealing with death," Mason explained. "We don't like to see it, or think about it, or deal with it. We pretend it's not there, but it is. Death is just another part of life and tissue donation is another part of death this country doesn't want to see or hear about. It's a godsend, though. Before the medical advancements in this area, people just suffered. If you blew out your knee cartilage, too bad. If you smashed your leg in a skiing accident, sorry pal. People don't want to know about where the tissue comes from, as long as it helps them."

"And helps everyone involved in tissue procurement, too?" Tom asked.

Mason Walcott didn't answer Tom. He crossed his arms over his chest again.

"We've researched what's available out there. Green Acres came up as a player in the trade. Patrick Smith is your main procurement specialist?" Harri asked.

"He's the only one. He's related to Jedediah Sumner, his brother I believe," Mason said.

"And what's your role in that part of the organization? You mentioned you're the embalmer, but bodies being cremated aren't embalmed, right?" Harri asked.

"Yes, I embalm bodies for funerals and burial," Mason explained. "On the procurement side, I get a bonus for each body I prepare."

"What does that mean? Prepare the body?" Tom asked.

"I wash the body and disinfect it if needed," Mason said.

"And you disinfect the procurement room, as well?" Harri asked.

"No, that's a service that comes in before and after a procurement is done," Mason said.

"What's the name of that company?" Tom asked.

"You'll have to ask Jed about that. I only clean, disinfect, and embalm," he said. "I don't even go in the procurement room. I do all my work in the prep room."

"Do you get the same amount each time you prepare a body?" Harri asked.

"I get a grand each time," he said.

"How often do you have to prepare a body?" Harri asked.

"Seems to be at least once every day," he said. "Sometimes there's more than one after a long weekend or a holiday."

"Is that not surprising to you?" Tom asked.

"I've worked with Green Acres for about eight years now. Before we were doing tissue procurement, Green

Acres wasn't the busiest funeral home and it still isn't for that side of things. Then Patrick joined up with Jed and that changed. The bonuses are great. Both my boys will be in sports soon and that's more than a nickel. They're both gonna be driving at the same time. I'm gonna have two kids in college at the same time. All that bonus money goes right into their 529 accounts. We were able to put a full twenty percent down on this house," he said.

Harri wasn't sure if he was explaining himself to them or his own conscience.

"Does it seem weird to you that so many bodies are being harvested at Green Acres?" Tom asked.

"What do you mean by weird?" Mason asked as he scratched his head.

"You tell me," Tom said.

"You've never felt something illegal might be happening?" Harri asked.

"Illegal?" Mason said in surprise. "No, never. This is all completely legal. The tissue bank we sell to is FDA approved, I'm sure everything is documented. There's a lot of demand for tissue out there. We're helping people."

Harri and Tom glanced at each other. Harri felt again that Mason was trying to convince himself what he did was a noble cause.

"What happens to the bodies after the tissue is harvested?" Harri asked.

"Alexander Marchand takes over and the remains are cremated and the ashes are given to their relatives," he said.

"Do you have any access to the bodies after you prep them?" Harri asked.

"No. I hand them off to Patrick and that's the last I

see of them," he said. "Just so you know, I don't go into the procurement room or the crematory. Those guys stay out of my room, and I stay out of theirs."

"Did you prepare this man's body for tissue harvesting?" Tom asked as he showed Mason Walcott the photo of Jared Atkinson.

"This looks like the guy we did on Sunday night," Mason said.

"Where did this body come from?" Harri asked.

"I have no idea. That's Juan Bindo's job. He's the one who takes the calls for whatever body needs to be delivered to Green Acres. Jedidiah approves it, so that's info Juan or Jed should have," Mason said.

"You're sure this is the man that you prepped on Sunday night?" Harri asked.

Mason leaned forward and took the photo from Tom. He studied it and then nodded. "Yep, that's the guy," Mason said as he handed the photo back.

"Have you seen the news at all?" Tom asked as he put the photo away.

Mason shook his head and chuckled. "You've met my boys. What do you think?"

"Would you be willing to give a statement to the fact that you prepped this man's body on Sunday night?" Tom asked.

Mason looked directly at Tom. "Is this the man that you found in the river?" he asked.

"Yes," Tom said. "He was an undercover cop."

Harri watched as terror moved across Mason Walcott's face.

"Oh, my God. Do I need a lawyer? They called me in special. They said they had a delivery, and I came in right after dinner. I normally don't work on Sundays," he said.

"Because it's a family day?" Tom asked.

"You must have kids," Mason said.

"I do but they're grown now and out of the house," Tom said.

"That day can't come soon enough," Mason said.

"Is there a window of time a body needs to be harvested within?" Harri asked.

"I don't understand your question," Mason said.

"How long can a person be dead for before you can no longer procure the tissue?" Harri reformulated her question.

"It should be done within the first 24 hours," Mason said. "After that, some tissue isn't usable and it's a huge job to sort that out."

"And did Patrick Smith do the procurement on this man?" Harri asked.

"Yes, he did," Mason nodded. "Right after I prepped the body. How did this guy end up in the river?"

"Don't worry about that for now," Tom said. "How was Patrick's demeanor that night?"

"His demeanor? He was pissed. I don't think any of us were thrilled to be there on a rainy Sunday night. That storm was wild."

"What time did you leave?" Harri asked.

"Uh, I'd say left around 9 o'clock?" Mason said. "I got in there, did my thing, and got out. Marlena had called me because the boys were acting up. I went straight home."

"We'll need you to come down to the station tomorrow and give us a statement," Tom said.

"Okay. What station?" Mason asked. He still had a worried look on his face.

"Someone on the team will call and set that up for you," Tom said.

They exchanged phone numbers and Tom put Mason's into his phone.

"One of the guys from my fraternity is a lawyer," Mason said. "Should I reach out?"

"If it makes you feel better, go right ahead," Harri said. "For now, though, we'd like for you to not speak about this to anyone."

"Except my wife, though?" Mason said. "She doesn't like it if I keep things from her."

"No," Harri said. "For now, don't tell her anything about this. For her safety."

"Oh, right. Okay, I see what you're saying. I understand. Mum's the word," he said.

"Thank you, Mason. You've been a huge help," Tom said. "We'll be in touch."

"I hope you figure out what happened to that guy," Mason said as he walked them to the door. "I'm so sorry to hear he ended up in the river. I don't understand how that happened."

They nodded and said goodnight. Mason closed the door and Tom and Harri hurried back to the car.

"We get Alexander Marchand to tell us what happened to Ethan Carle's body and we might not need Juan Bindo's testimony at all. We could have an arrest warrant for both Sumner brothers by tomorrow," Harri said as she buckled her seatbelt.

"That still doesn't help us with the missing women," Tom said.

"No, but we never thought these two cases were the same killer anyway. I'm hoping if we bring one down, we'll somehow find the other," Harri said.

She hoped to God that was true.

DAY 4 - NIGHT

The drive to East Hollywood was short and for that, Harri was grateful. Alexander Marchand lived in a house hidden by a tall fence and a cluster of surprisingly dense trees. Harri could barely see the windows of his home from the street. Adrenaline was keeping her awake, but barely. She was sure the caffeine wasn't even registering any more. Her excitement surged at the prospect of getting so close to the Sumner brothers and the truth of what happened to Ethan Carle. It also made her jittery as all get out.

Tom checked his watch. "It's almost 10:30 p.m. Think he's still awake?" he asked.

"I can see lights through the trees. I've never seen a front yard like this. It must be the oldest house on the block," Harri said.

The trees rustled in the wind and Harri shuddered involuntarily. The house had the look and feel of a neighborhood haunted house. It was the kind of house the children on the block would make up stories about and dare each other to sneak into. The tall trees and fencing masked the home, but Harri picked out details of the roofline and chimney that marked it as a Craftsman, likely built before the 1920s.

"This place is giving me the creeps," Harri said.

"I'm feeling it too," Tom said.

"Maybe it's just because it's so late," Harri said.

"You ready?" Tom asked.

Harri nodded and wondered what they were both sensing. Their excitement had turned to unease as they pulled up to the house.

They stepped out of the car and Harri unholstered her firearm. She wasn't sure why but did it anyway. She'd been on the job long enough to trust her instincts.

Tom opened the wooden gate, and they followed the dark path to the front door, using the light from the living room windows as a beacon guiding them forward. The front yard had at one time been meticulously land-scaped but now was overgrown and wild. Leaves rustled in the wind.

Every sound startled Harri just a bit. She breathed in deeply to calm herself and smelled the fragrance of roses, lavender, and sage. Someone in the past probably loved this house and the garden.

They had high hopes that Alexander Marchand would provide the missing pieces in the story of the Sumner brothers. Even if Juan Bindo wouldn't talk, his co-workers had given them enough information to bring Patrick and Jedediah in for questioning.

Tom stopped suddenly on the porch. He raised his finger for silence. His move was so sudden, Harri bumped into his back.

A garbled shriek erupted from the other side of the door. Harri heard something thud hard to the floor.

Tom turned the knob of the front door. He shook his

head no, indicating it was locked. The door was solid wood and Harri knew the hinges were probably wrought iron. They wouldn't be able to kick it in.

Tom pulled out his firearm and they both clicked their safeties off.

Tom gestured for them to go around back.

Harri's thoughts raced as she silently followed him off the porch.

Had they gotten it all wrong? Was Alexander Marchand the mastermind behind all of this? Was that even a possibility?

Or was he the limb killer and had Whitey and Rena on the other side of the door?

Tom took a left at the driveway and disappeared behind the house. Harri tried to see through the blackout curtains of the front window but the gaps were too small. She had an impulse to come crashing through the glass but knew that was a stupid idea.

They had no way to know what was happening in there.

She picked up her pace to catch up to Tom.

She rounded the corner and saw Tom quietly unlatching the back gate. On full alert, they made their way quickly past the rose bushes on their right while trying to see through any of the windows to their left, though the shades were drawn down, obscuring their view.

Tom quickened his pace and time seemed to stretch out for Harri. They'd arrived at the back door within seconds, but it felt like minutes.

Her blood was buzzing, and she became aware of a low whine in her ears. They were both prepared for the worst inside.

Tom twisted the knob to the back door. It was

unlocked. He opened the door and a loud squeak of the hinges made them both wince. They'd lost the element of surprise. No doubt about that.

Tom moved fast through the kitchen.

They had no time to spare.

He hid his body to the left of the door and cleared the hallway.

He nodded.

Harri rushed past him, through the hallway and into the dining room.

They only had seconds to spare if they had any hope of catching a killer in the act.

The dining room was empty.

Harri used the wall of an alcove to protect her as she peeked around the corner into the expanse of the living room. The tang of blood filled her nostrils, a unique metallic smell that was unmistakable. Too much blood was spilled in that room. Harri knew she'd find a body in there even though she couldn't see anyone inside.

The front door was now open.

Blood splatter marred the pale gray velvet couch and dripped to the wood floor where more blood was smeared. In the middle of the living room lay a man, face down in a pool of blood.

The living room was wallpapered with the most macabre artwork Harri had ever seen. It looked to be medieval and showed nude people fornicating with animals, being tortured, and then joyfully lounging in a garden.

Harri pointed to the door and Tom nodded.

Tom gestured to the staircase to his left indicating he would clear the rooms up there. The open door could be a trick to make them think someone had run outside.

Backup? She mouthed the word to Tom.

He shook his head no and pointed to the front door again.

Harri knelt near the man lying on the floor. She checked to see if he was breathing, though she knew he wouldn't be. He was dead.

She moved past him and stopped to clear the front door. She didn't need anyone ambushing her.

No one was on the porch.

She peered around the darkness of the front yard but saw no one there. She couldn't be sure anyone wasn't hiding in the bushes. She carefully checked behind each of the trees and made it to the front gate, which hung open. There was a smear of something wet on the door latch. Though she couldn't tell the color in the darkness, she was sure it would turn out to be blood.

Whoever just murdered Alexander Marchand had gotten away.

Harri returned to the living room to see Tom coming back downstairs. He was already on the phone calling in the coroner, the SID forensics team, and extra officers to canvass the neighborhood. This place would be lit up within minutes.

"He's dead," Harri said.

"I checked his pulse just in case. He's been stabbed multiple times," he said.

Blood was everywhere. On the furniture, on the wood floor, spattered on the walls and the nearest stack of books.

"That looks like arterial spray," she said.

"Wouldn't doubt it," he said.

"Check out this room," Harri said, slowly spinning to take it all in.

"You don't know this?" Tom asked in amusement. "This is Hieronymus Bosch's Garden of Earthly Delights Triptych," he said pointing at the wallpaper of the bizarre painting.

"Familiar with it?" Harri asked. "Religious art from your altar boy days?"

"I'm smart like that," Tom quipped. His expression turned serious as he went over to the built-in bookcase to take a look at the books on the shelves.

Harri came up behind him.

"He's a fan of Dante's Divine Comedy," she said.

Alexander Marchand had two shelves filled with various translations of Dante's work.

"Light reading," Tom said.

"Have you read it?" Harri asked.

"In college a long time ago," Tom said.

"So, he was a religious freak?" Harri asked.

"Not necessarily. Seems to have an interest in medieval studies," he said and pointed to several books on medieval crime and punishment.

"I didn't know there were so many experts on medieval torture," Harri said dryly.

"Wait a minute," she said and crouched down closer to a shelf lower on the bookcase. "Holy shit. It's the brand we've been searching for. Do you have that sketch you did at the river?"

Tom pulled out his little notebook out of his coat pocket and flipped the pages to the drawing he had made.

She pointed at the spines of four books on the end of the lower shelf. The exact same symbol that had been branded on the limbs was embossed in gold on volumes one through four of the series "The Complete Study of Medieval Torture Techniques."

"I'd say we found our limbs killer except for the fact that he's just been murdered," Tom said in frustration.

"Someone tying up loose ends? Neland Carrington is the author of these books," Harri read out loud.

"Marchand could be a fan," Tom said.

"Worth checking out this author," Harri said.

Sirens penetrated the silence. Tom left Harri in the living room as he went out to the front to direct the teams.

Harri stood in the deadly quiet of the house with the bloodied body of Alexander Marchand and listened as the sirens approached. Red and blue flashing lights broke through the cover of the trees out front and illuminated the grotesque artwork that covered the walls of the room.

It seemed unlikely that Alexander Marchand was the limb killer, but he must have been killed because he could lead them to him. What now?

. . .

Dr. Grimley examined the body of Alexander Marchand as Harri and Tom stood by watching.

"He died within the last forty-five minutes," she said, confirming the timeline and the noise they heard when they had approached earlier.

"Was it the cut to the carotid artery?" Harri asked.

"It could have been any of these twenty stab wounds," Dr. Grimley said. "This attack was frenzied. The cuts are deep."

"We interrupted him," Harri said. She now wished she had crashed through the window to catch the killer. Maybe they would have been able to save Marchand.

The century-old staircase squeaked and groaned as Paul Gibson, the SID forensic technician, hurried down from upstairs. Tom and Harri both reached for their firearms and Paul shook his head and held up his hand as he tried to catch his breath.

"I found something really weird. You guys gotta come upstairs," he said.

"Is it another body?" Harri asked, afraid he had found Whitey.

"No, Harri," Paul said. "That would be normal. This is...come upstairs."

Figures, Harri thought. This place was all about the weird.

Tom and Harri followed Paul upstairs and into the master bedroom. Once inside the room, Paul motioned them to a walk-in closet that had an open sliding door at the back which led to another room.

"How did you find this?" Tom asked.

"Completely by accident," Paul said. "I dropped my fingerprint brush and had to get on my hands and knees to find it under the bed. I saw light coming from under the back wall of the closet. I only saw that paneled wood wall. I figured there had to be some sort of secret door and it took me a minute to find the trigger to open it," he said.

"Where's the trigger?" Harri asked.

"Right here." Paul pointed to two black on and off buttons next to a shelf of expensive-looking leather shoes.

When Paul pressed the top button, the wooden section of the closet slid to the right and revealed a room behind it. The room was small, about the size of the walk-in closet, and Harri wondered if the room and the closet were originally a nanny's room, and the master bedroom was the nursery when the home was originally built.

The walls of the room were painted black, and it was lit like a gallery. In the center of the room was a museum pedestal displaying a book lit from above, like an objet d'art."

"You'd think he was displaying the Hope Diamond," Paul said from the closet.

"To him, it was," Tom said as he stepped inside the secret room.

"I can see what you meant by weird," Harri said as she followed Tom into the room.

Both Harri and Tom put on disposable gloves. Tom pulled a mini flashlight out and looked at the corners of the room.

Harri leaned closer and lightly ran her hand over the leather cover. It had the symbol on it. The same symbol branded on the limbs. The same symbol on Neland Carrington's books. The same symbol Jared Atkinson had shown her in that dream.

"This leather is different," she said.

She peered closer and saw something that sent a chill

down her spine. Harri's gasp filled the room and both Tom and Paul reacted.

Tom rushed to her side and looked where Harri pointed.

"What?" Paul asked from where he stood outside the sliding door.

"Tom," Harri's voice only came out in a whisper. "Tom, that's a mole. That's hair sticking out of that mole."

Tom studied the strange artifact and then took out his phone. He nodded at Paul and said, "Go get Grimley."

Paul nodded and moments later they heard him crashing down the stairs again.

Harri watched as Tom took several pictures of the book with his phone camera.

"This binding looks homemade," he said.

With his forefinger and thumb, Tom delicately opened the book to the first page.

The title said, *The Sins of an Evil Woman* with the now-familiar symbol below it.

Harri wanted out of the room immediately and tasted bile at the back of her throat. What had these women gone through?

"Does that look like dried blood to you?" Tom asked as he took more pictures.

Harri looked and recognized the dark brown pigment of the words on the page. Ink splotches marred the script. Someone had used a fountain pen without really knowing how. Or maybe that was part of the macabre experience? She learned in other investigations that blood didn't make a good ink unless it was thinned with something else. Otherwise, it would coagulate and clog the fountain pen's nib.

"What's after the first page?" Harri asked.

Tom turned the page and read out loud, "I am lazy and use drugs to escape who I am. I am a whore who sells my body for drugs."

He gingerly turned each page and they saw more of the same kinds of confessions. The pages were thick and looked like antique parchment or vellum. There were six pages in all.

"Did she have to confess her sins to the executioner?" Harri asked remembering the religious art and books they'd found downstairs.

"He skinned her and then wrapped her confessions with her own skin," Tom said quietly.

"Do you think the pages are skin, too?" Harri asked.

"What have you found?" Dr. Grimley asked from the doorway to the secret room. "Paul wouldn't tell me, just said I had to get up here."

Tom and Harri stepped away from the book and Dr. Grimley squeezed her way into the small room. She approached the book and Harri took that opportunity to press her body against the back wall. She stood next to Paul Gibson as Tom showed Dr. Grimley what they'd discovered.

"My god," Dr. Grimley said. "At first glance, this appears to be human leather. The pages seem to be human parchment. My god, look at this. That is a freckle right here."

Tom stepped out of the secret room and Harri followed him into the master bedroom.

"Where did Alexander Marchand get this thing if he wasn't the killer?" Harri asked.

"Could he have a partner?" Paul suggested. "Most freaks love it when they meet other freaks like them. Just thinking this piece must have taken some time and a certain level of skill to be able to..." His voice trailed off.

"Could be a partner, or a group," Tom said. "Let's hope not. Hate to think there's more of them out there. Smarter people than us should be able to tell us."

Harri knew he was thinking of the FBI and its team of profilers.

"This is the ultimate trophy," Harri said.

"Did you touch anything in that room?" Tom asked Paul.

"No, Detective," Paul said with a touch of defensiveness in his tone. "I did open the book like you just did with two fingers on the corner. I've been in my full gear."

Paul wore white coveralls over his clothes and hair. He wore surgical gloves and booties over his shoes.

Tom nodded in apology. "Go through this room with a fine-tooth comb. This is probably what our killer was after when we interrupted him."

"What about the book?" Paul asked.

"That'll go with Dr. Grimley. It's human remains," Tom said. "Need to find out whose."

"Do you know of anyone who could analyze something like this?" Harri asked. "We should be able to get DNA from the skin and the blood, right? Would tanning the skin get rid of the DNA?"

"I don't think so," Paul said.

Harri shivered as if the room temperature dropped by ten degrees. She stepped out of the master bedroom and into the hallway.

"Good job finding this, Paul," Tom said.

The crime-scene photographer moved past Tom and Paul and joined Dr. Grimley in the secret room. He took photos and the two men watched as Dr. Grimley placed the book into an evidence bag. Paul seemed to be having a hard time taking his eyes off the gruesome discovery.

"This is what's happening to the missing girls," Harri said from the hallway.

She didn't expect Tom to answer but felt that she had to say it out loud.

An image from the artwork downstairs flashed through Harri's mind. She'd seen something downstairs that now made sense.

"I think I've figured something out," she said.

She left the two men standing in the master bedroom and hurried down the stairs.

Alexander Marchand's body had been removed. SID forensic techs continued collecting evidence from every inch of the room. Harri carefully stepped over to one of the walls and stared at the image of a naked man being pulled over what looked like a ladder in the wallpaper painting. She stared at it trying to make her brain tell her what she'd noticed before her subconscious locked it away.

She turned her back to the image and thought of something familiar and ordinary. She pictured in her mind Jake's smiling face. In her mind's eye, Jake threw his head back and laughed. Harri quickly turned her head and looked over her shoulder at the image again. She was using a technique she'd been taught to unlock her memory. This time, the body looked like it was being stretched and Harri remembered some long-ago history class and the teacher, Mr. Carafano, who'd told her about the rack.

"Find something?" Tom asked as he came up behind her.

"I think I know how he's killing them," she said and pointed at the naked man being stretched on the painting.

Harri heard Dr. Grimley instructing Paul Gibson and

the crime-scene photographer as they all came down the stairs.

"Dr. Grimley," Harri called out.

"Just a moment, Harri." Dr. Grimley handed the evidence bag containing the book they'd discovered to Paul Gibson with a nod.

"You have a question for me?" she asked as she joined Tom and Harri.

"Could a modern-day rack contraption pull apart limbs in the way that we've seen? Around the wrists, elbows, knees, ankles?"

Dr. Grimley leaned forward, careful not to touch the wall. She looked at the image of the man on the rack that Harri pointed to. Tom leaned forward also and the two of them stared at the image with the same blend of fascination and horror that Harri felt.

"The rack," Tom said. "They used to torture people on those during the Dark Ages. They'd tie the victim up with their hands over their head and bind their feet and then harness the ropes to gears at each end. Every turn of the gear would tighten the ropes, slowly pulling the victim apart."

"That could absolutely cause the kind of damage we've seen on the limbs," Dr. Grimley said emphatically.

"He has Rena and Whitey now," Harri said to Tom.

Tom sighed heavily and pulled his hand through his hair. Harri recognized it as one of his stress responses when he tried to gather his thoughts.

"The author with the symbol, Neland Carrington. Cyndi says he lives in town. He's an adjunct professor at UCLA," Tom said.

"Well, isn't that convenient?" Harri said.

"I have Cyndi pulling everything there is to know

about him. She's updating me real-time," Tom said. "Where do the Sumner brothers come into this?"

"This isn't their style. They're in it for the money. This," Harri looked around the living room, covered in blood and macabre wallpaper. "This is something else," she said.

"So, how did Marchand and his killer know each other?" Tom asked. "Why did the killer come here tonight, right before we got here? Did the killer know we were on the way? Did he come to get the book? Yeah, most likely," Tom answered his own question. "But why?"

"Any evidence of a secret room to torture women in?" Harri asked the technicians.

"It's a big house, but no. No other secret rooms or hidden structures on the property. We've gone through all of it," Paul said.

"We'll get DNA back on that book. And stabbings always leave a ton of DNA behind. We'll catch him before he does it again," Harri said.

She wouldn't let Whitey or Rena go through this. Or any other woman for that matter.

DAY 4 - NIGHT

My plan was simple. I knew the man holding us captive was watching every move we made. We couldn't see in the dark, but we now knew exactly where the door was.

I was becoming weak. I hadn't eaten in over a day and the man hadn't come back to give Rena her daily bread and water. This scared me. He wasn't feeding us, which probably meant the end was near.

"All right, we should go over the plan one more time," I whispered to Rena.

"I'm gonna sit in the middle of the room with you to my right," Rena whispered.

"You're sure we can hear his footsteps before the door opens?" I asked.

"Yes," Rena said.

"The minute I hear the footsteps I'll get back to the wall to the right of the door. We'll be blinded by the light as soon as the door opens."

"How does that help us?" Rena asked.

"Oh, it won't. It'll bother us at first, so we have to

expect it. I'm hoping he'll focus all his attention on you and won't notice me."

Even to my ears, this sounded like a last-ditch plan, doomed to fail. It was the best I could come up with.

"Then I jump on him and use my body weight to throw him off balance," Rena whispered.

"And I'll be there messing with his feet, so he trips and falls. Once we have him down on the ground, we can kick him and slam his head on the floor as a way to knock him out."

"I don't know. He's a tall guy and I'm light. I'm not sure I can make him lose his balance like that. And what if he falls on top of me?"

"That's where we have the advantage. He'll be surprised because you haven't attacked him before, have you?" I asked.

"No, I haven't," Rena said.

"If you don't want to pull him down, then try to get him off balance by jumping on him and pushing him back. I can stick my feet behind his, so he trips over me and crashes down into the doorway. If we get lucky his head might hit the floor," I said.

That would be a lucky break, I thought.

"And then what do we do when he's on the ground?" Rena asked.

"You're going to kick him in the nuts as hard as you can and I'm going to pound his head into the cement floor to knock him out. Hell, if it kills him that'll work too."

"I don't want to die," Rena whispered and I could feel the fear in her voice.

"I don't want to die either, Rena," I whispered.

I squeezed the younger woman's hand in the darkness of our shared prison. This would be our one and only chance. If we failed, he'd kill us both in a heartbeat. This was it.

We had to make our stand and fight for our lives.

I'd been plotting for hours, and this was the best I could come up with.

"I think I hear him," Rena hissed.

I strained but didn't hear whatever she was listening to.

"Do you hear it?" Rena whispered. I felt her shaking beside me.

A deep fear settled in my belly.

I squeezed her hand again. "You can do this," I whispered to her and to myself.

I waited until the footsteps sounded right outside the door before I let go of Rena's hand and silently stood against the wall. I hunched my back against it, ready for my chance.

The door swung open, and light flooded into our prison.

I was temporarily blinded, so Rena had to be, too.

This was our only chance. It was time.

"Now," I yelled and threw myself at the man's feet.

I heard shuffling from Rena's direction and then a desperate cry erupted from her as she jumped towards us.

Her body thudded against the man.

He didn't budge.

She didn't have enough momentum to knock him down. I tried to scissor-kick his legs out from under him, but he kicked me off.

He grabbed Rena around the chest and heaved her up.

She screamed in pain.

I went at him with all I had, trying to get him to let go of Rena, but he was strong.

Too strong.

He swung at me and I didn't duck in time. His fist glanced on the side of my head, and I fell back, hitting the back of my head on the wall.

Stars exploded in my eyes and darkness seeped in from the edges. Bile rose up into my mouth as I sank to the ground.

He slammed the door shut behind him and carried Rena away. I could still hear her screaming and flailing against him. I was plunged back into the darkness. I closed my eyes and tears ran down my face.

My plan had failed miserably.

Instead of getting any sort of upper hand, I'd delivered Rena into his arms. I had no idea what he would do to her, but I couldn't keep the thought of the women's limbs that were found with Jared out of my mind. I was scared I would never see Rena again.

And then I would be next.

I'd been right to think he was starving us so we couldn't resist what was coming our way. We couldn't escape him. With my head throbbing, I lay down on the cold cement. I rolled myself up into a ball and cried like I hadn't cried in years.

I was going to die alone in the dark just like the trailer girls and no one would find me. This was a pathetic way to die. So what? My entire life had been pathetic up to now. Why should my death be any different?

⊕

How long had I been curled up on the floor? It seemed like an eternity. I sniffed and wiped my face with my hands. My tears had evaporated as I'd lain in a ball, cold and terrified.

I heard a clicking sound from somewhere up above me. I sat straight up, making my head spin. The dark made me nauseous now, too. Fear blossomed again from deep inside me.

Another click sounded and I was bathed in blue light. The sudden change of light blinded me again, and my head exploded with fresh pain. I moaned as the light ripped through my brain.

When the pain faded slightly and my eyes didn't feel like they were going to roll out of my head, I opened them and saw the horrible sight in front of me.

A large TV screen was mounted high up on the wall across from the door. I'd never noticed it before because I'd never run my hands that high up when I felt around the room. I squinted in the darkness and focused on the screen. I saw a naked Rena strapped to a strange wooden contraption.

Her arms were tied together at the wrists and pulled above her head. Her legs were spread and tied down at each ankle. There was a timer at the bottom of the screen.

This wasn't just TV, I realized. It was some kind of live feed.

The man wanted me to know what was in store for me.

Rena screamed and I felt warm pee running down my leg.

I had never been more scared in my life.

DAY 5 - MARCH 10, 2019 - 3AM

I t was close to 3 a.m. and Harri and Tom were still at Alexander Marchand's house overseeing all the evidence retrieval.

"Come here you two," Dr. Grimley said to Harri and Tom.

They joined her as she led them outside to the porch. Dr. Grimley sat down on the front steps and Harri and Tom sat down on either side of her.

"Have either of you ever heard of anthropodermic bibliopegy?" she asked.

Harri and Tom both shook their head in the darkness of the night as they looked out at the trees and overgrown front yard of the murdered man's house.

"No," said Harri.

"Can't say that I have," said Tom.

"It is the creation of books bound in human skin. Became popular in the 19th century."

"That's horrible," Harri whispered.

"It was actually fairly common. Many rural doctors at

the time made books from their patient's skin after they'd died as a memorial keepsake."

"This must be the same crowd that took photographs of the dead?" Tom asked.

"Life was closer to the land back then," Dr. Grimley explained. "People were more honest about death."

"What do you mean?" Harri asked.

"Most people in this day and age don't get their hands dirty with death. Back then, it was all around. People slaughtered their own dinner. Fathers delivered their own children a lot of times. The sick and elderly died at home in their own beds, not in a hospital or care facility. The photos and the books, it was grotesque but not uncommon."

"Did these books ever have the person's crime written inside?" Harri asked.

"I seem to remember something about books like this made after the French Revolution. Now, don't quote me on this, but I think with criminals who were sentenced to death, the executioners would write the criminal's confessions and list their crimes, which were transcribed in books made of their skin after the execution," Dr. Grimley explained.

Harri shuddered to think how close they'd come to facing this killer. They'd interrupted him. He hadn't had a chance to clean up, which meant he most likely left behind DNA.

Tom's phone rang and he picked it up. A curious expression crossed his face as he listened to the other person on the line. Tom left the porch and took the call out on the sidewalk. Harri had a hard time concentrating on what Dr. Grimley was saying as she watched Tom on the phone, pacing in front of the gate as he spoke to the caller.

Was it Richard Byrne trying to take over the investigation?

Was it another body?

Tom came back onto the porch with a smile on his face.

"That was county jail calling about Juan Bindo. Seems he heard the news about Alexander Marchand's death and never did get that lawyer. He wants to talk," Tom said.

"Excellent news! When?" Harri asked.

"Right now. He's awake and ready to get the hell out of jail," Tom said.

"He's not getting out of jail but he doesn't need to know that," Harri said.

Tom left instructions with the officers in charge of the crime scene and asked the forensic team how much longer they would be there. Everyone was sure they'd be gathering evidence for at least the rest of the day.

"I'll try to get this autopsy done by tomorrow morning," Dr. Grimley said. "We'll get on the processing of the book as soon as we can. If it's a match to one or more of the limbs, it shouldn't take long to confirm."

Harri and Tom were on their way to the county jail.

Juan Bindo looked a lot less cocky than the last time they'd seen him. He was sweaty, unshaven, and jittery. Harri wondered if he was detoxing off something, or if it was sheer stress. She also wondered about the lawyer. Had someone led Juan to think he'd be taken care of if he was ever picked up? Or had he just assumed so?

"We're here," Tom said. "Let's talk."

"What do you want to know?" Juan said.

"Tell us first about the limbs," Tom said.

"That's why I want to talk to you. Alexander's death is freaking me out. He's the one who gave them to me," Juan said.

"Alexander Marchand gave you the branded limbs that have been recovered?" Harri asked.

"They were in a bag. He told me to get rid of them," Juan nodded.

"So, you didn't pick them up anywhere?" Tom asked.

"No, he brought them in on Sunday."

"Alexander Marchand brought the limbs to you in a bag on Sunday night? Where was this? At Green Acres?" Harri asked.

"Yeah. At Glenoaks. On Sunday night after the procurement job," Juan confirmed.

"And you couldn't get rid of them because of the broken cremator?" Harri asked.

"Yup. That cop's body was already in the van. Alexander grabbed me on the way out and shoved that bag in my hand and told me to stick those in, too. I didn't know what was in there, and I didn't look," he said.

"Had you ever done something like that for Alexander before?" Harri asked.

"No. I'm just the driver. I pick up the bodies and bring them in," he said.

"Where did you pick up Ethan Carle's body from?" Harri asked.

"Who's that?" Juan asked.

"The undercover cop," Harri said.

"That was different. Supposedly that job was a favor Patrick had to do."

"What do you mean by a favor?" Harri asked.

"That's what I overheard Patrick telling Alexander.

He'd already harvested the body and when Alexander told him the cremator was broken, Patrick lost his shit. He didn't want to store the body and wait for the cremator to get fixed. So, he made me go out in that damn rain, and now here we are."

"Why did you run after you crashed the van?" Tom asked.

"I was scared," Juan said and looked down at his hands that were handcuffed to the table.

"Let's try that again," Tom said. "Why did you run after you crashed the van?"

Juan was quiet for a moment. Then he looked up and said directly to Tom, "Because I had some beers, okay? I wasn't expecting to drive anywhere in the rain. It was coming down like a bitch, so I sat in the office and had a beer."

"How many beers?" Tom asked.

"Almost two. I didn't get to finish the second one before Patrick started yelling and cussing at everyone about the cremator being broken," Juan said.

"Did you observe an uptick in tissue harvested bodies since Patrick came to work at Green Acres?" Tom asked.

"Uh, yeah. Everyone did. Before we only did two or three funerals a week and then it's like we're doing procurements every day."

"And who started that?" Tom asked.

"Patrick. He's the procurement guy."

"Where did the procurement bodies come from? Where did you pick them up from?" Harri asked.

"Well, that's the thing. I didn't always do the pickups. They paid me anytime a body showed up on the procurement table. Half the time I had no idea where those bodies came from," Juan said.

"You didn't think to ask?" Harri asked.

"They were giving me $100 a body. That's an extra $100 a day," he said.

"Why were they paying you if you weren't transporting the bodies?" Tom asked.

Juan shrugged. "Because I saw Patrick shoot up a guy and he died."

Harri and Tom paused and glanced at each other. This was unexpected news.

"You actually saw him using a syringe on someone who was alive?" Tom asked.

"I'd just done a pick-up. This was about a year and a half ago. I came back to Glenoaks and when I went to unload, I saw Patrick's construction van shaking back and forth. I went to see what was up. I opened the back door and saw him stick a needle in a guy's neck. The guy was out like Pacquiao after Marquez dropped him in their fourth fight. Then Patrick made me help him move the body inside."

"And the man was alive before the syringe went in?" Tom asked.

"He was thrashing around. Kicking and punching, but the guy wasn't that big, and Patrick got him," Juan said.

The detail about the syringe going into the neck was an important one for Juan to know about. It meant he corroborated what Dr. Grimley had discovered in the autopsy. Ethan Carle was killed in the same way.

"This happened about a year ago?" Harri asked.

"Yeah. Like a year and a half ago. That's when they decided to deal me in. Even if I wasn't bringing the bodies to Green Acres, I got paid $100 a pop."

"Meaning you knew your bosses were mass murderers, and you did nothing to stop them," Tom said dryly.

"Mass murder?" Juan shook his head. "I only saw that one thing. I don't know where all these other bodies come from. Not my business. Maybe what Patrick did was self-defense or something. I don't know," Juan said.

"Self-defense?" Harri asked. "Self-defense? You just told us that you witnessed Patrick Smith inject something into the neck of a very alive man, struggling against being assaulted, who then, how did you put it? Dropped like Pacquiao? How could that have been self-defense?"

"I don't know," Juan shouted. "Maybe it was like a lover's quarrel or something. I never saw anything else."

"C'mon, Juan. You knew the whole time what they were doing was illegal," Tom said.

"What's illegal? There were lots of dead guys showing up. So? It's a funeral home. This is a big city. Lots of people die all the time. I only ever saw that one thing. Anyway, after a person is dead, the body's up for grabs. All that tissue is worth a lot of money."

"But you only got $100 per body," Harri said.

"What do you mean *only*?" Juan asked. "That's like an extra two grand a month. Cash."

"Did you know Mason Walcott is paid ten times that? Per body?" Tom asked.

Juan's eyes got big on hearing that. Then they narrowed to slits and his mouth set in a hard line as he realized how cheaply his silence had been bought.

"Did Jedediah Sumner know where the bodies were coming from?" Harri asked.

"How could he not? He was in the game before, but when it was just regular business, Green Acres wasn't that busy. After Patrick came, it all started cranking. Jed has to know where the procurement bodies come from," Juan said.

"Why are you telling us all this now?" Tom asked.

"Because I made my phone call, and the Green Acres lawyers are blowing me off. Jed hasn't returned my call, either. I'm not gonna be the fall guy for those two," he said. "I did nothing wrong. I transported bodies to the funeral home from their places of death. That's it."

"Walk us through what happened Sunday night?" Harri asked.

"I don't know. The cremator at the Glenoaks location broke. Patrick flipped out. I'd already loaded the cop's body into the van. Alexander comes running out with this bag and forces me to take it. I did not look inside the bag. I didn't know what was inside the bag. And I didn't know at the time that the body was a cop or anything. As far as I knew, he was just a body being cremated," Juan said.

"And where were you going?" Tom asked.

"Green Acres has another location on Glendale Boulevard. I called ahead to make sure the cremator was working over there and it was. Right as I left, it started pouring rain again. Parts of San Fernando Road were flooded, and I was looking for another way to get over to Glendale and I lost control of the van. I jumped out right before it went over the side into the water. Broke my fucking arm. The river was insane. I could've died that night."

"And then what happened?" Harri prompted.

"I watched the van go down the wash toward the river. I'd lost my phone, so I walked all the way back to Green Acres. Patrick was still there. He was crazy pissed. I thought he was going to kill me. I managed to calm him down. I promised him the van would end up way far out in the ocean. I promised him the body would get eaten by fish or sharks or some shit. I was scared of Patrick that night, so I left. I've been looking over my shoulder this whole time," Juan said.

He looked scared shitless.

"Did he come after you?" Harri asked.

Juan shook his head. "I've been staying away from Green Acres, but I had to go pick up my check. Jed was there and he told me they were suspending the tissue harvest program for a while so I could stop thinking I was getting that $100 per. It was messed up because I need that money."

This guy was a piece of work, Harri thought. No wonder the brothers had chosen him to be part of their enterprise. He was as void of empathy and morality as they were. Harri tamped down her growing anger. They had Juan in custody and they would have the brothers soon, too.

"Will you testify to the fact you saw Patrick poison somebody with a syringe and witnessed his death?" Tom asked.

"I want immunity on any murder charges. I didn't kill anyone. I didn't know those limbs were in that bag. I'm not going down for anything those motherfuckers did."

"Fair enough," Tom said. "I'll see what I can do."

"Were the limbs harvested?" Harri asked.

"I said I didn't look inside the bag," Juan said. "Are you going to drop the murder charges against me?"

Tom took out his notebook and showed him the drawing he made of the brand. "Ever see anything like this?" He pointed at the brand that was found all over the limbs Juan had transported.

"What is that an owl or something? Nah, I've never seen that before. Should I have?"

"If you haven't, you haven't," Harri said.

"We're going to arrest Patrick and Jedediah. We'll let them sweat awhile and see what inconsistencies they provide with what you've told us. Once that happens, we'll come back and deal with you," Tom said.

"Fine, whatever. I didn't kill anyone. I didn't do anything wrong," Juan mumbled as Tom gestured to the prison guard to come get him.

After Juan was escorted out of the room, Tom turned to Harri.

"We have enough evidence to get warrants for Patrick and Jedediah. I don't think my judge is going to want me calling him at four in the morning. We should catch some sleep in the conference room and put the calls out in a couple of hours. Or would you rather go home?" Tom asked.

"Home's too far. A nap at the PAB will be fine," Harri said.

She wasn't sure she'd be able to sleep after all the coffee, sugar, and adrenaline she'd been running on for the last forty-eight hours. Harri wasn't going to miss bringing in those brothers, either.

"We should grab breakfast after our two-hour naps," she said with a smile.

Tom groaned when he registered how little sleep that was.

"What a case this turned out to be," Harri said.

"We aren't done yet," Tom said grimly.

"I can't stop thinking about Whitey and Rena. I hope they haven't run out of time," Harri said.

29

DAY 5 - MARCH 10, 2019 - 4PM

Harri dragged herself into the kitchen off the bullpen of Hollywood Division. She'd managed to get six hours of sleep because she and Tom decided to split up the work. She slept while he called his judge and got the paperwork together for the arrest warrants for Patrick and Jedediah Sumner. That took him almost all of the morning.

Once he had the arrest warrants in hand, Tom went to get his hours of sleep while Harri and Officer Cyndi Rodriguez arrested Jedediah Sumner at the Green Acres Funeral Home on Glenoaks Boulevard and served the search warrant for the business. They left a group of officers from their team to search for any and all financial paperwork. The SID forensic team was left to process the procurement room in the hope they would discover evidence of any as yet unknown missing homeless men who'd been victims in the tissue harvesting business, including Ethan Carle.

They placed Jedediah in an interrogation room at Hollywood Division. He'd sit there stewing as they went to serve the arrest warrant to his younger brother, Patrick.

Cyndi had finally found Patrick Sumner's address. He did live three doors down from his brother Jedediah in Studio City as Eleanor Dowd said. When they went to the home, Patrick was nowhere to be found.

"Well, this is disappointing," Harri said to Officer Cyndi Rodriguez.

"Do you think he knows we have his brother?" Cyndi asked as they headed back to the car. "Is he on the run?"

"I would be," Harri said. "But no. I bet Patrick Sumner's the kind of guy who always thinks he's the smartest one in the room. I'm more worried about him going on an evidence destruction spree. What's the next address?"

"The tissue bank," Cyndi said as she started the car.

"Let's go get him," Harri said.

Cyndi drove them down to El Segundo to the address listed for Cellmedtech Tissue Bank. The receptionist didn't want to let them through initially, but Harri wasn't going to let her give Patrick time to flee. Harri anticipated he might try running out the back entrance and had several officers posted there.

The receptionist was a slim woman who Harri thought resembled Eleanor Dowd. Creepy, she thought. The woman was condescending and Harri couldn't understand why.

"I'm sorry, I can't tell you if Mr. Smith is here right now and I can't possibly let you into the offices. Perhaps you should try calling him to make an appointment?"

"No. That's not how this happens," Harri said. "We have a warrant for his arrest and to search this place of business. You either step aside, or Officer Rodriguez handcuffs you and places you under arrest. The choice is yours. I have no preference either way."

The receptionist hesitated a few seconds too long and Officer Cyndi Rodriguez did handcuff her, despite the woman's shrieking protests.

Harri walked behind reception and caught the reflection in the window of a tall man running down a hallway. She inwardly laughed, knowing what was waiting for him.

In the moments it took for Harri to exit the rear entrance of the building, Officer Tony Diaz had pulled his firearm on Patrick and now had him face down on the ground as another officer handcuffed him. Harri knelt near Patrick's face.

"Hello there, Patrick," she said. "I'm Detective Harriet Harper with the Los Angeles Police Department. I have a warrant for your arrest, and we are currently conducting warranted searches of your home, as well as all of your places of business."

"I have nothing to say to you," Patrick replied in a strained voice.

"That's okay, Patrick. I have your driver and your brother in custody too," Harri said.

Harri left Officer Tony Diaz in charge of the search at Cellmedtech Tissue Bank. She let him decide if he needed to arrest the receptionist for interfering with a police officer. She was still handcuffed and crying when Harri and Cyndi drove away, following the patrol car that had Patrick Smith handcuffed in the back.

They arrived at Hollywood Division around three in the afternoon and placed Patrick in a room next to his brother. Neither brother knew the other was right next door. Harri's part of the operation lasted most of the afternoon, which allowed Tom to get some much-needed sleep.

When Harri and Tom reconvened, he looked like a

different man. It was amazing what five hours of sleep could do.

"Sounds like the arrests went off without a hitch," Tom said.

"Patrick tried running out the back, but Diaz had him on the ground by the time I got out there," Harri said.

"Quite the pair, aren't they," Tom said.

He'd taken a look into both interrogation rooms and noticed the same thing Harri had. The Sumner brothers were almost exact opposites in both looks and personality.

Jedediah was an average-height bald man in his mid 40s who looked like he could be an accountant. He wore glasses and frumpy dad clothes, even though he was unmarried without children. Everything about him was average and bland. If Harri saw him on the street she might not have noticed him. Her description of him would have to be average, bald, and soft. She couldn't think of anything else to say.

Patrick, on the other hand, was Jedediah's opposite. He was easily over six feet tall with a lean muscular build. He was also in his mid-40s and bald but wore earrings in both ears and looked like he belonged on Venice Beach working out with the other weightlifters. He exuded the aura of a jailbird. She wouldn't be surprised to learn he'd done time.

Patrick was not soft. His brother was a marshmallow.

"Looks like it would have been easy for Patrick to overpower pretty much anyone he came in contact with," Harri said.

"I wouldn't want to mess with him," Tom said.

"Who should we start with first?" Harri asked.

"I'm thinking Jedediah might be more willing to talk than Patrick."

Harri definitely agreed with that.

"Did you get enough sleep?" she asked.

"I can finally think again, so yes. Glad we did that," he said.

"I had my doubts I'd be able to fall asleep because of Whitey and Rena still being missing but I passed out," Harri admitted.

"It's good we're refreshed," Tom said. "We'll have to be sharp to interview these two."

"I dreamed of Whitey, but I did sleep," Harri said. "I'm ready to take on Mr. Marshmallow man."

"Marshmallow man?" Tom asked, his eyebrow raised.

"He looks squishy," Harri said as she pointed to Jedediah.

Tom nodded and they both stared at him. "They never look like the criminal masterminds we think they are," Tom said.

"No. They never do," Harri said.

"Ready?"

Harri nodded and they entered the interrogation room. Harri informed Jedediah they'd be recording the interview then turned the recorder on. She announced their arrival for the recording, including the date and time.

Jedediah looked up at them expectantly.

"I know this is about that undercover policeman. I had nothing to do with that," he said.

"How did Ethan Carle end up at your funeral home?" Harri asked.

"Patrick might be my brother, but I am not going to get tied up with all of this," Jedediah said.

"How did Ethan Carle end up at your funeral home?" Harri asked again.

"I don't know," Jedediah whined. "This is all Patrick's fault. He's been a sociopath since he was five. My parents made me take care of him all these years. I am done. I was perfectly happy running my funeral homes and then he blew into town and here I am, under arrest for murder," Jedediah said bitterly.

His face was flushed red, and his hands were balled up into fists.

This might be the easiest interview ever, thought Harri.

"You're telling us that Patrick, your brother, is the reason that Ethan Carle ended up dead at your funeral home?" Tom asked.

"Yes. That policeman caught on to the homeless men disappearing and figured out the connection to that organization called the California Unhoused Community Outreach project. That was where Patrick got his construction crews," Jedediah said.

"What happened to those men?" Harri asked. "Walk us through it."

"I didn't know what was going on until about two months ago. I told him to stop. I told him he'd gone too far like he always did. Patrick always gets too greedy. He always thinks he can handle whatever situation he creates and it's other people who suffer. It's always me that has to clean up his messes and I told him I wasn't going through that again. He threatened my life," Jedediah's face had turned tomato red. "He said he could get a good price for my tissue." He looked like a man who was about to explode.

"What happened to the men?" Harri repeated the question.

"He killed them. Patrick injected them with something. I didn't ask what it was. I didn't want to know," Jedediah said.

"How many men did this happen to?" Tom asked.

"I have no idea. It could be a lot. We made Green Acres a clearinghouse for other funeral homes because we had the procurement room set up. They sent us the cadavers for a fee. We have records for those. You'd have to separate those from our other clients and that should give you an idea," Jedediah said.

"What about their names? Do you have records of that?" Tom asked.

"No. Patrick faked all those."

"Didn't you do the books with him every Friday?" Harri asked.

"He did the books. I watched," Jedediah admitted. "Patrick is known for his dishonesty, so I insisted. I told him everything had to be on the up and up from the get-go. Look where I am now? I should never have let him back in my life."

"You're saying you were completely hands-off in the harvesting business?" Tom asked.

"Yes. I looked the other way," Jedediah said. "I let him do his thing to make him happy."

"Isn't it also true you made a lot of money from the harvesting business?" Harri asked.

"Take it. Take all the money. I don't want it and I don't need it. I want that guy out of my life once and for all," Jedediah Sumner said with a strangled sob as he threw his brother under the bus.

"Are you willing to testify that Patrick killed Ethan Carle? Do you have any information on the deaths of Arthur Sharpe or Davis Hines?" Tom asked.

"I don't know any names. Except for the policeman, Ethan Carle. Or Jared Atkinson. I heard Patrick talking on the phone with someone about Jared Atkinson. Someone else wanted the policeman gone," Jedediah said.

"Who was he talking to?" Tom asked.

"I don't know. And I didn't ask," Jedediah said.

"Walk us through how you purchased bodies for procurement from other funeral homes," Harri said wanting to circle back to the number of men they'd processed.

"Purchased?" Jedediah seemed offended by the word. "No, you can't purchase a body. The other funeral homes were paid a referral fee is all."

"Okay, so walk us through it," Tom said.

"We have a specialized procurement room for tissue removal. A lot of funeral homes don't want to take on the cost of that. We offered our procurement room and our driver to bring the cadavers to us and we paid them a referral fee," he said.

"So, these other funeral homes received payment for funeral services, but didn't have to take on the cost of an actual burial or cremation?"

"Cremation only," Jedidiah said. "We only accepted referrals that were to be cremated anyway."

"So, the other funeral home collected payment for cremation services, but didn't do the cremations?"

"Correct," Jedidiah said. "Those cadavers were diverted to our funeral home for harvest and then we performed the cremation."

"The other funeral homes were paid twice for one cremation they didn't even have to do?" Tom asked.

"Yes," Jedidiah said. "It's really win-win for everyone."

"And how many bodies would you say you received under those circumstances?" Tom asked.

"I'd say about one or two a week," Jedediah said.

"Your staff told us that you're doing at least one tissue procurement a day," Harri said. "That's five bodies a week."

"What about the bodies that came in through your funeral home," Tom asked.

"Patrick forged their records to make them donors. Half of them weren't. The relatives never knew."

Jedediah had just hung himself. Harri knew they'd be able to get him accessory charges, but with the record forgery, they definitely had him on fraud like Detective Fioranelli did in the case in New Jersey. Apparently, Jedediah didn't know about that.

"We do tissue procurement Monday through Friday and I didn't know where the other bodies were coming from. I was afraid to ask," he said.

"You're not close to your brother?" Harri asked.

"As I told you before, he scares me. I thought I was safe by moving across the country. I tried to get away from him. Then he lost his dental license and after that whole mess, he came to the west coast looking for me. Our parents are both dead and I'm the only relative he has left. He always comes back to me," he said with an exasperated sigh.

"Do you know when and where Ethan Carle was killed?" Harri asked.

"I have no idea. I was at Green Acres that Sunday and I kept my nose out of that business. I knew he was doing a special tissue procurement and I overheard it was Jared Atkinson," Jedediah said.

"Do you believe your brother killed all those men?" Tom asked.

"Absolutely. Can I prove it? No. I wouldn't know how. But he's my brother and I've known him since he was a baby. He's always lacked empathy. He's been a bully since before he was potty-trained. Our parents thought it was amusing. Now, as an adult he's no holds barred."

"Are you willing to testify against your brother in a murder trial?" Tom asked again.

"I will testify but you have to make sure to put him away. Forever. Otherwise, I'll be a dead man like all the others," he said.

Tom glanced at Harri and she saw his nod. They had what they needed from him to put his brother away. Harri suspended the questioning and announced the interview was over.

They left Jedediah in the room alone to discuss the next steps regarding Patrick. They hadn't anticipated that he'd cave so easily.

As they watched Patrick in the other room, Harri had questions. They had him for Ethan Carle. But who was the co-conspirator on the phone call? Someone else who wanted Ethan dead. Who could have power over someone as intimidating as Patrick Smith?

"I don't think Patrick will go down easy," Harri said.

"I'm betting he lawyers up immediately," Tom said.

"Then what's the question we want the most out of him?" Harri asked.

"First we ask about Whitey. Then we ask him about the man who sent him after Ethan Carle," Tom said.

Harri nodded. Those would have been her two questions as well.

They entered Interrogation Room A and Patrick regarded them with casual defiance. Harri informed him the interview would be recorded and turned the recorder on. She announced their arrival, date, and time for the tape and they sat down across from him.

"Where is Darlene "Whitey" Whiteman?" Tom asked.

"I have no idea who that is," he said.

"She lived next door to Ethan Carle at the Los Feliz river encampment."

"I've never been to that encampment, nor do I know that name," he stated.

"Who told you to target Ethan Carle," Harri asked.

Patrick narrowed his eyes. The question didn't scare Patrick. It made him mad. Harri knew his thoughts were running to figure out who'd snitched on him. If they didn't manage to convict him and put him away for good, Harri was sure Jedediah would be a dead man.

"What do you mean who asked me to target him?" Patrick asked.

"We know you were doing somebody a favor," Harri asked.

"I don't know what you are talking about," he said.

He was about to clam up, Harri thought.

"You're saying no one asked you to take out Ethan Carle," Tom said.

"That's not the way I work," he admitted.

"How do you work?" Harri asked.

"I use day laborers for my construction projects," he said. "I'm not the only contractor who does that."

"Are you the only contractor whose crew turns up missing after they've worked with you?" Tom asked.

"This conversation is over. I want my phone call. I'm not saying another word without a lawyer present," Patrick said.

Harri glanced over to Tom who nodded. Harri announced the interview was over and turned off the recording. They left him sitting alone in the room.

"You were right about that," Harri said.

"Did you see his expression when we asked about

Whitey? His face was blank. No recognition. His right eye twitched when you asked about Ethan Carle. He's definitely good for Ethan and all the tissue harvesting victims," Tom said.

"Arthur Sharpe and Davis Hines ended up the same way as Ethan Carle, but how can we prove that without bodies or records? He's not the guy with the limbs. And I don't think he's going to tell us who that guy is," Harri said.

"We have enough evidence to put them away and we can release them to booking. Jedediah on conspiracy, at least, and Patrick on murder. That's gonna take its time. We need to focus on finding out who took Whitey and Rena," Tom said.

"What's our next step?" Harri asked.

"I've already started that," Tom said. "Neland Carrington lives in Los Angeles. He's a professor at UCLA and lives in a big enough house for privacy."

"Do we formally interview him because of the symbol on the books matching the brand on the limbs?" Harri asked.

"We should watch him first," he said. "If anything looks suspicious, we'll move in."

"Where does he live?"

"Brentwood," Tom said.

"My new backyard," Harri said.

"It'll be an easy stakeout then. No crosstown driving," Tom said with a grin.

"We solved one case," she murmured, steeling herself for another sleepless night.

"We'll find her," Tom said.

Harri nodded. Tom went to talk with the officers about releasing the Sumner brothers to booking and sending them to county.

Harri checked her phone and saw she had a missed call from Jake and had several messages. She'd listened to the last one and knew Jake had made a breakthrough in the Wexler case, but she couldn't take her focus off finding Whitey. She decided to text him now and give him a call later.

He was concerned about her still working in the field and asked if she could come home. Harri knew if she did, it would pull her focus off finding Whitey. Harri didn't want that right now. The limbs case was finally moving forward, and she wasn't going to miss any of it.

30

DAY 5 - NIGHT

Tom had disappeared on Harri, so she decided to have some more shitty coffee from the bullpen kitchen. She'd waited for him for over an hour, reviewing updates from the teams still conducting the searches. Tom finally showed up with a scowl on his face and Harri's stomach twisted in anticipation of whatever bad news he had.

"You're not going to like this," he said.

"Something happen at booking?" Harri asked.

"Richard wants me to babysit this whole process," Tom said. "Wants to make sure there's no fuck-ups on paperwork and the brothers arrive at County Jail in one piece."

"Isn't that what we all want?" Harri said. "One of the team officers could handle that."

"That's what I told him, but he reminded me that a cop was murdered and said this case was too important to hand off to anyone else," Tom said. "I don't want you going to Carrington's alone, though."

"I can take Cyndi," Harri said, her heart racing. It

was so typical of Richard to throw a wrench in the works like that.

"Can't. I need her. She's busy on the paperwork," Tom said. The rest of their team was still busy with the search warrants, gathering evidence.

"I'll just go check out the residence. Get the lay of the land," Harri said.

Tom pursed his lips and acquiesced. "Don't do anything without backup."

"I won't," Harri said. "I'm leaving now then. Call me if you need anything."

"Harri," Tom started and then stopped, unsure of what to say next.

Harri was grateful when he didn't finish whatever he was about to say.

Instead, Tom shrugged and said, "Good luck."

Professor Neland Carrington lived on Saltair Avenue between San Vicente Boulevard and Sunset Boulevard. It was an old street with stately homes built in the fifties and sixties before Brentwood became synonymous with multimillion-dollar homes. From what Harri could see from the street, his home was a large, traditional Cape Cod with white siding and green shutters. There were large trees in front of the home and a white picket fence with a hedge running along the inside for privacy. The driveway led to a white rolling gate between two red brick pillars. The problem was that it was difficult to see much of anything past the privacy hedge. She had eyes on the front gate and the driveway but the house was well hidden.

She'd switched out the cruiser for her own Audi to be

more incognito and parked across the street and down a house. She'd seen other people parked on the street and hoped she fit in.

As soon as she was settled, she texted Jake and let him know what she was up to. She wanted to ask about his development on the Wexler case but didn't want to distract herself, so she kept it light. Jake wanted to know when she'd be home and she resisted the temptation to let him know she was only about ten minutes away. Instead, she told him she was safe and hoped it wouldn't be another all-nighter. Jake reminded her to be safe and told her he loved her. She said the same and that she would update him as soon as she could.

Harri watched the entrance of the home into the evening. From her vantage point across the street, she didn't see any lights go on as the daylight faded. She wasn't even sure if Neland Carrington was home.

But Tom had been right.

This house was roomy and had plenty of space for hidden rooms or a basement. There were no close neighbors to hear any screams. Although, if he was the limb killer, Harri was sure he would have soundproofed any room filled with so much screaming and pain.

Tom called several times to check in. She described to him the design of Carrington's home and that she couldn't see much. He told her to hold steady and reminded her to call in if she saw anything out of the ordinary.

Something out of the ordinary didn't happen until just after 9 p.m.

Harri had dozed off for nearly half an hour and dreamed again of Jared Atkinson and the owl. The owl shrieked and its talons were coming at her face when she woke up with a start. She was at first confused about where she was and then remembered she was watching Neland Carrington's home.

Her eyes adjusted to this new level of darkness. There were no streetlights on Saltair. The trees lining the sidewalk were dense and shaded the street from the moonlight. A movement at Carrington's property caught Harri's attention.

A shadow moved behind the front gate on the inside of Neland Carrington's front yard. Harri leaned in and studied the space beyond the white gate.

Was that shadow moving toward the house?

Her heart pounded as she remembered the way they had found Alexander Marchand. She couldn't take the chance that they'd lose another potential witness. She called dispatch and requested three units to come check out an intruder at the address on Saltair Avenue.

The dispatch told her the ETA for the backup units was five minutes.

Alexander Marchand died within five minutes.

Harri got out of her car as quietly as she could.

She crossed Saltair within seconds and quietly climbed over the front gate into Neland Carrington's front yard. She pulled her firearm from the holster and disengaged the safety to be ready for anything.

Harri found no one in the front yard. She checked the time. Four minutes until backup arrived. She looked down the driveway to the side of the house and saw that it was clear.

She moved quickly down the drive toward the garage and stopped at the corner of the house to check if the intruder was visible in the backyard. She leaned against the house and peeked quickly. There was no one in the backyard as far as she could tell.

Harri went to the back door and checked the knob.

It was open.

She looked around for any sign of the shadow she'd seen. When nothing moved, she stepped inside.

Three minutes for backup.

The back entrance was dark. Harri saw a laundry room to her right and moved forward past a pantry. The kitchen was dark, with only the glowing numbers of the appliances providing any light. Harri paused to listen for any signs of another person in the house.

She heard nothing but the faint hum of the refrigerator.

Could she have been wrong about the intruder?

She made her way through the kitchen and down the short hallway into a much larger space. A blue light filtered around the bottom and side of a door to her right. She sensed someone inside.

What if there wasn't an intruder and she scared the living daylights out of Neland Carrington in his own home?

She'd seen someone in the front yard, though. And another man died a gruesome death just this morning—a man who had probably known Neland Carrington personally. If she was wrong, so be it. She has cause to be here, and Harri wasn't about to let another key person to their case be silenced.

Her thoughts were interrupted by a scream of pain.

"I've told you everything. I didn't do anything else. Please. Stop. It hurts so bad. I'll say anything you want. Just get me off of this thing," the woman's voice pleaded.

"You must atone for your sins. True atonement can only come from pain. Confess. Tell me your deepest shame. Your sin," the man's voice commanded.

The woman screamed out in pain.

Harri knew she was in the right place. The door was ajar.

Harri crept closer and peered through the narrow opening. Inside the room, she saw a man sitting in front of a computer watching something in the dark. On the screen, a woman was on a large wooden contraption. Her arms and legs were tied to ropes attached to rollers with a handle and ratchet system, manned by a figure dressed all in black with a black hood over his head. Harri recognized Rena May's tortured face from the photo Heather had given her earlier.

Another excruciating scream erupted from Rena and Harri heard small pops as the executioner pulled at the crank on the machine that was tearing her joints apart.

Harri stepped into the room and pointed her gun at the man's head.

"Freeze," she said.

The man turned toward her, his mouth gaping and his eyes wide in surprise. His hand drifted toward the keyboard.

"Put your hands on the desk. I will shoot you if you turn that off," Harri said calmly.

He did as she commanded and put both his hands on the table.

"Who are you?" Harri asked.

"Neland Carrington. I live here," he said. "What are you doing in my house?"

"I'm Detective Harriet Harper with LAPD. I saw an intruder in your front yard. Your friend Alexander Marchand was murdered earlier this morning and I thought you could be next. Or maybe you're the one who killed him."

Harri was relieved to finally hear sirens in the distance, growing louder.

"I called the police for you. Just in case someone was coming here to kill you. But for now, I'm placing you under arrest for the murder of Alexander Marchand," she said.

Harri knew she was pushing it, but she needed a way to hold him for questioning.

"Is this live?" she asked.

Rena had been missing only a few days, but he could have been watching a recording of what he'd done to her.

Rena's body had angry red welts of that now familiar symbol branded all over it. Not just the limbs like they'd found on the river island. The killer tortured the woman into confessing by both ripping her apart and branding her body.

"It's live," Neland said. "It's a livestream."

"Where is this happening?" Harri demanded.

"I have no idea," Neland said. "None of us know."

Us? Harri was afraid to think how many people were tuned in right now. She pulled out her phone and recorded the computer screen. They would look over the footage for any clues as to where Rena was being held. Harri kept her eyes on Neland. She couldn't watch Rena's suffering anymore. The sounds were horrifying enough.

Harri doubted they'd be able to track the IP address of the livestream. She'd been on several cases which attempted to track a computer's IP address and it wasn't as easy as everyone thought it was. The tech world had developed sophisticated protocols for hiding a perp's location.

One last scream emitted from Rena. It sounded more like a gurgle and then she fell silent.

Harri kept her eyes on Neland, watching for any sign

of pain or disgust. Instead, she saw longing and excitement that she found revolting. He was sad it was over. He wanted more.

The screen went blank, and then a large timer filled the frame. It was counting down twenty-four hours.

"What was that?" she asked Neland.

"I didn't kill Alexander," he said.

"You just watched a woman get pulled apart on a livestream. You're a part of this, Carrington. You're going to tell us everything you know if you want to stay out of jail."

He nodded, eyeing the gun she still held pointed at his head with a terrified expression.

"Put your arms behind your back," she demanded.

He did as he was told and Harri zip-tied his wrists together and then to the back of the chair.

Someone banged on the front door. The backup units had arrived. Harri left Neland in his study and went to the front door to let the uniformed officers in. She held her credentials in front of her so they knew who she was.

"I'm Detective Harriet Harper with RHD. I called this in," she said as the door swung open to two sets of uniformed officers standing outside. They looked at her credentials and introduced themselves as she let them into the house.

"Hi, Detective Harper. You find the intruder?" Officer Ray Reeves asked.

"Not yet but the top floor hasn't been cleared. I was surveilling this residence and saw an intruder go over the front gate and around to the back. I called it in and followed him inside because we've already lost a witness on the case I'm working on this morning. I was afraid the resident would be next."

"No intruder?" Reeves asked.

"I haven't found him yet. I did find the owner of the house watching a livestream that's pertinent to our investigation."

"What investigation is that?" Officer Reeves asked.

"One of our own. Ethan Carle, the man found in the river after the rain," Harri explained.

"We heard about that," Officer Sam Finerman said. "What a tragedy."

"It is. I detained Neland Carrington on suspicion of murder and zip-tied him to a chair in his study. We need to clear the house to make sure the intruder isn't upstairs. Then we'll need to bring him to the nearest station. That would be West LA Community, right?" she asked.

"That's correct, Detective," Officer Reeves said.

"We might need more officers here. Can you assign a team to clear the house for any sign of an intruder and then also have a team transport Carrington to the station? I need to contact my partner and update him. I'll meet you guys over there for the interview," she said.

"Sure thing, Detective," he said.

He instructed the officers behind him and Harri walked back to the study. She stared past Neland Carrington at the twenty-four-hour countdown. She knew in her gut that was for Whitey.

"I'm bringing you in for questioning on the murder of Alexander Marchand and the murder we just witnessed onscreen. The officers behind me will read you your rights and then take you into custody," she said. "Officers are searching upstairs for the intruder. I'll be getting a search warrant for your place that I'll deliver to you at the station."

Neland stared blankly back at her.

"Do you understand what I said to you?" she asked.

"I understand," Neland said.

Harri turned to the officers and indicated that he was ready. The officers Mirandized Carrington and led the professor away.

Harri called Tom. "I took Neland Carrington into custody," she said when Tom answered the phone.

"What happened, Harri?"

"I watched this house for hours and didn't think anybody was even home. Around 9 p.m., I saw someone jump the front gate and I was afraid he'd end up like Marchand. I followed the intruder into the back yard and when I didn't see anyone there, I tried the back door which was open. I went inside looking for the intruder but instead, I found Neland Carrington watching a livestream of Rena being pulled apart. I watched her die, Tom," she said.

"I'm so sorry, Harri. I wish you hadn't seen that. Did you find the intruder?" he asked.

"I called for backup before I went in. They're still searching the house," she said.

"Did you say livestream?" Tom asked.

"Yes, I recorded his computer screen on my phone. After she died, the screen went blank and a countdown began for 24 hours. It's still going. I feel certain that's got to be for Whitey," she said.

"Uniforms still on-site?" he asked.

"The officers are clearing the house, just in case the intruder is upstairs. They also took Neland Carrington to West LA for questioning. I had him arrested for the murder of Alexander Marchand," she said.

"Bit of a stretch," Tom said.

"I know. But he has to know who's killing these women. He had a front seat to Rena's death and it can't have been his first time. If it was live, then he can't be our limb killer, because whoever killed her was there on the screen," she said. "I'm leaving an officer here to watch the countdown. We need another search warrant."

"Judge Abraham is gonna love me tonight," Tom said dryly.

"Can you meet me at West LA?" she asked.

"I should be there within the hour," Tom said.

They hung up and Harri looked around Neland Carrington's home. She wouldn't search for anything until the warrant came, just in case he somehow was the killer and she'd stepped into something she didn't fully understand. The last thing she wanted to do was set a killer free because of a technicality. It was bad enough the officers hadn't found anyone upstairs.

"Officer Reeves, could you have two of your men stay in that room watching the countdown on the computer screen? Call my cell if anything changes." She gave him her cell phone number. "We should also have two officers stationed at the entrance of the house until my partner can deliver the search."

"Yes, Detective," Officer Ray Reeves said.

She left the officers standing guard and headed to her car. She fought against the panic rising in her chest. She recognized the signs of a PTSD episode. She stood at her car and breathed in deeply to keep it at bay. She couldn't afford to have an episode now. Whitey was running out of time. She'd discover what was going on from Neland Carrington. As far as she was concerned, he was another marshmallow she was willing to roast to get what she needed.

31

DAY 5 - NIGHT

I watched as the man in black stretched Rena more and more. There was no way to drown out her screams. Even after I shut my eyes against the terrible sight hours ago I couldn't escape her pain.

I heard his voice commanding her to tell him all that she had done.

Her every sin.

The man droned on about atonement and how she would ascend to heaven because of the journey he was taking her on.

The guy was weirdly religious and totally insane.

Rena told him everything. Every detail of her life he had no right to ask about.

I didn't want to hear anymore.

I didn't want to know all her dark secrets.

And most of all, I didn't want to hear her scream.

Her torture lasted hours.

I heard the pops.

The squeak of the wheel turning.

And then her muffled little cries.

I had no concept of time left so I counted.

I counted the seconds and then I counted the minutes and then I counted the hours. I tried to focus on the voice in my head counting and not the whimpers, the pleading, and the overwhelming pain that surrounded me.

I was also ashamed that I peed on myself.

I was more terrified than I'd ever been. How did I end up in this place?

I worked so hard to get clean and find a way off the streets. I thought it was hopeless and would never happen. I thought I was doomed to live in a tent until I backslid inevitably into my addiction and woke up dead. Instead, I got a neighbor named Jared Atkinson and he changed my world in more ways than I could ever have imagined.

I'm not sure if I'm happy I met Jared. Not after this. Not now.

Jared was a kind and giving friend, but was that worth dying over?

It was my own fault I ended up here.

I could have given the cops his notebook right when I'd found it. I didn't need to go searching for answers on my own. Why had I done such a stupid thing?

I'm still not sure why the man grabbed me because the trailer girls hadn't told me anything I didn't already know from Jared's notebook.

My brain stopped on that thought. Jared's notebook ended Sunday morning and he met his killer soon after. I sat up, putting two and two together.

Everyone knew he carried that notebook around and wrote everything down. What if his killer thought Jared wrote down he was meeting with him that Sunday?

What if that's why he came after me? Because I'd been telling the trailer girls things he'd written down in his notebook. I would not be in the least bit surprised to hear they'd sold me out in some way. Or Miguel did.

Jared's notebook landed me here. Now, I was going to die from my mistake.

Maybe it was better this way. I wouldn't have to worry about staying clean or where I was going to live or what happened to my stuff. I would be like the stars in the ether, knowing nothing and knowing everything at the same time.

I was not a religious person and didn't know what I thought happened when we died. I definitely didn't think I was going to end up at the pearly gates.

I was an addict. I wasn't sure I even deserved forgiveness.

Rena howled in pain above me, and I squeezed my eyes tighter.

That's going to be me after he's done with Rena, and I won't last as long as she has. I was never very good with pain. I flinched when anyone touched me, forget them actually hurting me.

I was going to have a medieval torture device used on my body. I'd rather die a quick death and get my body harvested than this. Figures the creep was only taking women, too.

Why was it that creeps always took women? Because they were too weak to stand up against a man?

I wish I'd taken those self-defense classes my friend Jeanette told me about all those years ago. I could've come up with a better plan to get Rena and me out of here. My idea had been terrible. I probably pissed him off more and now he was making both of us pay, and her in the worst way.

I wished for Rena's death right now.

No one deserved to go through this kind of torture. It didn't matter what they'd done in their life. And who made him God anyway, I thought.

Rage took over from my despair. I felt all the hot anger coming.

He might come for me, but I wouldn't make it easy for him.

I would scratch his eyes out and kick him in the nuts. I'd do whatever I could to make him hurt. It wasn't even about my survival anymore.

If I left this earth knowing I'd hurt him in some way, I think it would make my passing easier.

This monster deserved all the pain I could give him.

32

DAY 5 – 11:45 PM

Harri and Tom sat across from Neland Carrington in an interrogation room at the West LA Community station. The room was hot and cramped and perfect for cracking a criminal.

Neland Carrington was a handsome man in his 40s with curly brown hair, wide-set brown eyes, and a sprinkling of freckles over his nose and cheeks. He was the kind of man who would be called boyish well into his fifties and he sat across from them with beads of sweat on his brow and above his lip.

It had taken Tom closer to two hours to get to West LA and Harri made sure that Neland Carrington was not offered anything to eat or drink while they waited.

Instead, he sat in the interrogation room with his hands cuffed to the table, dripping with sweat. When Harri and Tom had first entered the room, the smell of body odor hit them so hard they both recoiled. Neland Carrington saw their reactions and hung his head. This was a man who wasn't used to such humiliation.

"March 5th, 2019, 11:45 p.m. Detective Harriet Harper

and Detective Tom Bards entering interrogation room three to interview Neland Carrington in connection to the murder of Alexander Marchand," Harri said to the recorder.

"State your full name and date of birth," Tom said.

Neland did as he was told.

"Neland Carrington, have you been read your rights?" Harri asked.

"I have, but I've done nothing wrong," he said.

"You watched a girl die in real-time," Harri said. "She was under the age of 18, so you're being charged with knowingly viewing pornographic content of a minor, aiding and abetting the assault and battery of a minor, and aiding and abetting murder. You do know if you get caught with child pornography that's a felony," she said.

"That wasn't pornography," Neland Carrington said.

"We'll let the prosecutor decide," she said.

"I don't understand how you got into my house," he said.

"Your home was under surveillance because of your connection to Alexander Marchand. He was murdered earlier this morning and we thought you might be next," Tom said.

"I saw someone behind your front gate and figured they meant you harm," Harri said.

Neland laughed. "Well, isn't that so convenient?"

"I was trying to make sure you weren't found dead with twenty stab wounds to your torso," Harri said with an edge to her voice.

"Did you know Alexander Marchand?" Tom asked.

Neland hesitated, then nodded. "Yes."

"How did you meet?" Tom asked.

"We met in an online medieval forum. He's a, he *was* a student of medieval literature and was deeply into the symbolism of the Divine Comedy by Dante. I offer classes on that literature, so we connected that way," Neland said.

"When was the last time you saw Alexander Marchand?" Harri asked.

"I would say about a month ago," Neland said.

"Do you know what this symbol means?" Tom asked as he slid a photo of the symbol they'd discovered on the amputated limbs across the table.

"It's an owl. An evil entity from hell that watches over the humans in this realm," he said.

"I thought owls were associated with knowledge," Harri said.

Neland Carrington sighed, and his voice took on a slightly condescending tone.

"If you look at any painting from the medieval era portraying the soul's transformation or transcendence from earth to heaven or hell, you'll see that an owl is in every single depiction of Hell or Purgatory. It was a manifestation of the evil in all of us."

Harri looked at the sweat dripping from Neland Carrington's upper lip and forehead and wondered how he could maintain his smugness.

"Is that the reason you have it on the spines of your medieval torture book?" Harri asked.

"That was a decision made by my publisher," he said tightly.

"And who is your publisher?"

"Orbis Strix," he said. "Emmanuelle runs it and applauded my work connecting Dante and his commentary on what he witnessed in contemporary Europe. I have a new perspective on Dante's work and the methods used to torture people in the name of crime and punishment."

"That's fascinating, really," Tom said dismissively.

Harri wanted to laugh. Tom had noted the condescension in Neland Carrington's voice and wanted to let him know they weren't impressed with him.

"Have you seen this?" Harri asked and pushed a photograph of the human skin book in front of him. Neland gasped when he saw it and leaned forward to get a better look.

"Please don't get any perspiration on that photo," Tom said. "It's the only one we have."

"Where did you get this?" Neland asked.

"Do you know what it is?" Harri asked.

"It's a Confessional. You can find them sometimes on auctions on the dark web. They're made from the skin of the confessor."

He looked at the photo as if the photo itself was a precious thing.

"Who initiated you into this death torture livestream club?" Harri asked.

"It was Alexander Marchand. We'd been dancing around our obsessions for months and finally, he invited me over to his house for dinner and we watched one of the previous livestreams. I'd never seen anything like it, and I couldn't get it out of my mind. He did it on purpose."

"What do you mean by that?" Harri asked.

"He wasn't just looking for a friend with similar interests. He wanted to get my perspective, as an academic, on Dante's deeper meaning. He'd read all my books and everything else out there on Dante and he had his own theory. He wanted my help in fleshing that out. He had me watch the livestream so that I would be complicit. After that, I was sent my own login for the livestreams."

"What was Marchand's theory about Dante?" Tom asked.

"That he was into S&M and hated himself for it," Neland said.

"Who sent you the login?" Harri asked.

"I don't know. It was a text. I deleted it after I got into the livestream."

"How often do you watch this man doing the torture? Do you know his name?" Harri asked.

"He calls himself The Scholar," he said.

"Why The Scholar?" Tom asked.

"Because he knows Dante better than all of us put together. He's a genius," Neland Carrington said with pride in his voice.

Harri couldn't believe this man was so separated from reality. "And how often do these livestreams happen? How do you know when they're scheduled to go live?" she asked.

"We get a text message with a link five minutes before the time."

"How often does this livestream happen?" Tom asked again.

"It's been one every couple of weeks, but another one starts in less than 24 hours. We've never had a count-down so soon after the one before."

"Does The Scholar make these books?" Harri asked.

"I always assumed so, but the two things aren't necessarily connected. You have the confessional books and then you have the livestream. The Scholar might be making them himself, or he could be outsourcing. I have no way to know that for sure," Neland said.

"Did you know that Alexander Marchand had such a book?" Harri asked.

"He didn't!" Neland Carrington was astonished.

"How did he get one so fast? I've been trying for months. He said he hadn't been able to locate one either and had been outbid twice," he said with fury in his voice. "I've never even had a chance to bid."

Harri and Tom couldn't help looking at each other in shock.

"Why did you want the Confessional so badly?" Harri asked.

"It's a part of living history. To get my hands on such an artifact with so much care and knowledge in its creation would be an incredible honor," Neland Carrington said. "How could I not want one?"

This man is batshit crazy, Harri thought. If she hadn't witnessed him watch Rena die while sitting in front of his computer, Harri would be positive he was the one torturing and dismembering the women.

"Why do you think Alexander Marchand was killed?" Harri asked.

"I have no idea. He was in way deeper than I was, so I don't know," Neland confessed.

"We have a search warrant for your house and the team is going through it right now for any signs of a missing woman named Darlene "Whitey" Whiteman."

"She the one that's coming next?" Neland asked.

Harri ignored his curiosity.

"Have you ever had any contact with The Scholar?" she asked.

"No, haven't had the privilege," he said in all seriousness.

"You have any idea who he could be?" Harri asked.

Neland shook his head no.

"What can you tell us about him that we don't already know?" Harri asked.

"He's a genius. He's the greatest expert on Dante to

date. He's classically educated, so most likely Ivy League, probably Europe. If we weren't talking about women missing in Los Angeles, I would believe The Scholar was somewhere in Europe. I mean the device these women are on," he said. "It's almost a perfect replica of a rack that I saw in a museum in Paris."

"Does The Scholar ever appear on camera?" Tom asked.

"He always has an executioner's hood over his head. So, yes, he does appear on camera but he's dressed in black from head to toe."

"Do you have any idea as to his ethnicity, nationality, accent?" Harri asked fishing for information. She'd only seen The Scholar briefly on the screen and wasn't able to pick up anything that would provide information on his identity.

"He always wore black. I was more interested in the women and the procedure," Neland confessed.

Harri wasn't sure if there was anything else he could provide. He was a participant in the private livestream of what was basically a real-time snuff film. They would charge him under the child pornography act, but she didn't think he knew who The Scholar was.

"Can I get some water?" Neland Carrington asked. "I've been here for hours, and nobody's offered me anything to drink."

"Sorry you're dissatisfied with the service here. Someone will bring you some water," she said. "Interview ending at 12:36 a.m. Detective Harri Harper and Detective Tom Bards leaving suspect Professor Neland Carrington."

Harri and Tom went to find their suspect a bottle of water.

"He didn't kill Alexander Marchand," Tom said.

"I don't think so, either. I used that as a way to get him into custody so we could interrogate him about the livestream."

"He doesn't know who The Scholar is either," Tom said.

"Did you buy that Alexander was the one who introduced him to the livestreams?" Harri asked.

"It's a possibility. Did you see the kind of obsession at Carrington's we saw at Marchand's? Update. The forensic team is still going through Marchand's house with a fine-tooth comb. They found some kind of workshop behind the garage where he was attempting to try his hand at tanning skin into leather," he said.

"Human skin?" Harri asked.

Could Alexander Marchand have been The Scholar and someone killed him? No, that didn't make sense with the livestream she'd just seen.

"From what they found it looked more like a squirrel hide," Tom said.

"That's disgusting," Harri said.

"A regular Ed Gein, that one," Tom said with a grimace.

"Is that the one that made furniture out of people's skins?" Harri asked.

"You're learning your serial killers," Tom said.

"Alexander Marchand didn't have the expertise to make that confessional book. Neland Carrington is a professor of medieval studies and likes to watch women being tortured, but he gave that up too easily. He doesn't know he's a freak. He thinks he's better than the rest of us. He's not a sociopath, just a narcissist. He looks up to

The Scholar. Thinks he's a genius. Marchand must have, too. Did Marchand rope Carrington into this because he wanted to collaborate on his Dante S&M theory? Bring it to life?" Harri asked.

"Possibly. Probably. We're getting closer to him, The Scholar. I can't believe it's a coincidence the brand on the limbs is the same symbol as on the spines of Carrington's books. Are we dealing with a chicken or the egg situation?"

"What do you mean?" Harri asked.

"Did The Scholar see the brand on the book first? Or did The Scholar create the brand and then it was used on Carrington's books?" Tom opened the fridge and grabbed three bottles of water.

"If it's the first one, then we're no closer to finding this guy than we were before we found Carrington. But if it's the second, then Carrington has a connection to The Scholar and might not even know it," Harri said.

"We should put Cyndi on researching who published those books of his. If we can get the name of the artist who put the book cover together, we'll be closer to the answer," he said.

"Whitey has less than nineteen hours left," Harri said as she glanced at her watch. She'd set a timer on her phone to match the countdown. "We need to get back to Neland's house. Find the connection to that brand. It's the key."

"I've sent some of the nerd techs to Carrington's to see if they can track anything from his devices. This computer stuff is complex. Not sure how far they'll get in the next nineteen hours," Tom said.

"What about Marchand's?" Harri asked.

Their team was now spread so thin over so many

locations that everything was taking longer to complete, which was the opposite of what they needed.

"The teams were done with Green Acres and the tissue bank earlier tonight. I assigned all of them to canvas Alexander Marchand's neighborhood for any witnesses that might have seen a man in bloodied clothing running through their streets. So far, no updates. He must've had a car nearby he jumped into."

"Do we have any available SID forensic techs to send over to Carrington's?" Harri asked.

"We've been offered a skeleton crew. Because of Rena's death, and your recording of the livestream we got our search warrant," he said.

"What should we do with him?" Harri asked.

"Let him sit in jail overnight. That takes him out of the game. As you said, we have less than nineteen hours to find Whitey. One of these two likely came across The Scholar in real life. You don't get to watch a woman be tortured and murdered without a personal connection. That symbol showed up in both their homes. That's not a coincidence and it's not just their shared fanboy love of Dante. We know The Scholar is in Los Angeles because of his victim pool," Tom said.

"I'll bring him the waters," Harri said.

"He can have one water," Tom said. "These other two are for you and me."

She took the bottles out of Tom's hands. "I'll meet you out front. Maybe we can take the same car this time," she said.

33

DAY 5 – AFTER 9:30 P.M

The horrible image above me was finally silent.

I opened my eyes and saw the lifeless form of Rena and her misshapen arms and legs.

The torture had lasted hours. My soul ached for her. I hoped she was finally at peace wherever she went to.

My head cleared up slightly and I wasn't as dizzy and lightheaded as I had been.

The panic attacks kept rolling through me. He was coming for me next.

The man hadn't given me any food or water since he brought me here. I had no idea how long I'd been down in the darkness, but it must be days now. I no longer sweat and when I cried no tears ran down my cheeks. I hadn't peed in a long time, either.

My thirst was unbearable at first, but then it subsided along with the hunger. My stomach stopped growling. It must have figured out no food was coming. I tried to do some push-ups and sit-ups to get my blood flowing. When he came for me, I had to fight back. I wouldn't just submit and I wanted some power behind my desperate bid to survive this.

My mind kept going from being convinced I'd be able to take him on, believing I could defend myself, to absolute despair.

This wasn't going to be a fair fight.

The man wanted to destroy women. Especially sinners like me. He was starving me to make sure I was powerless, and he had all the control.

Women like me didn't fit into his sick version of the world. Or maybe he simply hated women. I'd heard about killers who hated their mothers so much they kept killing her over and over and over again. How men could do such evil things to women would always be a mystery to me.

I used the wall to prop myself up to a standing position. My legs were wobbly. and my head swam. I needed to find my balance. I wanted to give myself a chance.

Then I swayed, and my body betrayed me. Being on my feet was too much for the condition I was in. I fell back to the ground in a heap. I cried my waterless tears and curled up into a ball. Maybe if I got small enough, he wouldn't find me.

DAY 6 – MARCH 11, 2019 - 1:31 AM - HOUR 18

I nstead of going directly back to Neland Carrington's house, Tom and Harri decided to stop at Alexander Marchand's first. They were grasping at straws. They knew the key to finding the Scholar was that brand. The image that was popping up everywhere. But they didn't yet have the intersection between Carrington and Alexander when it came to the symbol. Tom had suggested they search Alexander's property one last time for any other instances of the brand.

They arrived at the house after midnight and ducked underneath the crime-scene tape. When they walked into the living room, their noses filled with the familiar acrid, metallic odor. The blood spatter had ripened and taken over the macabre living room. The crime scene techs had dusted fingerprint powder everywhere and Harri could see traces of it on every surface. The smell of chemicals fought for dominance over the smell of blood.

"I see several owls in the wallpaper," Harri said as she pointed to the particularly dark scenes of people being tortured from the Bosch painting.

"I see some on this wall too," Tom said.

"Owls on the wall. That's number one," Harri said.

"Let's go through any notebooks, files, loose sheets, and the garbage," Tom said.

The crime scene techs wouldn't know the drawing of the owl was so important to them.

They put on disposable gloves and quickly searched through all the paperwork they could find in the living room and bedroom. There were no signs of the crudely drawn owl symbol.

"He didn't doodle the owl. I don't see that symbol anywhere. Is it a logo? Should we call it a logo?" Harri asked.

She was trying to lighten the mood but the lack of evidence in Alexander Marchand's home was frustrating.

"It's a logo for The Scholar, I suppose," Tom said as he moved to the bookcase.

All of Neland Carrington's books were still on the shelf.

"Let's shake these out," he said.

They each took a book and shook it out, observed its front and back cover, and flipped through the pages for anything inside. They then flipped through all four Dante books and the three medieval torture books that remained on the shelf. There were no inscriptions and no notes or loose papers inside any of them.

"This logo looks like it belongs to the publishing house and not to Carrington," Harri said. "Orbis Strix. Is that Latin?"

"Sounds about right," Tom said. "Orbis means 'the'. That much I do remember."

Harri pulled out her phone and opened a translation

app. She typed in Orbis Strix and the app translated it to 'The owl'.

"The owl," Harri said.

"The owl what?" Tom asked.

"That's what orbis strix means in English," Harri said.

"And the logo does look like an owl," Tom said.

"And Carrington, the professor of medieval studies, said that the owl was known as the harbinger of evil. So, the publishing company is announcing itself as the harbinger of evil? That doesn't make sense. Unless The Scholar is the publisher. If the scholar is actually running the company, why would he announce himself like that?" Harri asked.

"Maybe he's daring us to put it all together," Tom said.

"I wish Mitzi or Jake were here right now to answer that question for us," Harri said.

"Why don't you call Jake and ask him to join us?" Tom asked.

Harri knew why she hadn't called and talked it over with Jake. He was so involved with the Jerome Wexler case that it was hard to pull his mind onto anything else. He'd cleared his slate of projects to focus solely on the sound file they'd received. Harri didn't want to distract him from the file, just like she didn't want to be distracted by it while she worked this case.

"He's tracking down a lead on the Jerome Wexler case. We really don't have the time anyway," Harri admitted.

"Makes sense," Tom said and left it at that. "I think we're done here. I'm not seeing what else we can do until we get all the science back on this place."

"Agreed. Let's search Neland Carrington's home," Harri said.

"One of these two met this guy in real life," Tom said. "I know it in my gut. We just have to find the proof."

35

DAY 6 - 1 A.M. - HOUR 18

I was in way worse shape than when I was with Rena making my grand plan to escape.

My new idea was to pretend I was dead already.

In playing possum, he'd have to stoop down to lift me up and carry me. If I got him into such a compromised position, I'd have the advantage of balance. He'd be off balance and I could try to hurt him in some way.

Maybe if I was closer to the wall, when he bent over, I could spring up and throw him toward the wall. I knew the only way this could work was to knock him off balance. I wouldn't even need to hurt him necessarily. If I got him off balance, then I could make a run for it.

I wouldn't make the same mistake we'd made the first time.

I hadn't realized how big he was. When Rena went rushing at him, he didn't move. Her weight was nothing compared to his. But if I made him come to me, then I had the advantage. He was tall and would have to stoop down. His center of gravity would be lowered.

That would be the moment I could crash into him. Even in my weak condition, going up against him as he was leaning forward would give me the advantage to knock him back and off-balance. His guard would be down if he thought I was asleep. Or passed out. Or near death.

Maybe he'd hit the wall with his head. I imagined his head cracking against the concrete. I would enjoy that.

I'd only have a few seconds, but it would be enough to give me a head start. I doubted he'd pass out from hitting a wall but he might get dazed enough to allow me to run away.

I wanted that chance to live.

I wanted a second chance.

I would make a real go of it if I got a second chance.

I was ready to start living life again.

My determination couldn't completely overcome my fear and they competed within me. I was scared of that contraption, and I was scared of that man. But I had nothing left to lose. Why not die trying? I'd rather die fighting in this room than tied up to that thing Rena was killed on.

My head pounded in pain again from all my thinking and plotting. I was sure I had a concussion because my brain wasn't working properly, and I was sleeping a lot.

Maybe I didn't want to be awake anymore.

Not in this room at least.

I laid down on the floor again and curled myself into a ball and remembered my grandparents' house in Silicon Valley. My brother and I'd been so happy when they took us in. My grandmother baked cakes almost every week and she cooked us her favorite meals. My grandparents had both been teachers and they always stressed the importance of a good education. They read to us and took us to museums and concerts. They were excited about the bright future my brother and I had.

Yet here I was homeless and about to die at the hands of a lunatic.

36

DAY 6 – 2:49 A.M. - HOUR 17

Neland Carrington's yard looked different than the first time Harri had seen it. The street she worried was too dark for her to see anything while surveilling the house was now lit up with the blue and red of the silent flashing lights from two of the cruisers.

The house behind the hedge was ablaze with light, too. They'd received word on the drive over that the rest of their team was on scene. Tom made the executive decision to designate Carrington's home as a satellite command center because they had to watch the countdown on his computer for any updates.

The computer whiz, Ritchie Jones, advised them over the phone that they wouldn't be able to leave the IP network nor turn off the computer without losing the connection because of the way the chat room was run. The best place for the team was in Carrington's study.

They had the SID forensics team go through the study first to make sure all the evidence had been cataloged before the team set up shop there. Then forensics worked their way through the rest of the house looking for any evidence that connected Carrington to Alexander Marchand or any of the limb killer's known victims.

Cyndi Rodriguez, Tony Diaz, Donald Chow, Gerald Moore, and several new additions to the team all had their laptops in front of them and were seated around the room, even on the floor. The ominous clock ticked down from 17 hours.

It was hard not to look at it with a sense of dread.

"We didn't find any other images, or logos that look like the crudely drawn owl symbol, in Marchand's home outside of the books themselves. What we did uncover was that the name of the publishing company, Orbis Strix, means 'The owl'. Our new working theory is the publishing company was the first place the logo was used," Harri said.

"And, if we want to extrapolate further, we're thinking the publishing company wants us to know this logo is who and what they are. Is The Scholar taunting us to make that connection?" Tom asked.

"I've been looking through that company," Gerald Moore said.

"What have you found?" Harri asked anxiously.

"Orbis Strix is owned by a company named Tenebris Malum LLC," he said.

"Tenebris Malum? What is it with these Latin names?" Harri asked.

"Tenebris Malum means dark evil, or maybe darkest evil," Tom said.

"Who owns that company?" Harri asked.

"I haven't been able to find out," Gerald said. "It's another one of those shell hierarchy like you showed us before."

Harri sighed. It was after two in the morning, but she had no other choice but to call Harvey Berger. He answered after four rings sounding groggier than Harri had hoped. She explained what she needed, and he said he'd call her right back. Harri hoped he wouldn't roll over and go back to sleep thinking her call for help had been a bad dream. To everyone's amazement, he did call back within fifteen minutes.

"Tenebris Malum LLC is owned by Mortifer LLC. And Mortifer LLC is owned by Achlys Multimedia." Harvey said. "I just emailed you everything I could pull up. Need anything else, Detective?"

Harri said no and let the man go back to sleep.

"Another man playing the shell company game to hide his identity," Tom observed.

The door opened and a deeply-tanned blonde man who looked like he enjoyed surfing walked in carrying two computer cases.

"You must be Ritchie Jones," Tom said. "Our computer whiz guy, everyone."

"Welcome to the team Ritchie," Harri said.

Introductions were made all around and Ritchie sat down where Neland Carrington had sat watching the livestream hours before. The countdown number of 16:29 glared in the room.

"Is this what I need to trace?" he asked.

Harri nodded.

"We know the location is somewhere in Southern California. Our guys told us the IPs are pinging all around the world. We need to get to the source," she said.

"I'm on it," he said as he unpacked his gear.

He cleared off the right side of Neland Carrington's desk and set up two PCs next to each other.

Harri turned her attention away from him and typed on her phone.

"Mortifer means bringer of death," she said.

"How do you know that?" Cyndi asked.

Harri held up her phone.

"Translator app. The last one is Achlys and it's Greek. It means darkness," Harri said.

"Well, they're staying on theme," Cyndi said.

The name trail convinced Harri the publishing company was associated with The Scholar.

"Tony, could you start going through Carrington's paperwork? We need to find his contracts for the books he's put out with Orbis Strix. There's something to this company. He's laughing at us," she said.

"I'm on it," Tony said and opened the study's closet.

Harri was grateful to see the closet was organized with a three-drawer filing cabinet to the left and banker's boxes on the floor.

"Cyndi, you've been going through Marchand's contacts?" Harri asked.

"Yes, I have his phone records and I've been back-tracking all the numbers to everyone he called in the last week. Looks like he was in close contact with Patrick Sumner because that number comes up the most frequently," she said.

"Patrick couldn't have killed Alexander because he was in our custody," Harri said.

"Right. So far, I'm not seeing any other calls that stand out. We haven't been able to get into his emails, but we did find his calendar and it doesn't look like he had too many appointments. Or friends," Cyndi said.

"Maybe he kept all that information in the cloud," Harri said.

She wasn't sure if focusing on Alexander Marchand was the best use of their time. She felt like he was a dead end.

"Will you be able to track down the location of the IP address in time?" she asked Ritchie.

"It depends on what VPN service he's using," he said. "That's the most stable way to keep the connection open while hiding your identity. Unfortunately, the company he's using is in Russia so we're not going to get much help from them," Ritchie said as his fingers flew over the keys. Harri had never seen anyone type so fast.

"Is there any way you can keep searching in the background while you look for some other information?" Harri asked.

"I could try. What am I looking for?" he asked.

"We need to find out who owns Achlys Multimedia," Harri said as she showed him the information Harvey Berger had emailed her.

"I'm on it," he said.

Harri turned to Tom who was on the phone. He held up his finger as he listened, said uh-huh, uh-huh a few times, and then hung up.

"That was Dr. Grimley. Alexander Marchand had the same brands on his chest as the limbs did. It's that same owl symbol. However, the brand does not look fresh so that's something to consider. He was also stabbed twenty-one times and it appears he likely bled out from the cut to his carotid artery."

"Did she have any information on that skin book?" Harri asked.

"She did. The analysis found hCG, a pregnancy hormone in the skin. She figured it could be Marpessa Roberts, the missing pregnant girl Jared Atkinson was looking for. The SID forensics unit found some relatives of hers down in San Diego and they're waiting on the DNA results."

"God, what happened to that baby?" Harri asked.

No one in the room answered her.

37

DAY 6 -2 P.M. - HOUR 5

I tried to keep awake so he couldn't take me by surprise. But in the darkness and with no idea of the passage of time, I kept slipping in and out of consciousness. Each time I was awake, I did my meager push-ups and pathetic running in place even though I felt dizzy and confused.

I was no longer hungry or thirsty, but the headache wouldn't go away. I didn't know how much longer I could last like this. It wasn't going to stop me from trying to be as strong as I could be against him. But I wasn't sure if he'd find a corpse when he finally came back for me.

I remembered some breathing exercises one of my drug counselors had taught me when I had a real bad urge to drink. I used the technique to protect my mind against the fear that kept inching its way closer and closer to the surface.

If I stopped focusing on my breath and let my mind wander, the images I'd seen of Rena being pulled apart made me freeze and panic.

I had cried and I had screamed until my throat was raw.

I had spent all of that energy already and yet the fear kept coming back. I felt like a little girl who had no control over anything that was going to happen to me. The helpless feeling was so overpowering I almost wished he would come in and get this over with. The waiting was agonizing.

With each minute, each hour that passed, the fear threatened to swallow me up.

It made me want to curl up into a ball and go to sleep forever.

I couldn't do that.

I would never forgive myself if I didn't fight him one last time.

I'd survived the streets of Los Angeles and I'd survived an alcohol addiction, and I'd survived right up until this moment.

I would survive this evil asshole, too.

38

DAY 6 -2 P.M. - HOUR 5

Harri stared at the countdown clock despondently. It was after 2 p.m. and they had only five hours left to find Whitey before the broadcast began.

After numerous runs for coffee, their team looked beaten. Cyndi had come to a dead-end on Alexander Marchand's contacts. She couldn't find anyone out of the ordinary he'd called in the days before his death.

Ritchie had also been unsuccessful in pinpointing the IP location of the livestream on the countdown. Harri and Tom had discussed with Ritchie about hacking into the Russian VPN company that was hosting the chat room. Ritchie had the skills and equipment, but they all agreed they weren't ready to take illegal steps in finding the location. Something like that could make all the evidence inadmissible in court and Ritchie wasn't sure how far the Russians would go in retaliation.

Harri and Tom had considered it seriously, but in the end, they didn't want to jeopardize the case or the careers of the other people on the team. Tom made a good point that if The Scholar had hidden himself in so many shell corporations then he most likely did the same with the VPN service.

Ritchie tried to mimic the algorithmic program the VPN was using to make the IP bounce through different compromised computers around the world. The best he could pinpoint was The Scholar was in California, information they already knew.

Meanwhile, Harri, Tom, and three of the team members had spent the entire night searching Neland Carrington's home from top to bottom. They looked through every closet, through every drawer, and all the papers and books throughout his home. They found no other instances of the owl logo.

Tony Diaz searched Carrington's calendar for associates and friends. He had few listed and they were mainly connected to his job at UCLA. None of the names had come up in their investigation. Harri handed off the calling of all his contacts to one of the officers in charge of canvassing. One of the extra uniformed officers Lieutenant Richard Byrne had thrown at them went for a lunch run. The lack of sleep wasn't helping anyone keep sharp and Harri noticed eyes closing.

"We have five hours," Harri said rallying the team. "We haven't failed yet."

"I've put tracking the IP address on hold while I dig into Achlys media," Ritchie said.

"Is it hidden inside a blizzard of shell companies?" Harri asked.

"It is but I'm tracking bank accounts now. The company brings in revenue and its main bank is a Wells Fargo here in Los Angeles. But then the money gets transferred out to a smaller bank called California

Community Bank and I'm trying to see where it goes from there," he said.

"How do you know its main bank is a Wells Fargo?" Harri asked.

"That was from me," Gerald Moore said. His head poked out of the closet. "I found some royalty checks from a branch on Wilshire."

"I won't ask how you know about the California Community Bank," Harri said.

"I have some ways to get that information," Ritchie said. "We just need a name, right?"

"If we get the information illegally we won't be able to use that as chain of evidence for bringing the guy in," Tom said.

"Let me see if I can at least point us in the right direction," Ritchie said.

The timer was ominously ticking down and Harri nodded.

They needed another direction.

"Cyndi, have you been able to get into Alexander Marchand's emails yet?" Harri asked. Her question startled Cyndi awake.

"I haven't been able to find a password for them yet," she said, smiling sheepishly. Harri winked at her and gave her a thumbs up to let her know it was all okay. The night and day had been a marathon already.

"Marchand must've had a personal connection with The Scholar because he was the one who had the limbs at Green Acres. Which means he had to have agreed to get rid of the remains for The Scholar. How was that agreement made?" Harri asked the room.

"Is there a chat function on that countdown window?" Tony asked.

Ritchie checked the window of the countdown and nodded. "There is a chat and a question area," he said.

"If it's so hard to track where the chat room is then we have to assume The Scholar feels it's a safe way for him to communicate," Tom said.

"But how did they find out about the chat room? If Carrington found out about it from Marchand, then who did he find out about it from?" Donald Chow asked.

"Could have been anywhere. Marchand looked to be familiar with the dark web and with his obsession with Dante and Hieronymus Bosch, maybe someone in one of those places where people like him hang out mentioned the chat room? Or The Scholar made contact that way. Having a cremation specialist on hand to finish his dirty work would have been good for him," Tom said.

"We can't just sit here twiddling our thumbs while the clock counts down," Harri yelled.

"Let's take a walk outside," Tom said.

Harri's stress permeated the room, and she knew she wasn't helping anyone by letting her anger and frustration get the best of her. "Sorry everyone," she said and followed Tom out of the room.

"You know, this is a posh house for a single man who works as an adjunct professor at UCLA," Tom said.

They had stepped out onto a deck overlooking the back garden and were treated to an expanse of green lawn and brightly colored snapdragons bordering the wooden fence. There were chairs set up under an umbrella table. Harri sank into one of the chairs and stared into the lush greenery.

A sweet breeze ruffled the umbrella and Harri noticed to the left of the deck was a massive climbing rose. That's where the smell must've been coming from. The last three days seemed almost like a dream to Harri.

"He's probably from a rich family," she said. "They always set their kids up with nice houses. It's a great way to park their money and keep the cash away from the taxman."

"We still have time to find her," Tom said quietly as he sat down across from her.

"We've been banging our heads against the wall all night long," she said. "We searched two different houses and still came up empty. We have a list of over fifty names to still go through, none of them even close to familiar from the investigation. Our only link to him so far is that damn clock. He holds all the cards. All the control."

They'd gathered the names of all the individuals that had come into these two men's lives in the last year and sent out officers to speak to every single one of them for any sort of clue. But Harri felt they were tossing spaghetti at the wall to see what would stick.

"The problem is these guys were so deviant that no one in their normal lives knew about it. Marchand ended up working around a bunch of shady people so we happened upon him," Tom said.

"But we're not going to find the same thing with Neland Carrington. He's a professor, and he would need to keep this part of his life completely hidden. He'll be thrown out on his butt from UCLA when this gets out," Harri said.

"I'm convinced we're on the right path. Our central premise is that one of these men crossed paths with The Scholar. But in real life, under his real name. We just have to find out where," he said.

"We only have four hours left," Harri said.

"I know," he said.

They both watched a hummingbird as it hovered

above a rose to the left of them. It decided against the rose for some reason and flew away.

Harri wished it could take her with it.

39

DAY 6 - 4 P.M. - HOUR 3

A strange, fuzzy feeling enveloped my mouth. I wondered how long before the thirst and hunger would return. Before the man returned? I knew I didn't have much time left. I'd fallen asleep again on the cold concrete floor and every muscle I tried to stretch out cracked.

I was sore and exhausted. What if he was just going to dehydrate me to death? It didn't sound like a pleasant way to go but maybe it was better than what happened to Rena.

I scrunched myself back into a ball again and took stock of my weakened state. I wouldn't be able to fight him now, no matter how much I wanted to.

A shuffling sound came from the other side of the door. Every sense in my body suddenly went into high alert. I was wide awake as the door slowly opened, and light flooded into the darkness.

"Hello, Whitey. I think I've starved you long enough. It's time for you to go to confession," the man said.

He walked into the room and grabbed me by my hair.

I unfurled and sprang up with the last bit of energy I could muster.

He laughed at me and pulled my hair harder. He never lost his balance and because he was so much taller than me, he could pull me even higher. I screamed out in pain as my hair ripped out of my scalp.

I knew this was only the beginning of the pain he would inflict on me. I opened my eyes and stared at his face.

"Wait. I know you. I know you. What are you doing here? You're the one?" My voice came out in a raspy croak. My brain scrambled in recognition and the betrayal I felt was absolute. This man had helped me in the past.

This was the man who was going to end my life? The enormity of my feelings overwhelmed me, and all the fight left me. I slumped against him.

"That's a good girl, Whitey. The best way forward is not to fight the journey. Embrace it. When you come out on the other side, you will be clean and whole again. You won't have to live like an animal. You won't have to suffer anymore," he said.

His voice was soothing and hypnotic. My body, starved of food and water, went totally limp. All the fight was gone. He was going to take me and tie me up to that contraption. At this point, I didn't even care anymore.

He dragged me down a dimly lit hall, our movements curiously muffled. It was like walking in a dream. A very quiet and still dream. I was too exhausted to even feel the telltale signs of fear. I closed my eyes and let the blackness take me.

I woke up to goosebumps on my bare skin.

I was completely naked. My arms were above my head and my wrists were bound with rough rope. I tried to move my legs and they were tied up at the ankles.

My brain conjured an unwelcome image of the contraption Rena had been tied to.

I was on the rack now and soon I'd be screaming in agony, too.

No one could help me now.

I was all alone with my confessor, my torturer. I felt oblivion seeping in at the edges of my awareness and figured maybe that was for the best. My brain was trying to protect me from what was to come, and I wasn't going to fight it.

I did not want to be awake for this, either.

40

DAY 6 - 4 P.M. - HOUR 3

Harri and Tom searched in every book, nook, and cranny of Neland Carrington's house for other stashes of paperwork besides the one that Gerald Moore was working through. It was better for Harri to not be anywhere near the countdown clock. Cyndi was monitoring it in case it changed in any way. Harri knew they were quickly running out of time and she could feel her anxiety mounting with every moment. What if they failed? What if they didn't find Whitey in time?

"I found them," Ritchie called out.

Everybody stopped working and gathered around him.

"Been going down the rabbit hole of Achlys Multimedia. Through ways that I will not talk about here, I found out Achlys is owned by SK Trust," he said.

"What is that?" Tony Diaz asked.

"In this case, it's a financial vehicle for rich people to hide their money," Ritchie said. "SK Trust is connected to Melanis Pharma. You guys heard of them?"

"Is that the company that manufactures the cancer drug that was recalled?" Tom asked.

"Ten points to Tom Bards," Ritchie said. "Just scanning through lots of reporting about that recall, I discovered Melanis Pharma is a privately held company that is fully owned by the Sklar family."

Harri felt every hair on her body prickle and stand on end as her brain fought through her memory for something. She knew better than to force it. It would come. It was right there...

"Aren't they those reclusive billionaires nobody knows anything about? They supposedly own everything. Belinda Sklar was on an Olympic Equestrian team for a minute, right?" Cyndi asked.

"I read somewhere they fund super PACs on both sides of the aisle," Ritchie said.

"So, the whole family owns Achlys Multimedia?" Tom grabbed Cyndi's laptop and did a quick internet search for a list of Sklar family members. He clicked on a gossip site following billionaires.

"Wait a minute," Harri said. She felt like her throat was lined with cotton. "What was the name of that guy we met at CUCO headquarters?"

"Raymond. It was Raymond Sklar." Tom said.

Nervous energy filled the room as they finally found the next step forward.

"Hold on everybody, I think I found our smoking gun," Gerald Moore called out from the closet he hadn't left since the night before.

"Take a look at this." He came out holding two pieces of paper. One was the size of printer paper and the other looked like a check. He turned the larger piece around to show the logo, the brand, of the owl. It had Neland Carrington's signature at the bottom of it.

"Carrington was the one who designed the logo for the publishing company," Gerald Moore said.

"Who paid him? The Orbis Strix company?" Tom asked.

"No. It's a personal check from Raymond Sklar," Gerald Moore said as he handed the check to Tom.

"Damn," Cyndi said, flipping through her notebook. "He's the big philanthropist who owns CUCO. I've also seen his name on some of the Smith Construction documents, too."

Harri turned to Tom. "He's the one who lawyered up on us when we asked for a copy of the intake form."

"That son of a bitch," Tom said. "We know who The Scholar is. Now we have to find out where he is right now."

The team fell silent for a moment as the weight of their discovery sank in.

Ritchie was the first to speak. "The Sklar family owns six residences in Los Angeles. Four of those residences are owned by the family trust. However, there's one that is owned by Raymond Sklar himself. It's on Bel Air Road, next to the Stone Canyon reservoir."

Harri looked up the address on a real estate app. It was a massive estate.

"This has to be the place," she said.

"Real estate blogs just love to give helpful information in their articles," Ritchie said as his fingers flew over the keyboard again. "Here we go. The house was listed before he bought it. It has nine bedrooms and 21,000 square feet of living space. It boasts a cellar and underground garage, and basement storage big enough to fit a medieval torture device. Just perfect for broadcasting livestream murders to all your friends. Okay, I made up that last part, but it does have all those underground rooms."

"We have the check. It's payment for designing the brand he's put on all his victims. It can't be Neland Carrington since Harri was here with him when Rena died. Sklar has connections in the homeless community and he knew Patrick Sumner personally. He must be the one who had Patrick take Ethan Carle out. Ethan must have stumbled onto Sklar somehow when he took Rena," Tom said. "That was the favor Patrick did for his good friend, The Scholar."

"Are you making the call?" Harri asked.

She knew how much the LAPD did to avenge one of their own. Even against someone as powerful and rich as Raymond Sklar.

"Richard Byrne needs to make that call," he said. "This is going to take some massive political clout, but I think we have it."

Tom dialed Richard. Every cop in the room waited with bated breath to see if the brass was going to allow them to avenge their own and save Whitey.

DAY 6 - 6 P.M. - HOUR 1

The politics of getting an arrest warrant for Raymond Sklar played out behind the scenes. Lieutenant Richard Byrne had to pull in favors to get the warrant approved for someone as wealthy and well-connected as Raymond Sklar, and Harri couldn't help feeling that if a cop hadn't been one of the victims, it wouldn't have happened at all.

Finally, the District Attorney had approved the arrest and was convinced that if they caught Raymond Sklar in the act, with all the evidence that brought the police to his doorstep, he would be able to convict. To Richard Byrne's credit, despite all the hoops, he had a warrant ready within the hour of Tom's call. Enough time to make it to Raymond Sklar's house before the torture show would go live.

There was always one thing that turned out to be the big error in a case. Raymond Sklar's huge mistake was to instruct Patrick to go after Ethan Carle. Had Detective Carle not been killed, who knows how long it would have taken to crack this case.

They hadn't put together all the pieces of the puzzle yet, but Harri knew that once Raymond Sklar was in custody Patrick Sumner would rat him out. He was just that kind of guy.

Lieutenant Byrne was coming to serve the arrest warrant himself and Harri was glad for that. All the gloves came off for a dead cop and she was more than happy to not have to mug in front of the cameras when the shit hit the fan. That was the Lieutenant's thing. He loved to take credit and get his picture taken. She just wanted to get the job done and that was it.

Her goal had always been to become a detective in the Robbery-Homicide Division and work on complex cases. Hard work and determination had gotten her there and Harri had no problem letting Richard Byrne have the politics and public relations. Without him, she wasn't sure if they'd have gotten the warrant in time.

Lieutenant Byrne decided on ten additional cruisers with two officers in each to assist in the arrest. All of the team working the case already would be joined by a SWAT team with a battering ram to open the gates and doors, if necessary. Harri requested Officers Reeves and Finerman to watch the Carrington residence with Ritchie Jones as she and Tom joined Lieutenant Byrne and another detective in RHD named Amanda Marscone.

The moment the Bel Air Security Force saw the caval-cade approaching they, of course, stopped the first unmarked which had Amanda and Lieutenant Byrne inside.

"Richard is telling them if they alert the media, he'll rain hell down on them," Tom said.

"You've seen this show before?" Harri asked. They were in the second unmarked car, traveling right behind the Lieutenant's with the rest of the crew behind them.

"It's Richard. I recognize one of those guys as a retired cop. Vincent something. Luther, maybe? He'll keep everyone in check," Tom said.

Whatever Lieutenant Byrne said worked because the security detail waved them through.

Harri thought the number of officers was overkill and it would take too long to organize, but everyone was ready within thirty minutes of the warrant.

Ritchie Jones had been texting a photo of the countdown to Harri every thirty minutes since she'd left Neland Carrington's house. They had twenty-five minutes left.

Lieutenant Byrne had decided he didn't want Raymond Sklar alerted to their presence since they needed to catch him in the act. Harri wasn't sure how breaking down the massive iron gate wouldn't trip the alarm. When she had mentioned that Tom said they'd made calls to the security company that monitored Raymond Sklar's home and had them put the alarm system in test mode so that nothing would be tripped.

The resources and strategies Lieutenant Byrne gathered in such a short time both impressed and bothered Harri. She wondered again how many people in this town owed him favors. But it could save Whitey and that's all that mattered. This would be a huge media coup for the Lieutenant and he wanted to make sure everyone knew it was he who came for Raymond Sklar. They finally crested the hill and the estate spread out in front of them.

Richard pulled to the side of the drive and the SWAT vehicle, a HUMMER, bumped the gate to get it open. The first bump bent the gate and on the second try, the gate ripped away from the hinges and the HUMMER dragged it to the side. The SWAT team led the way, and the line of police vehicles invaded the stately drive.

The mansion sat perched on the edge of a hill with a gorgeous view overlooking the reservoir. Stone steps led up to a cream-colored Mediterranean-style mansion. Light blazed in all the windows.

Lieutenant Byrne pulled on a bullet-proof vest with RHD emblazoned on the back and stepped out of the first vehicle. He motioned to the four SWAT officers holding a battering ram to get going on the front door.

Harri and Tom pulled on their bullet-proof vests and watched as the battering ram bumped the massive wooden doors right open and police streamed inside. Lieutenant Byrne took up the rear with Harri and Tom right behind him.

"He has to be in that cellar," Harri said.

They'd studied the video of the livestream from her phone and took note of the concrete walls and floor. The space that held the rack looked bare and windowless. Ritchie Jones had pulled the floor plans for the property from the permit records. There was only one way down to the cellar.

"The staircase to the cellar is through there," Harri pointed to the right of the main foyer. The staircase was off the kitchen behind the formal dining room. Harri, Tom, and Richard, weapons at the ready, marched down the hall and through the kitchen to the cellar door. Richard opened the door and Harri exhaled, not realizing she was holding her breath.

They were rewarded with an enclosed concrete staircase leading down to another door. Harri's phone buzzed in her pocket. She took it out and saw the photo of the livestream.

She showed the others her screen. They had fifteen minutes left.

They moved down to the second door. Harri held her breath again as Lieutenant Byrne tried that door and found it locked. Byrne quietly requested the SWAT Team to come to the cellar staircase. The rest of the team was clearing the upper levels at the direction of Amanda Marscone.

Harri's heart pounded as she set her watch to count down the remaining minutes. The SWAT Team showed up at minute twelve. It took them only twenty seconds to get that door open. With all the noise happening on their side of the door, Harri was surprised no one came to see what was going on. She hoped this meant they still had the element of surprise and she assumed that everything was soundproofed on this level of the property.

A dark hallway dotted with pinpoint lights stretched out in front of them. There were two doors on the left and three doors on the right with a larger door at the end of the hallway. All of them had deadbolts on the outside.

Harri checked her watch.

Eight minutes.

She flashed eight fingers at Tom. He nodded in understanding and took the lead in opening the first door on the left.

The room was windowless and dark, essentially a concrete box with a bad smell.

"What is that?" Harri pointed to a glass rectangle inset into one of the concrete walls about seven feet off the floor.

"It's a screen. Maybe he forced his prisoners to watch the livestreams too," Tom whispered and Harri inwardly shuddered.

They opened the other three doors and the rooms

were exactly the same. Concrete boxes with a drain in the middle of the floor. The fourth door was a closet storing a hose and cleaning supplies.

Lieutenant Byrne took the lead and approached the last door, his gun in both hands. As they followed him, their footsteps barely made a sound. The hallway was soundproofed, too. Harri's head buzzed with the lack of white noise. Byrne tried the handle, and it was also locked.

He motioned to the SWAT officers behind Harri and they moved forward and did their thing with the battering ram again.

The door swung open to reveal a scene of absolute horror. A large wooden structure filled the cavernous concrete box of a room. It almost looked like a big ladder. It was tilted on an angle and Harri recognized the rack from the livestream she'd recorded on her phone. It was the same device that Rena had been tied to, being stretched and tortured until she took her last breath.

A naked woman was bound by her wrists and ankles to what looked to Harri like a rolling pin. Harri recognized the woman immediately as Darlene "Whitey" Whiteman. A tall man stood near a crank. Raymond Sklar hadn't put on his executioner's hood yet and Harri saw that his expression was a mixture of shock and panic when he turned to see them entering the room.

The torture chamber smelled of sweat and burnt skin. A camera was set up to the right of the door and cables ran to a laptop that sat on a small table beside it. The camera and laptop were so ordinary looking that for a moment Harri thought it couldn't be real. The whole scene looked like they'd walked in on someone making an amateur film. Except that Whitey was bound to an authentic medieval torture device and the burnt skin Harri could smell was hers.

"Don't you move!" Lieutenant Richard Byrne of the LAPD Robbery-Homicide Division screamed at Raymond Sklar. "Hands in the air and on your head," Byrne yelled as he moved toward The Scholar with his gun drawn. "Turn around!" he growled and pointed his gun directly at Raymond Sklar's head. So did Harri Harper and Tom Bards.

The Scholar saw the three guns pointed at him and did what he was told. Harri ran over to Whitey and saw that she was shaking and crying, and thankfully, still alive.

"Did he start, Whitey?" Harri asked.

Whitey shook her head and lifted her chin to her left. Harri's eyes followed Whitey's and saw the brand already on her left arm. The symbol of the owl stared back at her.

"He branded me."

"Just the one?" Harri asked.

"Yes," Whitey's voice was weak. "I can't believe you found me. I tried fighting but I couldn't..." Her voice trailed and her eyes rolled back as she passed out.

"We need the medics," Harri cried. She heard running footsteps behind her, but she didn't leave Whitey's side. Two of the SWAT officers worked with Harri to release Whitey from the ropes that were cutting into her wrists and ankles.

ONE WEEK LATER - MARCH 19, 2019

Detective Harriet Harper drove out of the parking lot of the PAB for her one-week vacation. She'd been called back from her last vacation attempt on the first day, when Ethan Carle's body had been found on an island in the Los Angeles River after a rainstorm. They had been able to bring the man who was responsible to justice over that week, but she hadn't slept much, and Lieutenant Richard Byrne had given both Harri and her partner, Detective Tom Bards the next week off. Of course, the way it always worked, it took them another week to button up their case and process all the paperwork involved.

As Harri predicted, when Patrick "Smith" Sumner heard that Raymond Sklar had been arrested in the middle of his torture session, he flipped on his friend and sang like a bird.

In exchange for the death penalty being taken off the table, Patrick Sumner confessed that on the Sunday afternoon that Ethan Carle died, Raymond Sklar had called him and told him that Jared Atkinson was actually a cop working undercover. Patrick stated that Ethan Carle had discovered Raymond's penchant for young prostitutes and had followed Rena to her meeting with Raymond.

Patrick Sumner told them Raymond Sklar was afraid Ethan Carle had tracked down the car he drove when he picked up Rena and, therefore, had to be neutralized. So, Patrick Sumner called Ethan Carle and offered him a job for that night. When he showed up, Patrick injected him with a drug cocktail that stopped his heart.

Ethan Carle's body was harvested for tissue per the agreement Patrick Sumner made with Raymond Sklar, who didn't care what happened to the body after Ethan Carle died, as long as it was disposed of completely. In what seemed to Harri as divine intervention and seemed to Tom Bards as luck finally running out on two serial killers, the cremator at Green Acres Funeral Home broke that night.

If it hadn't been for that, Ethan Carle's body would never have been found. The limbs The Scholar gave to Alexander Marchand to incinerate would never have surfaced next to Ethan Carle's body. They would never have read Ethan Carle's notebook and found out about the women that Raymond Sklar branded, tortured, killed, and then skinned for his growing enterprise of confessional books that were auctioned off for hundreds of thousands of dollars on the dark web. All of it would have remained another dark secret as Ethan Carle's body and the limbs were cremated and turned to ash.

But it didn't happen that way because of a surprise rainstorm that Sunday night. It was a strange confluence of events. Like someone once told Harri, Los Angeles is blue skies every day, but when it rains the city turns into a vengeful bitch.

As for Raymond Sklar, he'd been immediately

disowned by the entire Sklar family. There had already been dozens of articles and press pieces in the last week as the family's crisis PR team went into action to spin how Raymond was the mentally unsound black sheep of the family and they'd tried to get him help for years. They assured the public that if any of them had any idea of what he'd been up to, they'd have cut off his financial resources and forced him into a psychiatric facility where he could get the help he obviously desperately needed.

Raymond Sklar had personal funds and had hired the best criminal defense lawyers to represent him. There was hardly anything they could do except mount an insanity defense since he was found with the brand iron in his hand and a naked woman on the rack. Not to mention Ethan Carle's police badge that Patrick Sumner had given him to prove his problem had been handled had been found in Raymond Sklar's tannery workshop. It was bittersweet for Harri to watch Tom Bards return Ethan Carle's badge to his partner.

The FBI was now involved, working on tracking down the people who'd watched The Scholar torture and kill his victims in the private chat room. At some point in his dark descent into utter depravity, Raymond Sklar realized that part of his fantasy was to have an audience like the medieval executioners and had hired a team of Lithuanian experts on the dark web to set up his livestream operation.

That little piece of the puzzle Neland Carrington had offered up as part of his plea agreement. He'd realized what Raymond Sklar was up to when he saw the brand on the women the first time he watched one of The Scholar's livestreams. He'd designed it at Raymond Sklar's request, after all. But he decided to ignore that because he also realized watching an executioner torture a victim to confess her sins made Neland feel all the closer to the medieval era that had been his obsession since he was a young boy.

Neland Carrington had been charged with conspiring to commit murder for his role in creating the brand and participating in the livestreamed snuff films. The DA was trying to use the child pornography act to put him away for longer since watching pornographic abuse images of minors was a factor as Rena was not yet seventeen when she was killed.

The police tore Raymond Sklar's mansion apart and found his leather tanning workshop with four more books ready to be auctioned off. They'd sent the books off to Dr. Grimley in the hopes that she and her team could extract DNA and somehow match it to missing persons.

As to the death of Alexander Marchand, they'd found Raymond Sklar's DNA mixed in Marchand's bloodied clothes. It was a needle in a haystack moment because the police never recovered the knife that had been used to stab Alexander Marchand twenty-one times. Harri wondered if it was at the bottom of the reservoir.

Raymond Sklar refused to say anything to anyone except that he would like to speak to his attorney, so their interviews with him went nowhere. The current theory was that Raymond Sklar needed to clear up loose ends when the Sumner brothers were going down for their tissue harvesting business. Raymond Sklar realized that Alexander Marchand had gone from being a useful idiot to an unacceptable liability who knew way too much, and therefore had to be neutralized. He couldn't call Patrick Sumner to do his dirty work this time, since that hadn't worked out so well the time before, so Raymond Sklar decided to do away with Alexander

Marchand himself. But Raymond Sklar was not a common murderer. He was an executioner, and Alexander Marchand was not some weak, young girl bound to a medieval torture device. He fought back. As a result, Raymond's saliva and hair were found mingled with Marchand's blood in Alexander's macabre living room.

Jedediah Sumner was indicted on fraud and that case was moving forward rapidly. The DA was confident he would be convicted and sentenced to five to seven years, like the perpetrator in the similar East Coast case.

Patrick Sumner was beginning preparations for his own murder trial. The DA had agreed they would not seek the death penalty even though he'd surpassed the grim record for the city and become one of the most prolific serial killers in LA history by murdering at least two men a week from the homeless community. At least, according to the records from Green Acres Funeral Home.

Darlene "Whitey" Whiteman survived the ordeal and was released from the hospital four days ago. Harri worked with the social worker assigned to Whitey and made sure she was receiving the psychiatric counseling she needed. Harri helped Whitey hire the best victim's recovery attorneys in the city. The DA had approved protective placement for Whitey as Raymond Sklar had unlimited resources and every reason to neutralize any witnesses.

Whitey had been allowed to call her the day before and told her she was in a safe place that was beautiful and had a big TV and a comfortable bed. Harri was overjoyed to hear the warmth in Whitey's voice. If a nice television and soft bed made Whitey feel this way, what could suing Raymond Sklar into permanent destitution do for her well-being?

Harri pulled into the drive of her new home and saw Jake standing in their front doorway. She got out of the car and smiled. "I finally have my week off. All the paperwork is done, and we can finish unpacking. And I can sleep. I don't ever want to see paperwork again," she said.

"I hate to tell you this," Jake said as she reached their front door.

Harri's stomach dropped. Now what?

"You know how the FBI was digging in that plot of land I told them about above Pointe Dume Beach?" Jake asked.

While Harri had been investigating this last case, Jake had made quite a bit of headway into the Jerome Wexler sound file that had been delivered to their home. He'd discovered that embedded in the sound file was a map to a piece of land at the edge of the peninsula. It was a burned-out desolate place amongst multimillion-dollar homes that for some reason wasn't being developed and nobody wanted to go near because they were spooked.

He'd called in the FBI a week ago and they'd searched the plot for anything relevant to the Jerome Wexler case. Last Harri had heard they'd struck out, but by the look on Jake's face, they must have found something.

"What is it?" she asked.

"We found three bodies there," Jake said.

Harri's heart raced at the news. She wouldn't be having her vacation after all. However, they were closer to uncovering what Jerome Wexler had been up too since he killed her sister and the other kids on the island.

"You did it, Jake. You cracked his code," Harri said and walked into his hug.

Thank you so much for reading The Skin Hunters!

I hope you enjoyed Detective Harri Harper solving this intricate case. Find out what happens when Harri and Jake team up with the FBI to identify the three bodies found by Point Dume and Harri is called to a family massacre in Venice Beach in The Little Deaths.

PRE-ORDER The Little Deaths now so you don't miss it!

ABOUT DOMINIKA BEST

Dominika Best is the author of the Harriet Harper Thriller Series and the Los Angeles Ghosts series.

For more information:
www.dominikabest.com
hello@dominikabest.com

Made in the USA
Thornton, CO
03/30/23 18:14:12

797f52d1-eb14-4229-90aa-bc4f3389ef82R01